The Last Days of
Alfred Hitchcock

The
Last Days of
Alfred
Hitchcock

A Memoir Featuring the Screenplay
of "Alfred Hitchcock's
The Short Night"

DAVID FREEMAN

The Overlook Press
Woodstock, New York

Acknowledgements

Many friends and colleagues helped in the preparation of this book. Among them were:

Sandra Archer, Robert Bookman, Jon Boorstin, Leo Braudy, Merle Browne, Jay Cocks, Joan Cohen, Lawrence Dietz, Lee Eisenberg, Mark Gompertz, Jeremy Kagan, Bill Kerby, Anne Mandelbaum, Michael Mandelbaum, Philip Moffet, Stephen Paly, Tom Pollock, Lynn Povich, Peggy Robertson, Roger Simon, Gordon Stewart, Donald Spoto, Amanda Urban, Steven R. Weisman, Daniel Yergin, and Jeff Young.

I would also like to thank MCA and the Academy of Motion Picture Arts and Sciences.

791,4309
HITCHCOCK

First published in 1984 by

The Overlook Press
Lewis Hollow Road
Woodstock, New York, 12498

Copyright © 1984 by David Freeman
A portion of this book first appeared in *Esquire*
Photos courtesy of The American Academy of Motion Picture Arts and Sciences,
The Museum of Modern Art, Larry Edmunds and Steve Paley.

The publisher wishes to thank Merchandising Corporation of America and Laurence Pollinger Limited for their assistance in the publication of "The Short Night," in this volume.

Design by Joe Marc Freedman

Library of Congress Cataloging in Publication Data
Freeman, David,
The last days of Alfred Hitchcock.
Filmography: p.
1. Hitchcock, Alfred,   . 2. Moving-picture producers and directors—Great Britain—Biography.
I. Title.
PN1998.A3H5469 1984   791.43'0233'0924 [B] 84-42672
ISBN 0-87951-984-3

Contents

For Judith Gingold

The Last Days of Alfred Hitchcock

"Now my charms are all o'erthrown. . ."

—Prospero, *The Tempest*

I

A man sits in a car holding a bouquet of chrysanthemums. It's evening, getting dark and raining. The car is a Humber Hawk and it's parked on a cobblestone service road, next to a high brick wall. The man with the mums is listening to a voice we can't quite make out. It could be the car radio, but his ear is cocked slightly toward the flowers.

The camera moves toward the windshield, descending slightly as it dollies forward peering into the car, about to show us what the man is doing with those mums. But when the camera arrives at the car, it surprises us, and further piques our interest, by panning off the windshield, over the wet cobblestone road, toward the brick wall. As the camera climbs the rough red bricks, going steadily higher, inducing dizziness in the viewer, the voice we've been hearing becomes clearer, as if the camera were hunting it. It's an angry voice, an upper-class Oxbridge accent. "I'm here . . . hurry on now . . . can you hear? I said, I'm here." When the camera is at the top, and before its descent, we get a glimpse of the surroundings on both sides of the wall. But instead of clarifying, it only serves to tease us more. In our one glance, from this height, we can see that inside the wall is a prison. There's a tower, a few searchlights, and rude-looking cell blocks. On the outside, beyond the service road, we glimpse another large institution and a sign that says "Hammersmith Hospital." But before we know what to make of that, the camera, our guide, moves down the wall toward the voice.

Inside, a tall, imperious man, dressed in prison garb, is huddled against the wall avoiding the lights and speaking urgently into a primitive walkie-talkie. "I'm here, damn it. I'm here. Now move." The camera cuts to the outside (the very first cut in the scene) to the interior of the car. The driver speaks soothingly into his flowers. "That's right then, I'm here. You'll be fine . . . stay calm." He starts to get out of the car, but his eyes register surprise and he stops talking. Across the service road, another car has parked and its headlights have gone off. There's a young couple in the front, and they're embracing feverishly. The man in the Humber Hawk mutters "Damn . . ." into his flowers and the voice from the other side, desperate now, says, "What is it? What's the matter?"

"It's a bloody lovers' lane." He silences his flowers and then flashes his headlights at the second car, leering at the couple. They pull apart quickly, frightened by the light. The woman averts her eyes and her thwarted lover scowls and drives away. The mums are turned on again and a torrent of abuse comes from inside the prison. "Where the bloody hell are you? . . . You've bollixed it. You bloody Irish ass. I'm not going back. I'm not. I'm not going back."

It could only be Hitchcock. Daring, outrageous, and complicated. Several things are happening at once, each component of the scene both clear and mysterious. It's what Hitchcock liked to call "pure cinema." By that, he meant a telling of a story in a way that has no effective equivalent in written narrative. It's an emphasis on the visual, rather than the verbal. In the scene just described, the camera is doing one thing—traveling toward the mysterious mums; then before we can know what the flowers are, and who that fellow in the car is, the camera moves toward and then up and over the prison wall toward the angry voice. Now the sound track contains two unexplained voices, one desperate, the other soothing, while at the same time, the exact location of the activity is teasingly unclear. There are cars, a prison, a hospital, searchlights, and a rainy night that makes it even harder to know what we are being drawn toward. That all these things can happen simultaneously, and before we're more than forty-five seconds into the picture, is unique to the medium. Pure cinema. In fact, it was to be the opening of Hitchcock's fifty-fourth film. Mortality intervened.

Those of us in the various imaginative dodges often spend our time puzzling about the nature of genius. What does it mean, what's it like?

Do we have a touch of it? Does this one or that one? I'm not talking about somebody with a bright future, or a good book or two on the shelf, but a flat-out, form-giving master. In his assistant's office there was a stack of books on Hitchcock, maybe twenty-five volumes in many languages. And new ones arrived frequently. There was an industry of critics surrounding him, with scholars popping up all the time with yet another gloss on "Strangers On A Train," or a new theory of "Vertigo."

I spent six months working on a script with Hitchcock, from December 1978 to May 1979—the last screenwriter to work with him before his death in April 1980. The time we spent together was always decorous, frequently pleasant, occasionally tense. I can try to tell you a bit about him as I saw him, but I warn you, in the end, to me at least, he was ultimately unknowable. It was a bit like the Eiffel Tower. You hear about it all your life, and when you finally see the damn thing, it looks so much like the postcards that it's difficult to see it fresh. With Hitchcock, his public self was so distinct that it was often impossible to know if you were dealing with the corporeal man or the invented persona. I think he sometimes got it confused, particularly in his story telling. He was a well-known raconteur, and some of his stories were widely known and repeated—often by him. There were times when he seemed to feel obliged to tell Alfred Hitchcock stories. Sometimes he was at the top of his form and did it well; other times, less so. I was aware of it some of the time, and as I came to see, so was he. With his high-waisted black suits—the trousers rested above his enormous belly, leaving just a few inches of white shirt exposed and with a black tie tucked into his pants—he looked positively fictional, from Dickens perhaps or a banker by way of Evelyn Waugh.

When I was working with him he was seventy-nine years old and sometimes lost in the solitude of great physical pain, mostly from arthritis. He moved in and out of senility, and yet for all that, he seemed in no hurry to finish his work, even though his life was clearly limited. There was always time in our work sessions for stories and anecdotes. One minute the script, the next a discussion of the tailor of some long-dead matinee idol or the steamer schedule in and out of

Tahiti in the thirties. Sometimes the talk was without apparent purpose, but other times some shred of casual chatter would turn up in a story idea. It was an odd mixture of an obsession with detail and a slow, meandering style.

Hitchcock had the historical good fortune to have worked from silent films through television. At his best, he was an inventor of part of the modern cinema's grammar. But unlike any other film director, he was an identifiable public figure, recognizable as any president or movie star. Television did that for him—but long before his TV show he was popping up in all his movies for the tiny cameo appearances that audiences loved. He exploited a body that most would hide away and try desperately to diminish. He wasn't crazy about being fat, but he saw it as a tool to use in making his career. He always claimed that "in England everyone looks as I do, and no one would remark on it." Maybe, but he exploited his profile as effectively as any pin-up.

Those of us who grew up in the late fifties and early sixties and who now peer down the long corridor toward middle age, cannot remember a time when these films didn't exist. They seemed like a permanent part of the mindscape, the way mountains or rivers are part of the physical world. They were beyond criticism (the French *nouvelle vague* critics were news to us). That they had a creator was not a surprise. After all, he was on television every week, telling macabre stories and frightening us all. And even though an older generation had also grown up on Hitchcock's films, those pictures—from the English period mostly, or the early Hollywood ones—were more polite, scary but decorous. Then came "Psycho" and "The Birds." They were a private teenage preserve. There was nothing polite about them and nobody's parents approved. Later, rock music was to fill that slot in our lives, but for a few years, when Hitchcock made "Vertigo" (1958), "North by Northwest" (1959), "Psycho" (1960), and "The Birds" (1963), in succession, he was our mountain and our river, curled permanently inside us.

I'm to be at his bungalow at Universal at 12:30 for lunch, to meet him for the first time, going to see a man about a job. Are we going somewhere else? Do we eat in his office? I don't ever recall seeing him in the commissary, and who would forget? I remember that he's a food and wine maven, and rather formal. Should I wear a tie? Oh stop it; I've been to script meetings beyond count, so just put on your regulation screenwriter's drag and go to lunch with the man. I settle for a sweater and jacket and throw a tie in my briefcase just in case it turns out to be the prom. I arrive at 12:25 and the secretaries are in a tizzy. It seems that Mr. H is not only expecting me, he's expecting Thom Mount, the head of production at the studio. Mount has not been informed of this. After much frantic buzzing about the lot, Mount is located and changes his plans at the last minute—somebody's long-planned luncheon is canceled, and Mount is on his way. I'm ushered in. The office is standard Universal issue, sort of pseudo-English-manor-house. To call it a bungalow is to understate the case a bit. It's a bungalow the way summer houses in Newport are cottages. This bungalow has two levels, a screening room, a dining room, many offices, an art department and cutting rooms. Then he appears in the doorway. He's short, five feet five inches or less, with almost un-wrinkled skin. He's very fat. The famous deadpan eyes that stared out so opaquely, so unrevealingly on television, permitting only drollness to be perceived, seemed a little more relaxed now, less guarded, less contrived. A hopeful sign. We shake hands and he immediately begins a monologue about prison breaks and South America. It makes very little sense. If anyone else were telling it, I'd be looking for the door.

Mercifully, Mount arrives and lunch is announced. We move down several steps to the dining room. Hitchcock remarks that he fell on these steps a few days ago. Now there are rails. He needs them. The table is set with three Universal commissary steaks and coffee. As we eat, he continues to deliver various monologues. It's all interesting, but the sort of stuff you read or hear if you spend any time in Hollywood. The truth is I'm starting to get uncomfortable. I begin to think he doesn't know why I'm here. Does he think I've come to interview him? The steaks are eaten when Mount, who has some skill in these areas, brings up the movie. He lets it float over to Hitchcock with a calm directness that I admire. But it doesn't do any good. Hitchcock's going on about English pork butchers and how to best prepare pork cracklings. It's clear that if we're going to talk about the script at hand, I'm going to have to lead. So I just plunge in, and sure enough, things turn around. He stops the monologues and we begin to chat about the script, some of it general, some of it quite specific. It's about love and spies. He has ideas, I have ideas. We agree here and disagree there. His face lights up and he sounds a hell of a lot better. It's amazing. A minute ago I was convinced this wasn't going to work, and now I can feel a script forming. We plan to meet again on Monday. A deal is made by the end of the next business day. Deals aren't usually made that quickly at Universal—or anywhere else, for that matter. A request from Hitchcock is taken *very* seriously. We're rolling.

For about ten years, Hitchcock had been interested in the case of George Blake, the English spy who escaped from Wormwood Scrubs Prison in London in 1966, and disappeared into the Soviet Union. Hitchcock acquired the film rights to two books: a novel, *The Short Night*, by Ronald Kirkbride, based on the Blake case; and *The Springing of George Blake* by Sean Bourke, a fellow prisoner who helped in the escape.

The screenwriter Ernest Lehman, who among other films wrote "North by Northwest," wrote several drafts of a script, based mainly on the novel, and worked on the project until he and Hitchcock had a falling out. Hitchcock asked Universal to find him "a younger man." That must have galled Lehman, who was twenty years younger than Hitchcock. At that time, I had been doing a lot of script rewriting, some of it for Universal, and so I was asked to dance. That Lehman, Hitchcock's collaborator on a film as enduring as "North by Northwest," and a man well skilled in Hollywood navigation, could run aground was a caution to me.

The general agenda of our working sessions was similar in form to those I was used to with other directors, producers or writers. That is, we discussed character, motivation, situation and story continuity. But with Hitchcock it was different in one important way: "First you decide what the characters are going to do. Then you provide them with enough characteristics to make it seem plausible that they should do it." My God, he thinks of the action first, *then* the characters? This is a heretical view and if it were left at that, I don't think much good would come of it. The traditional wisdom is "action is character," and their evolution is one, with a slight edge to character. But when Hitchcock does get to the characters, he discusses and analyzes their motives and their goals in enough depth to make his stated procedure meaningless. He might talk about the "what" first, but it's the "who" that's on his mind. The real work in our story meetings was on character in a very traditional way. Hitchcock was criticized for years for paying more heed to form than content, and his stated working procedure would certainly seem to confirm that criticism. The trick to it, of course, was that the thoroughness and penetration with which he attacked characterization was sufficient to create the reality of the characters that run through his films. In the end, the procedural question of situation before character is rendered moot by the results. It's as if the chicken and the egg arrived simultaneously.

The opening of the picture is to be the prison escape. The central thrust of the sequence is drawn from historical fact. Blake escaped from the Scrubs, hid out near the prison, and then made his way across Europe to Moscow. Lehman's script began after the jailbreak, focusing on the hero of the picture, an American who pursues Blake. My script will start with the escape. We make this decision together. The idea is to show how determined the hero's adversary is, and because it follows a narrative device Hitchcock has used to good effect in the past: a story begins one way, proceeds, then stops abruptly, allowing the main story to begin. And of course, because a prison break offers rich theatrical possibilities.

We discuss the escape in physical terms—how high is the wall, what is the geography of the prison yard, what sort of uniforms do the convicts wear. Hitchcock has a few preliminary ideas for camera moves and I make a few proposals about characterization and dialogue. Once Blake (to be called Brand in the film) is over the wall, Hitchcock wants to see maps to study possible routes. London street maps are obtained, enlarged, and mounted on cardboard. He holds them on his belly and studies them with a magnifying glass. He's obsessed with the topography, demanding to know where the stop lights are, if there are any roundabouts, and just what the traffic patterns are in the evening. He wants to know every external detail, even if it's all to be shot on a soundstage. It reminds me of Stanislavski's dictum about stage sets: A living room might be all the audience sees, but the director and the actors must know what's in the hypothetical offstage rooms, right down to what's in the linen closets.

This need to imagine the complete place and lives of the film is ironic in the face of Hitchcock's celebrated shooting procedures. He has taken evident pride in his ability to build only the parts of a set that the camera will see. If he can make a scene by shooting only a corner of a room, he plans ahead and builds only that corner. "The public sees what the lens sees. It's wasteful to have more." The lens might be limited to two boards and a passion, but Hitchcock's mind's eye doesn't stop where the room stops. If Blake is to make his escape at dusk, what times does the sun set? When do the street lights go on? The questions are beyond what is needed for the film, and it won't make any difference to the audience, but it makes a difference to him. Hitchcock enunciates these questions slowly, carefully, as if each one is the key to unlocking the mysteries of the script.

"Tell me, Da-vid, if it's a rope ladder Bourke uses in effecting Blake's escape, do you feel he made it himself?"

"Well, we know he's a resourceful fellow and we've seen he can keep a secret. Buying a ladder would leave a trail, so maybe he did build it in private."

"Umm. Then when we arrive at his flat in Highlever Road in Shepherd's Bush following the escape, perhaps there ought to be remnants of the ladder. Bits of jute lying about."

"Fine."

"Umm. Da-vid, where do you suppose he got the jute?" I, of course, have no idea where he got the jute. I'm not even exactly certain what jute is. Rope, I guess. But Hitchcock likes the sound of the word, so jute and its acquisition bounces around the room, like a small rainstorm. I figure if he just says "jute" enough times, it will all pass and we'll get back to the scene. "Would he have been careful enough to clean and destroy the odd pieces of jute you've left so messily about?"

"Maybe so, Hitch. But he's not without faults—we've seen him forget detail and just improvise solutions."

"Hmm. Then the question is, jute or no jute."

A question more germane to the scene, at least to me, is coordinating the prison break with the change of shift at the Hammersmith Hospital. The two institutions, prison and hospital, sit side by side in the best English manner. I suggest we have the hospital change its shift to suit our convenience, that is, almost, but not quite botch the prison break. We can give Blake just a few precious minutes between the two, then have it go wrong. This does not seem like a profound bit of dramaturgy on my part, and he agrees with it; he just doesn't like getting to it so quickly. When he doesn't like an idea about a character or a story point, he says, "No, no. That's the way they do it in the movies. Let's do it the way it is in life." Of course, then he'd usually do it the way it's done in the movies anyway. Only better. The problem with most movie direction is not so much the inability of the directors to move the camera. Although there are some successful directors who show little gift for photography, the real problem is stale observation. Hitchcock always saw human behavior fresh, even in a tired form like melodrama. The lucidity of his eye in contrast to the conventions of the form is part of the source of the power his films generate, the reason for their grip on our emotions. The detail seeking is compulsive and probably a little nuts. Part of it, at least, is to avoid actual script writing, but it's also so he can know what can be known about the background and fabric of the scene. He's immersing himself in it, creating the density of felt detail, from which fine performances emerge. Hitchcock moves from the general to the particular in his script preparation exactly as he does in the celebrated sequences of his films. Truffaut has remarked on this in his long interview with Hitchcock done in the mid-sixties. That splendid and endlessly instructive enterprise, *Hitchcock*, discusses all the movies through "Torn Curtain" (1966) and most of the interesting shots. The party sequence in

"Notorious" illustrates the principle. It begins with a wide shot from high above the top of the stairs, the glittering party below. Ingrid Bergman stands talking with Claude Rains. The camera begins its descent, moving closer, agonizingly closer, to Bergman, until it's tight on her fist which we know contains the key to the wine cellar, which Cary Grant must have in order to . . . Hitchcock sometimes called this "from the farthest to the nearest" as in the opening of "Psycho." First a wide shot of the city, then one building. Then one window in the building. Then inside.

After several days of looking at photographs of the Scrubs Prison, more map studying, and a lot of telexes back and forth to London, we talk about Blake's character and the nature of English spies. Kim Philby in particular. Hitchcock's method is becoming clearer. First the place (if it's unusual), then the people—much of the discussion wide-ranging and speculative—then the details about the people that will drive our story forward. Sure enough, the general to the particular, the farthest to the nearest.

Our schedule has settled into: 11:00 till 12:30, story conference; 12:30 till 1:45 or so, lunch in his dining room. Then after lunch either more story meeting, a film, or my own work session, alone. He arrives about 10:00, does his mail, and answers the few phone calls he gets, till 11:00. No one seems to have the nerve to call him and he's usually pleased when an old friend does. Occasionally Lew Wasserman, the chairman of MCA and one of Hitchcock's oldest friends, rings up just to see how he is. From time to time another old chum, Lord Bernstein, the producer and head of the Granada chain of cinemas, rings from London.

One morning I had arrived about nine to prepare for our 11:00 meeting. I stayed in my office till 11:00 working and didn't hear him arrive. When I did walk down the hall to see what he was up to, he was closeted with Peggy Robertson, his assistant since 1949, and my interpreter of mysterious Hitchcockian doings. Their offices adjoin, and the doors were closed. Peggy Robertson played a unique role in

Hitchcock's operation. She started as script supervisor on "Under Capricorn" and stayed as a permanent assistant to the boss. What there is to know about making movies and about Alfred Hitchcock, Peggy knows. Occasionally imperious, sometimes girlish, she was aware and almost always in control of every slip of paper and phone call that shuffled through the office. In another time she would have been called a producer. As it was, she functioned as chief of staff, frequently as plenipotentiary, keeper of the keys, and one-woman story department. The fact that she, like Hitch, is British and living in a strange land gave her additional leverage with the maestro. I hung about reading the *London Daily Telegraph*—Hitch subscribed so he could check the West Ham soccer scores—and chatting with Sue Gauthier, Hitchcock's secretary of many years.

At about 11:30 the door opened. Hitchcock looked dazed and Peggy was trembling. The two of them looked as if they'd just been in a car wreck. He motioned for me to come in.

"Da-vi-id. Good morning." The more syllables he put into my name, the worse his physical condition.

"Good morning. How are you feeling?"

"Knees . . . my knees." He looked his age, which was seventy-nine, and it looked to me as if not much work was going to get done. Normally I would spread out my note cards, remind him where we had left off the previous day, review the last scene, and then we'd plunge into my index cards, proposing changes from the Lehman script, or suggesting something be let to stand; debating and examining. It's slow and arduous, and takes great concentration under the best of circumstances. With Hitchcock, the pleasure and occasionally the problem was just letting his mind roam, and ever so gently tugging it back to the script when he began to repeat himself. I had two areas on the table for discussion. The first was relatively routine. Some cuts, a few slight character changes, an idea or two about putting some humor into the script. Nuts and bolts and not much glamor. The second section dealt with the nature of the love affair at the center of the script. The man looked so weary that I decided to skip the dull stuff and get to the heat.

Hitchcock lived the life of a good burgher. He dressed like a banker and never did anything irregular. His roots were in the nineteenth century and his childhood was Edwardian. He once told me that he only vaguely understood "the mechanical aspects of sex" until he was in his early twenties. It wasn't that I was interviewing him—after all, my purpose was to write a script, not collect personal data about a senior colleague. And in fact with Hitchcock, when we weren't tending to business—that is, our script—and the conversation was casual, Hitch still set the agenda. It was certainly friendly enough, but I couldn't mistake him for one of my cronies. His personal myth and too many years separated us. And yet, he would occasionally be remarkably revealing—sometimes in a logical context, other times private thoughts would just bounce out and flutter in the air. The remark about not understanding sex till he was in his twenties, is a tough one to reply to—"Oh, that's odd, I knew all about it by the time I was ten." Or, "Don't worry, you didn't miss all that much." Of course not. Someone else might have reacted differently. I tried to smile politely and if a question occurred to me, I'd ask it. In the six months I spent with him he told me astonishing things about himself but rarely asked about me. I don't mean he was impolite, he tried to ask personal questions now and then—Was I related to the Freeman who used to run Paramount? (No) What other Universal pictures had I written?—that sort of thing. Mostly the questions were mildly curious; the remarks about himself, intimate. Below the decorous surfaces of many of his films, rude, angry sex simmered; cool, icy blondes were tied up, handcuffed, humiliated. It was clear to me that at least at the end of his life, the Dionysian streak was trying to get out. So I changed our morning agenda and moved to the love story. I began talking about the nature of the love affair in the script. Sex and passion: compulsive, life-changing, soul-altering sex—all to be made more explicit than any scenes in his past films. Now I genuinely believed that some spelling out of the passion was necessary for the film, and in fact, I had been brooding about how to bring it up. I sailed on, but I didn't have to sail far. The talk of love was a tonic for him. "Yes, yes. That will work. Very exciting." It was as elaborate as praise ever got: He was saying "I will put that in my movie." He was off and running.

"The lovers are seated across the room from each other," he began in his deliberate tones. "Their robes open as they look at one another." He stopped, savoring the scene, repeating that the robes were open. He was starting to sound suspiciously like a schoolboy with a copy of *Penthouse.* "Outside, on the bay, a tiny boat is approaching, coming over the horizon" (the scene takes place in a cabin on an island off Finland). "The lovers know the husband is approaching. They can hear the sound of his boat's motor, growing louder as it comes over the horizon. They stare at each other and begin to masturbate, each of them. The camera moves closer to their eyes. The sound of the motor grows louder as their eyes fill the screen." He's grinning now and actually stretching his legs, his cane has fallen away with the lovers' robes. "Then, after orgasm, the man must take an ivory comb and comb her pubic hair." Now he didn't actually intend to put this in the film. It was a private vision, playful and from the heart, a true home movie.

This led to a general chat about pornography. I told him about the Pleasure Chest—a Hollywood shop that sells sexual paraphernalia. I told him San Fernando Valley housewives walk up and down the aisles with supermarket baskets buying vibrators and dildoes. God knows if it's true, but it astonished him, and he loved being astonished.

This was a Tuesday and that meant Hitch had his regular lunch with his agent, Herman Citron. So Peggy and I went off to the commissary. I was pleased with my decision to avoid the routine script problems in favor of the spicy stuff. I was more right than I had known. Peggy told me that before our story meeting, he had been in tears, complaining bitterly about the pain and saying she should call Lew (Wasserman) and say it was off, that he couldn't continue. she said he kept repeating, "When do you think I'll go? When?"

Hitchcock had a pacemaker. Once a month he had to attach a device to his chest, clamp metal bracelets on his wrists, and hook the whole thing up to a telephone. An electrocardiogram was taken over the phone and then sent to his physician for perusal. "Come on, Da-vid. Let's play with my pacemaker." It was as good a reason to stop working as any, so I put aside my note cards and watched while he took great pleasure in demonstrating the monitoring procedure. After everything was in order, and the call had been placed, Hitch picked up the receiver and said, "How do you do?" in his slow and deliberate voice. The technician on the other end was probably in a laboratory a thousand miles away. "Today," he intoned, "I have attached our little device to the electric typewriter. How is its heart?" He also said he intended to attach it to the dog. The little disks on his wrists resembled handcuffs. Hitchcock's fear and fascination with handcuffs is well documented; they appear over and over in his films, along with ropes and chains. He seemed quite taken with the idea of being taken.

Ten days of story meetings at the Hitchcock house in Bel Air. At first he announced he wasn't coming to the office because it was raining. Then it stopped raining, but he still wasn't coming in. I suspect it was his wife. She'd had two strokes in the last few years and until her death in 1982, she was a semi-invalid. She worked on many of the films and I don't think she liked being left out. So off I went, driving into Bel Air in my twenty-year-old Porsche with the occasional windshield wiper, for the occasional rain.

The house is simple by Bel Air standards, an area given to mansions with swimming pools, tennis courts, and grounds tended by platoons of gardeners. The Hitchcock house, the only one they ever owned in Los Angeles, is a bungalow looking out on the fairways of the Bel Air Country Club. One of its few concessions to the luxe standards of the neighbors is a long, winding driveway that keeps the house hidden from the road.

We meet in his study, where he sits waiting, in his black suit. There are paintings in the study and throughout the house: Vlaminck, Rouault, Utrillo, Soutine, and several Klees. The books in the study include a set of Shaw's plays with the first volume inscribed to Hitchcock from GBS. The furniture is all solid department store good taste; except for the art and the large number of books, it might be the house of a well-to-do businessman. A good burgher indeed.

Hitchcock was a man of considerable wealth. In the early sixties, his friend Lew Wasserman helped Hitchcock arrange the sale of his portion of the rights to the "Alfred Hitchcock Presents" television series to MCA in exchange for stock. Hitchcock said as a result he owned more than two hundred thousand shares, which made him the third largest shareholder in the company, presumably behind the late Jules Stein, the company's founder, and Wasserman. In addition, he had made prudent investments and except for his wine cellar, did not live lavishly. As for the wine, he told me that he had in storage at Bekins, a local furniture-moving concern, two cases of an 1875 Mouton-Roth-schild, and in the basement of the Bel Air house, several cases of a 1921 Cheval Blanc. He had no plans to drink any of it.

Working here is easy, and at first he seems more relaxed than at the studio. Story meetings with my peers are usually a matter of tossing out many ideas until the right one is there. The trick is being able to recognize the right one when it comes along. Hitchcock identifies the good stuff quickly, and his own ideas are almost always right. So, good ideas are in the air, and as we plunge into a knotty section, he leans toward me in a conspiratorial, almost lascivious way and says, "Let's pile on the menace."

Hitchcock does not seem to be by nature generous. He doesn't offer a drink until he wants one, the same with his supply of Cuban cigars. I don't think he's stingy, just self-absorbed. It took me a day to figure out the drink ritual. By 2:30 on the first afternoon we worked at his house, I was longing for a cup of coffee but felt awkward about asking. Finally, he said, "Would you like a cup of tea or something?"

Too quickly I answered, "Yes, I'd like some coffee."

He rang for the nurse (the Hitchcocks kept round-the-clock nurses but no servants) and announced darkly, "Mr. Freeman will have coffee." I got my coffee and the day was clearly over. The next day, about the same time, he said, "Would you like a cup of tea or something?"

"Umm," I answer. "That would be nice. Tea or something."

"Maybe a glass of wine?" he asks. I nod and he rings for the nurse. "Two vodka and orange juice," he announces deadpan. And we start belting them down. I learn by the third day to tell the nurse privately to make mine mostly orange juice. Hitchcock gets potted and the day's work is over. I try to stay sober enough to maneuver back to West Hollywood.

The next day it's vodka and orange juice time again. But this time a substitute nurse is there. She doesn't know that I don't want the vodka, so I'm getting smashed and Hitchcock, as usual, is complaining that his drink is too sweet, which means that the glass is cluttered with ice cubes and orange juice. He's drinking them down, ringing bells and demanding more. The substitute nurse says to him in a stage whisper, "You know, the doctor says no vodka." This woman in addition to being a lousy bartender, is a fool. Hitch picks up his cane, pushes her aside with it, and laboriously tries to get to his feet, saying, "I'll do it myself." I quickly appoint myself bartender and make the man a drink. I never saw that nurse again.

After a work session, as Hitch and I make our way along a corridor toward the kitchen, he stops near his bedroom and says he wants to show me something. On the bureau opposite his bed there are about fifty bottles of pills, all set out out on a silver tray, mostly from Schwab's drugstore. Hitch stares at the array of vials for a moment and then says, "You know, the thing is, there are half as many again in the nurse's room."

"Are you meant to take them all? Every day?" I ask.

"Oh, I don't know. I suppose. Shall we have a drink before you go?" I nod yes and we have another drink. The amount of medication in that house is overwhelming. I'm sure that unless a nurse brings him a pill, he just ignores the whole business. It would be reason enough to drink.

Alma Hitchcock, the times I saw her, was a frail, birdlike woman who looked angry to be infirm. Her opinion was of great importance to Hitchcock. He called her the Duchess, and if the Duchess didn't like something, then it was of no value. That was a court from which there was no appeal, and no appeal wanted. In "Vertigo" there's a strange jump cut in the first bell tower sequence. At one point Kim Novak runs away from James Stewart, across a wide expanse of field. She starts running, then cut, she's across the field and Stewart has caught up with her. It's disconcerting since there are no other jumps of this sort in the picture. Hitchcock said that when the picture was finished, he took it to New York to screen it for the Paramount executives. Hitch hadn't seen the film in about ten days, it had been in the hands of George Tomasini, the editor. Hitch, Alma, and several others were to watch the final cut before they showed it to the studio. When the screening was over, Hitch asked Alma what she thought. She said, as Hitch recalled, it was fine, but "of course you're going to do something about that shot."

"What shot?" he asked nervously.

"Why that shot of Kim running. Her legs are so fat. It looks awful."

"Alma hates the picture." And then the order to Tomasini: Cut out the run. The result is in the finished print, Alma's criticism answered, Kim Novak's heavy legs protected and all logic left on the cutting room floor.

By the second week of our story meetings at their house, Alma was used to my presence, and Hitch asked if she would like to sit in on a story meeting. To his delight, she said yes. She had to be helped back to the study where we worked, by her nurse. She sat on a sofa, sipping tea, looking hopeful. Hitch seemed thrilled. The woman had had two strokes and was generally in a dark frame of mind. This was like an outing for her, and he wanted to make it a good one. He began to perform, going over his favorite scenes, repeating sequences and acting out dialogue as if he'd just thought of it all that minute. Since he didn't have to impress me, it was clearly a little show for Alma. I think he wanted to show her how clever he was, and more importantly, how well it was going, that there was hope, a future. And he desperately wanted her approval. Each time he would mention a story point or repeat an exchange of dialogue, he would glance up at her to see if she was smiling. I felt as if I were intruding on someone's first date. At that time they had been married more than fifty years.

At the end of one of our sessions I joined them in their kitchen for yet another drink. Hitchcock is very proud of his kitchen, and he's comfortable here. It's quite elaborate with a walk-in freezer and several ovens. There's a large red banquette with an oval table. On the side bar, above the table, there's a miniature of an old-fashioned stove, a child's toy. It was a gift from Truffaut and it used to have a tiny doll in it. The freezer is filled with meat, sides of beef and slabs of specially prepared baby lamb, packed in dry ice and flown down from a favorite butcher in San Francisco, met by the chauffeur and rushed to Bel-Air—where it hangs cooling, no one hungry for specially cut baby lamb. Occasionally the nurses cook a bit of the meat, but if the Hitchcocks want food, they call Chasen's and Mrs. Chasen sees that dinner is sent over. This is a service that I assume is reserved for very few. Chasen's is known for its catering but not for take-out. When they do dine at home, the Hitchcocks sometimes use Limoges china marked "Plaza Athénée." They seemed to have service for eight of these elegant blue and white plates. Alma had admired it during a stay in Paris some years ago. Hitchcock dropped a note to the hotel asking if it would be possible to buy some. "I had in mind a teacup or two. Perhaps a saucer." A crate of the stuff arrived at the studio, compliments of the Plaza Athénée.

Around his kitchen table, with his wife having a good day, Hitchcock relaxes a bit, asks me a few almost personal questions, and talks a bit about other directors. He says he likes Truffaut's work but is hard pressed to think of a title. I suspect that mostly he likes Truffaut. He finds a grudging word of admiration for Buñuel. He can barely speak the titles, but manages to let "Tristana" and "That Obscure Object of Desire" pass from his lips. He's a hard man. As far as I can see, no one else's work interests him; and except for his current work, he's happiest when he's reminiscing. I would not presume to say what is in anyone's heart, but I suspect that the streets of London at the turn of the last century and life in his father's house, are very much on this man's mind now.

II

Alfred Joseph Hitchcock, the son of a London greengrocer, was born in 1899, and like the movies, he grew up with the twentieth century. His father, William Hitchcock, prospered and his business grew from a small shop to a wholesale and retail business, with several shops, an enterprise of some substance. By all accounts, Alfred, the youngest of three, was a well-behaved boy who took pleasure in pleasing his father, who, Hitchcock said, always referred to his youngest son as "my precious, spotless little lamb."

The family was Catholic, and Alfred, like his brother William, who was nine years older, and his sister Nellie, who was seven years older, was raised in the faith, educated by Jesuits. Alfred went to various Jesuit boarding schools, and near the end of his life, the memories of corporal punishment at the hands of his teachers were vivid. "First you would be told how many strokes you could expect. Then you were left to consider that amount until such time as *you chose* for the blows to be administered. A boy would naturally put it off and that only increased the agony. One was beaten with a cane made of gutta-percha, which was similar to hard rubber. The sting was absolute. I can feel it now."

His father died in 1914, when Alfred was fifteen years old. William Hitchcock, Jr., the oldest son, took over the family business, and Alfred, in the confusion following his father's death, withdrew from school, and declaring an interest in engineering, was enrolled in the School of Engineering and Navigation. "I liked mechanical things, but I might as easily have said masonry or medicine. I was very young and it was not a considered decision."

At eighteen he took a job with the W. T. Henley Telegraph Company, as a sort of apprentice mechanical engineer making working drawings of electrical fittings. Possibly because of his weight, he had been excused from service in what we call the First World War, and Hitchcock, like others of his generation, usually called the Great War. Instead of the military, he joined a volunteer corps of the Royal Engineers, and received training in explosives. He was given a uniform about which the only thing he could remember was that he could never get the puttees wrapped properly and permanently around his legs.

As to how he became interested in the movies, he was never absolutely certain. His parents were regular theater goers, a habit their son happily inherited. The cinema wasn't quite as acceptable a hobby as the theater, and perhaps it was with a tiny bit of rebellion that Alfred, by the time he was seventeen, was a frequent movie goer. Sixty years later, he couldn't recall any of the films he had seen, only that he felt a strong urge to figure out how they were made. "The stories weren't much, you know," he recalled. "But it was a wonder to watch them."

In 1919, before Alfred was twenty, Famous Players-Lasky, the Hollywood company that was eventually to become Paramount Pictures, built a studio in Islington, where they planned to make pictures. Hitchcock recalled reading that Famous Players planned a film called "The Sorrows of Satan," based on a popular novel. He bought the novel and produced a set of title cards for it. At that time, the title cards, in addition to the wooden dialogue, often contained illustrations. So Hitch illustrated "The Sorrows of Satan" and with his heart in his mouth, took the results to the studio. It was Alfred Hitchcock's first lesson in the unreliability of studio executives' announcements. By the time he got his title cards to Islington, Famous Players had scrapped "Satan" in favor of a new project. So Hitch designed another set of title cards. They didn't want those either but were impressed enough with his persistence and enthusiasm to hire him. By the age of twenty, Hitchcock was no longer an apprentice engineer but a title card designer. Over the next three years he did the titles for all the Famous Players-Lasky films made at Islington. Some of the cards were quite complex, with elaborate illustrations and borders as well as hand lettering.

From that came jobs writing scenarios and as an art director and assistant director. The mechanical drawing business was put aside. During his early attempts to become a director, he met Alma Reville, an English girl just one day younger than himself. She was already established in the movies as a script girl. At that time the script girl also cut the film, a task that seemed simpler than keeping track of the shots as they were made.

By 1925 Hitchcock had established himself as a jack-of-all trades for Famous Players-Lasky at Islington. He went to Berlin to work at Ufa's Neubabelsberg studios as part of an English-German coproduction deal. Going from the tiny, financially shaky Islington operation to Ufa, one of the largest studios in the world, must have been dislocating, but Hitchcock seems to have managed. He wrote the scenario, designed the sets, and was assistant director to Graham Cutts on "The Blackguard." Later that year, he went back to Germany, to Emelka's more modest facilities in Munich, but this time he went as a director. He made "The Pleasure Garden," a melodrama about a chorus girl, which was a modest commercial success but a great showcase for the director. Hitchcock recalled that the *London Daily Express* ran a headline "describing me as 'the young man with the master mind.'" Also, in Germany, he made "The Mountain Eagle," which was set, Hitchcock recalled, "in old Kentucky, wherever that might be." The film is now lost.

While he was in Germany, Hitchcock saw the work of, and probably met, F. W. Murnau, the great German film maker. It's impossible to say with certainty what influences directly shape an artist's work, but at Ufa, Hitchcock worked under the same roof with Murnau—the earliest master of what the Germans call *stimmung*, the bleak light and shadows and extreme angles, that characterize German expressionist films. Today, Murnau is more watched in the academy than in the theater, but two of his films, "The Last Laugh" and "Nosferatu," with their stark and arresting images, look like the source of at least some of the visual style of "The Lodger" (1926), the silent picture that is generally regarded as the first true Hitchcock film. In Germany, Hitchcock also met Fritz Lang, who like Murnau, was later to work in

Hollywood. Hitchcock was in his mid-twenties. He was abroad. His sensibility was forming; it was partly shaped by the German expressionist masters. It was the right place at the right time.

"The Lodger, A Tale of the London Fog" was the first film that seemed to come from Hitch's heart. In it one sees the seeds of the themes that were to dominate his mature work. It's a story based loosely on Jack the Ripper, set in the London of the twenties. There have been a series of murders of attractive blondes. Each one has been strangled on a Tuesday night and a calling card marked "The Avenger" left under the victim's skirts. London is frightened and mobilized. The film fairly basks in the pleasure of showing the police, the press, and various concerned citizens trying to solve the murders. A mysterious man steps out of the fog, looking for a room to let. He seems aloof and aristocratic and very troubled. The Lodger, who has no other name in the film, is played by Ivor Novello, a matinee idol of the day. The Lodger falls in love with the daughter of the house, a pretty blonde model whose beau, a detective, is infuriated. The Lodger is not the Avenger—although everyone suspects him of the crimes. There's a happy ending and along the way some spectacular Hitchcock film making, clearly the work of a cinematic visionary. The most famous shot in the film is of the Lodger pacing in his room. Hitch built a glass ceiling, so the audience sees the pacing, the swaying chandelier on the floor beneath, and, simultaneously, the effect on the worried people below. There's also an elaborate circular staircase. As the Lodger descends the darkened stairs, we see only his white glove on the rail, until he steps out into the foggy night. Thematically, the story is about a man wrongfully accused. And in the film, handcuffs, with all their hints of sadomasochism, figure prominently.

It would seem now, with the vantage of over half a century, that Hitchcock's power would have been self-evident. On the strength of the domestic detail, or the picture of London in turmoil, one would think any viewer might have known an extraordinary artist had burst upon the world. But it wasn't to be so easy. While C. M. Woolf, who financed and was to distribute it, watched "The Lodger," Hitch and Alma (who were engaged to marry) wandered about London, worried about their future, anxious about Woolf's opinion. Woolf, apparently an early pathfinder in the tradition of movie executive blind stupidity that continues to thrive in our own time, felt the film was hopeless and unsalable. He shelved it for several months. But there's a happy ending: Finally, after some recutting, it was deemed barely releasable and shown to the press and public. The response was ecstatic and the film was a hit. By the end of his life, Hitch could smile at the troubles of his youth. But the pain at the time must have been very great. It's hard to say with certainty, of course, but I suspect Hitch's faith never wavered. The man was put on earth to make movies and he must have known it even then. In his maturity he disowned some of the more outlandish cinematic shenanigans of "The Lodger," including the glass ceiling, saying a simple swaying chandelier would have been better and simpler. That might be, but the real point of it all is that Hitchcock was young and he had a chance—not some nonsense about Kentucky shot in Bavaria, but a morally ambiguous yarn about sex and murder set in his own London. This was not the time to be shy, so Hitchcock lit up the sky and showed the world everything he had. And once past C. M. Woolf, the world said "More, please." Hitch never looked back.

Hitchcock made the transition from silents to sound with "Blackmail" (1929) which was his and Britain's first talkie, although it didn't have much talk. "Murder" (1930) was Hitchcock's first sound era commercial success. During his English period he also made his first version of "The Man Who Knew Too Much" (1934), "The 39 Steps" (1935), "Young and Innocent" (1937), and "The Lady Vanishes" (1938).

The former apprentice engineer retained a lifelong interest in the way things worked. His most elaborate camera maneuvers seemed almost diabolical in their complexity. Cineastes have commented endlessly on the bell tower sequence in "Vertigo," the shower sequence in "Psycho," the long takes in "Under Capricorn" and "Rope," among others. Some of Hitchcock's English films now feel dated, but they all have touches of greatness. "Young and Innocent" contains an astonishing crane shot. The camera takes in a large ballroom during a crowded tea dance. The pair we're watching (in this case it's Nova Pilbeam and Edward Rigby) are searching for the murderer, a man whose only identifying characteristic is a compulsive twitch. They believe he's somewhere in this huge ballroom. The camera begins to make its way across and high above the room, the dancers below, the music in the distance. As the camera works slowly toward the music, it descends and dollies closer and closer to the orchestra, which we can now see is made up of musicians in blackface. The camera is headed for the drummer in the back row. He's drumming frantically, his arms flailing. The camera glides in tight until it frames his twitching eyes. Cut. It's a sequence of breathtaking virtuosity; but the most one can say for the racial politics is that it's from another time.

There were other successes during his English period: "Blackmail" (1929), "Murder" (1930), and "Secret Agent" (1936). But it's "The 39 Steps" and "The Lady Vanishes," that pair of espionage films that today seem joined in a permanently looped double feature, that are surely the glories of Hitch's and England's thirties. So great is their forming influence on all the subsequent international intrigue pictures—including his own "North by Northwest" (1959)—that no one can see, let alone make, a spy picture without, knowingly or not, building on Hitch's foundation. Even in the butchered versions regularly shown on television, and despite the black and white photography and the dated wardrobe, the intricacies of the scripts and the emotional grasp of the performances will probably always seem contemporary.

By the late thirties, Hitch's problem was not his own abilities, or even the possibility of war in Europe; rather it was the British film industry, which was small and helter-skelter. No one could doubt that Alfred Hitchcock was an Englishman, and an Englishman was what he would have been quite happy to be for the rest of his days. But he knew, and his British colleagues knew, that by 1939 there was only one place to make movies. Hitchcock came to the United States to live and work when he was almost forty. He and Alma were parents and he was already an international figure. He came at David O. Selznick's urging, and together they made "Rebecca," "Spellbound," and "The Paradine Case." Hitchcock came to Southern California with some trepidation. He had a flat in London that he enjoyed and a country house in Shamley Green. He leased them so that if it didn't work out in Los Angeles, he and his family could always "come home" as he put it. But after a taste of Hollywood's facilities and technicians, the Hitchcocks made California their physical home, if not their emotional one. He bought a house, sent his daughter to American schools, and most importantly, made Hollywood movies. His English period had been rich and vital, but it was in the United States that the succession of masterpieces was made. Yet for all his success in Hollywood and despite his enthusiasm for the American film industry, he remained forever an expatriate. Even after he became a citizen in 1955, he was an Englishman abroad. He always dressed formally, and in recent years his wardrobe never changed. He had a tailor who ran up dozens of the same suit in different sizes to account for slight variations in his weight. The only surprise was his left collar point which was allowed to curl. It looked accidental, but it wasn't. A portrait of him was done once in which the collar point was made to sit in its proper place. He hated the painting and wouldn't have it around. In his black suits and with his formal demeanor, Hitchcock always looked as odd as he probably felt in the bright California sun.

In the early fifties Hitchcock became the subject of serious critical scrutiny by a group of French film critics, mostly associated with the journal *Cahiers du Cinéma*, and known loosely as the *nouvelle vague*. Some of those critics, notably Truffaut, Chabrol, and Eric Rohmer, later became film makers of international repute. In 1953 *Cahiers* devoted an issue to Hitchcock including an interview conducted by André Bazin, the editor of the magazine. In 1957, Rohmer and Chabrol's *Hitchcock: The First Forty-Four Films* was published in France, and has only recently been published in English. The critic Robin Wood wrote of the book in 1966, that it "constitutes a very serious attempt to account for the resonances his films can evoke in the mind." Hitchcock's reputation before the *Cahiers* group was not exalted. He was regarded as one of the very finest commercial directors. His still-developing oeuvre was divided, within the movie business, into hits and flops. That he was engaged, even unwittingly, in anything like the formulation of a moral vision would have seemed highly unlikely to a movie goer or many reviewers. The first of Hitchcock's American films, "Rebecca" (1940), from the story by Daphne du Maurier, was called "the first mature Hitchcock work . . . a complete vision of the universe," by Rohmer and Chabrol. In addition, in the forties, he made among others "Shadow of a Doubt" (1943), "Notorious" (1946), and "Under Capricorn" (1949). By the fifties and early sixties, he seemed to turn out a master work every year.

The price of the critics—even if it's only a small band of French critics—shifting their view of Hitchcock from clever popular entertainer to Significant Artist, is that a critical counterrevolution is bound to form. In Hitchcock's case, the negative view is probably best summed up as "form at the expense of content," or anything for the flashy shot.

Hitchcock himself rarely answered these charges directly. But he did speak to the issue of the razzle-dazzle camera moves, at least indirectly. We were discussing "Lifeboat" (1943), a film of his that takes place almost entirely in a small boat adrift at sea. "People believe that the cinema has to, by necessity, be horizontal in its form. That is, go to a great many places and locales. That is not so. It should be possible to make an interesting film in a closet with the door shut. The idea is to reveal human nature and behavior with your camera moves. If the camera is still, but in many places, the result will be tedium spread out. If the camera is surprising and you, if I may say so, are in a lifeboat, then the film will be interesting. This presupposes, of course, an interesting story and characters with something worth revealing."

One looks to the man's life in an attempt to understand his accomplishments. Did something happen that opened the floodgates of art so that in a fifteen-year period, roughly the fifties and early sixties, a successsion of films that were popular and enduring works, were made? Consider: "Strangers on a Train" (1951), "Rear Window" (1954), "Vertigo" (1958), "North by Northwest" (1959), "Psycho" (1960), "The Birds" (1963), and "Marnie" (1964). Hitchcock laughed at that kind of Freudian-aesthetic detective work. "The same things happened that had always happened," was all he would say on the subject. And from all accounts, that would seem to be so. Production got easier as Hitch's skills became common knowlege. He didn't have to use himself up persuading people to work for him, or convincing moguls to finance his films. Surely that was a help in allowing him to focus all his energies on the work itself. But that really only deepens the mystery—and deepening the mystery was his favorite activity— because in the heyday of the studios, he was a master of studio politics. When financing changed, Hitch changed with it. He put up the money for "Psycho" himself, eight hundred thousand dollars. Paramount distributed it, and Hitch kept the profits less a distribution fee. And I think if a period had arrived in which films were financed with green cheese, Hitch would have effortlessly cornered the lunar market, saying something like, "Well, you know, groceries really were the family business."

One looks through this life for some sign of the price, of some Faustian bargain. But he lived the life he set out to live, happily married, a man able to enjoy the small domestic pleasures of home and family. The only scar seems to be his weight—and surely the misogyny that runs through his films is the fat boy's revenge. He intimated to a number of people that his marriage, although certainly the center of his personal life, a lifetime of profound devotion and intimacy, had been without passion for forty years. Was it true? He said it to John Russell Taylor, his authorized biographer; and one raw winter morning in his office, when our story session had bogged down and he didn't feel like chasing narrative details, he said it to me. Pushing the script aside, Hitch started musing on the Moral Rearmament Program in Los Angeles in the late thirties. That led him to a woman who wanted him to make a film about the life of St. Francis. I suggested that it was because she had seen "The Birds." He laughed and made his own joke about St. Francis the sissy. Maybe he didn't like my upstaging his story with a joke, or maybe it was one of his unique, unfathomable segues, but from St. Francis the sissy, he went directly to "You know, Da-vid, that Alma and I do not have relations. Haven't for years." It was such an unexpected remark, that at first I didn't understand it. I almost blush now to admit it, but I thought the man was talking about relatives. He said nothing more and my face must have been quizzical until the actual meaning dawned on me. I stumbled a bit and then managed to say "I'm sorry to hear that."

"Oh, don't be," he said airily and then turned back to the script. Now Hitch was always making strange turns and spins in his conversation, but this was surely the oddest. I wasn't certain of the connection between Moral Rearmament and the St. Francis lady, let alone to the sexual temperature of his marriage. Those conversational surprises always made me think that if I listened more closely, or was more clever or more subtle, I'd grasp the connection. Sometimes the logic of the transition became clear later, but often it only seemed to be his mind darting here and there. Trying to follow it in a linear way was usually a mistake. In this case, even if the remark appeared to be offhand, it wasn't. I doubt that he meant such a thing casually. I had told him that I was keeping a journal of our work and that I might someday write about it. He hadn't acknowledged it, but I think he heard me. Whether the remark about his marriage was true or not, only the principals could say for sure. But it's clear that's what he wanted the record to say. To say to the world that sex and passion, the absolute fundament of his work, was not a part of his marriage, was surely to be trying to say: "I am my films, my films are me. If you want to know either, look at them, my spiritual legacy, not at my odd, misshapen corporeal presence. There is no other me." It is said that after making love, Balzac always said, "There goes another novel." I think Hitch must have believed it.

Most of Hitchcock's films are filled with eroticism and none more than "Vertigo" (1958). It is a puzzle within a puzzle that proceeds both by logic and by dreams. It is made all the more powerful by the casting. James Stewart, whose every performance is animated by a straightforward decency, is here filled with necrophilic sexual longing that all but consumes him. We've seen Stewart in love many times, but never before or since has that most American of American actors been in such absolute heat.

"Vertigo" is adapted from *D'Entre les Morts*, a novel by Pierre Boileau and Thomas Nacejac, the authors of *Les Diaboliques*. According to Truffaut, *D'Entre les Morts* was written with the express purpose of luring Hitchcock into buying the film rights. Quite a gamble, but it worked.

The story: Scottie (James Stewart) is a San Francisco detective who has acrophobia, the result of a ghastly rooftop accident (the opening of the film). He's retired. He's asked by Gavin Elster (Tom Helmore), an acquaintance, to follow Madeleine (Kim Novak) who is Elster's wife. He's afraid she's about to kill herself.

Scottie follows her and falls in love. He saves her once, but then later, she throws herself off a church tower while Scottie, with his fear of heights, is unable to stop her. Scottie has a nervous breakdown and is nursed to health again by Midge (Barbara Bel Geddes), an old friend who is in love with him.

Sometime later, on the street, Scottie encounters a woman (Judy) who bears a great resemblance to the dead Madeleine. Judy, however, is a trashier version of the more elegant Madeleine. Scottie pursues her compulsively, reforming her, redressing her, turning her into a living version of Madeleine. The truth is they are the same woman. Madeleine was Elster's mistress, not his wife, and the two of them tricked Scottie into apparently witnessing a suicide as part of an insurance swindle.

When Scottie realizes what has happened, he takes Madeleine back to the church tower, the scene of her false death, to make her confess. At the top of the tower, she accidentally falls to her death.

That's the skeleton, the bones. The flesh is eerie and shimmering, full of dreams and mystery and all the themes of Hitchcock's canon: love and guilt, murder, pursuit, retribution, and desperate, impossible love. In "Vertigo" treachery consumes the treacherous and finally only death and emptiness are left. The film ends with Scottie standing at the top of the church tower, stunned to see Madeleine dead beneath him and the church bell tolling behind. His vertigo is apparently gone, but his shaky grip on reality seems shattered forever.

"Vertigo" takes a great and daring leap in its narrative. Judy's real identity is revealed to the viewer, soon after she's introduced, before

Scottie learns it. Now that is highly unorthodox. The more traditional way, would be to save the news for the slam-bang finale. Watching Scottie remake Judy into the lost Madeleine, creates a new and highly charged question: What will Scottie do when he finds out? It is, as Hitchcock said, "the difference between surprise and suspense." What he does, is try to drive Madeleine/Judy to a confession. He drives her, instead, to her death.

There are three razzle-dazzle set pieces in "Vertigo": The first bell tower sequence for which Hitchcock made a model of the tower, set it on its side and tracked backward with the camera, while zooming the lens forward. The result, when projected upright, is, well, vertigo.

The second is Scottie's nightmare. After he's visited what he believes to be Madeleine's grave, he has a dream in which a series of seemingly disjointed images flow in and out of his mind. The sequence has the tone of a nightmare, but it also hints at the final revelations of the story. Scottie's subconscious knows Madeleine is a fraud. That sleepful terror so upsets him, that he dreams he's falling into his own grave. Dream sequences and nightmares, like melodrama itself, is usually employed when invention fails. It's usually a cheap trick. In "Vertigo" it advances the psychic story. We learn, or almost learn, since the clues go by fleetingly and ambiguously, what Scottie's subconscious knows. We can't grasp the real meaning until more events unfold.

Thirdly, after Scottie has made Judy over, back into Madeleine, they kiss deeply. As they do, the background of the room revolves and the hotel room seems to change into the stable at the church where Madeleine apparently committed suicide. The effect is not only of physical vertigo, but of a sort of emotional dislocation and vertigo as well. The past and present glide in and out, truth and lies merge until Scottie at the height of his passion begins to sense the truth.

And yet, the richest sequence in the film does not depend on tricky camera moves, but on acting and ideas. When Scottie remakes Judy into Madeleine, that is, makes her into what she really is, the film becomes charged and erotic. Our expectation is that when Scottie's through playing Pygmalion, he'll see her true identity, that it will be clear to him. But he's too far gone; his lust overwhelms and defines ——

him. And Judy/Madeleine has surrendered her own sense of identity to him, so that now she is neither woman and both. It's as overtly a sexual scene without a bed that has ever been shot.

"Vertigo" has an odd flaw in a secondary scene. During the early, dreamlike pursuit of Madeleine, it's suggested that she believes herself to be the reincarnation of Carlotta Valdes, a nineteenth-century woman who went mad. As Scottie pursues her from a cemetery where she sits by Carlotta's grave, to a museum where she sits by a portrait of Carlotta, he becomes almost hypnotized by her beauty. He follows her to a hotel, where he sees her sitting in a window. When Scottie goes into the lobby, he's told she's never been there at all. And in fact, when he looks, her car is gone. It's an eerie moment that sends shimmering thoughts of reincarnation and madness through the viewer. It confounds Scottie. Unfortunately, the theme is discarded. It remains unexplained in a film full of mysteries that are finally explainable and explained. I asked Hitchcock about it, but never got a satisfactory answer. He retreated into "Yes. Yes. Very strange isn't it. Quite mysterious." It was my experience that whenever Hitchcock felt on shaky ground, he retreated into tiny physical particularities or intellectual generalities. When he was sure of himself or his position, he was always specific and to the point, just as he was in his films. If one insists on coherence in narrative—on a moment-to-moment basis at least, and not just thematically—then the hotel window scene in "Vertigo" is a mistake.

For a while, "Vertigo" had a different ending. An additional scene was shot and perhaps shown in preview. But it was never in the release print. It was back at Scottie's apartment, after the death of Judy/ Madeleine. Scottie and Midge are listening to a newscast on the radio. The radio was a large-scale prop. The intent was to fill the screen with it. The news they heard was that Gavin Elster, who had perpetrated the initial crime had been caught. Justice was going to be done. The further implication was that Scottie and Midge were going to get together for what promised to be a tepid romance. It sounds like the kind of scene that only a film studio would think appropriate—in some dim way to tie up the loose ends of moral ambiguity.

"Vertigo," with "Rear Window," the American version of "The Man Who Knew Too Much," "The Trouble With Harry," and "Rope" were all kept out of distribution for many years and have only recently been rereleased. The reasons for this are unclear. For a while Hitch said "Rear Window" was tied up in litigation about the underlying rights. The film is derived form a Cornell Woolrich novella. It's hard to believe that if such a problem existed, it couldn't be resolved in under twenty years. Then for a while a theory was floated that keeping the films off the market was meant to increase the public's appetite for them. Keeping an interested public away from the films for a generation seems an odd marketing ploy. During the time of its darkness, "Vertigo" became much sought after and discussed, with scratchy, usually mutilated 16mm prints and later video cassettes of it circulating. It was shown on television once in the early seventies, but for the most part, "Vertigo" has been more discussed than seen. By early 1984, when Universal began releasing all five of the films, there was certainly an audience for it, just as there had been for years previous.

From time to time Hitchcock intimated that "Shadow of a Doubt" (1943) was the film of his he liked the most. I suspect this view changed and that it had a lot to do with the smooth working conditions he enjoyed with Thornton Wilder, who wrote the script. Hitchcock liked working with Wilder, but not so much that when Wilder was finished and on his way to Washington, D. C. ,for the duration of the war, Hitchcock didn't replace him. "I had to bring in Sally Benson to put in the neon." In this case the neon was some rowdy teenagers. One moment Hitchcock would be praising Wilder for his penetrating sense of small town life (the film is set in Santa Rosa, California) and the next minute dismissing him as "schoolteacherish" and saying the script was just an extension of "Our Town."

The writing of the script might have been smooth, but there were some problems shooting it. Joseph Cotten wasn't cast until after the shooting had begun. There's a shot in the picture, near the beginning, that had to be done early in the schedule. It's a high angle long shot of a man walking away from camera. Hitchcock shot it three times: with a short man, a medium man, and a tall man. When Cotten was finally cast, Hitchcock picked the footage that most nearly matched Cotten and put it in the picture.

In "Shadow of a Doubt," Teresa Wright plays a young woman named Charlie—she's been named for her Uncle Charlie (Joseph Cotten) who, at the start of the picture, has come to visit his family in a small California town. Uncle and niece are connected by more than their shared name. There's a deep, almost telepathic communication between the two. Young Charlie adores her uncle. Her suitor, a detective (MacDonald Carey) has come to town in the belief that Uncle Charlie is the murderer of several well-to-do widows. The film explores this bizarre set of circumstances without ever losing its hold on the daily routine of small town life. It's full of elegant, subtle characterizations as well as mystery.

In "The Short Night," the script I worked on, a man pursues a woman in order to trap her husband. In each story, a man pursues a criminal and falls in love with a woman connected to that criminal. Hitchcock was fascinated by this observation and considered it at some length. That was unusual. He seemed to me always interested in connections between real events, but connections between films usually struck him as bookish, the province of critics. Critics are fond of pointing out that transference of guilt is a recurring theme in Hitchcock's films. In "The Short Night," it's not guilt that gets transferred but love. It does not, however, take a French film critic to see that love and guilt are closely linked in Hitchcock's work.

Hitchcock read speculation about his mind for so long that I suspect he just decided to go along with it, probably because it seemed like good publicity. He was always ready to tell a story that seemed fraught with significance. The all-time winner is how at age five (or six, or seven—it varied) for some forgotten childhood misdemeanor, his father had little Alfred put in a cell at the police station for a few minutes to be shown "what happens to naughty little boys." Hitch told that story all his life. It may even be true. From it, critics, friends and enemies have derived their theories about his fear of the police and his obsession with handcuffs. In that little tale many a woolly critic has found the embers that created the smoky hints of sadomasochism. Hitchcock repeated it all, but his voice lacked conviction. He always sounded like a schoolboy parroting his teachers. It was as if he were saying, If I give them a little Freud, maybe they'll let me alone.

One could no more imagine Alfred Hitchcock undergoing analysis than one could picture him anorectic. He never got visibly angry—his feelings could be hurt and he might sulk or seek retribution, but he'd never raise his voice. Those who knew him longer than I've been alive say it just never happened. It's obvious that in place of anger and self-analysis, Hitchcock made movies. The very finest drama never makes statements, never declares itself. Its meaning is its action. Hitchcock went along with the speculation about his mind, but in his work he usually let the meaning come sliding out in indelible images that have no explanation, save their existence. I don't know if Hitchcock would have agreed with this. At the height of his powers, two of his greatest films, "Psycho" and "The Birds," each has scenes in which an incidental character is trotted out to tell us what it all means. In "Psycho" it's a psychiatrist (played by the young Simon Oakland) who tells us what we've seen. It doesn't matter. What we, a collection of Peeping Toms ourselves, have seen is Tony Perkins peering at Janet Leigh through a tiny hole in the wall as she prepares to take her last shower. What we, voyeurs alone in the dark, have seen is a spectral mother, knife in hand, come to join Janet in that shower. No explanation can match that. In "The Birds" the action is stopped so an elderly ornithologist (played by a very old Ethel Griffies) can tell us how many birds are in the world. Hitchcock always insisted the scene was important, that "the public has to have the facts." He really believed that enumerating the bird population gave understanding and that explaining psychiatric theory revealed character. I think he's wrong, that in these dramas, as in all dramas, information is not emotion; facts are futile. Real understanding and actual truth accumulate more insidiously. I believe it's a measure of the depth from which Hitchcock's art came that he disagreed. We are all guilty all the time and retribution will come for our unnamed sins. The birds will seek us out and they will use no logic we know. They will destroy us and be still and then destroy us again. No matter what Hitchcock said, what he did was to photograph our fears and make palpable the invisible. His film is not about how many birds are fluttering about but about the unknowable terror that is everywhere all the time. It's about the delicate fabric of the universe and how our fragile insides crumble when that fabric is torn. It never explains these things. It is these things.

"Psycho," it would seem, has been written about almost as much as it's been seen. It's a film with an apparently enduring grip on our libidos and probably all of our emotions. On the surface it's really a rather straightforward melodrama. A woman, desperate to marry her lover who is impoverished by alimony and his father's debts, has temptation, in the form of forty thousand dollars, put in her path. She steals the money and goes to her lover. On the way she has a change of heart and is about to return and try to straighten it all out. But the man who unwittingly helps her change her mind, an odd, lonely motel keeper, murders her. Her sister and her boyfriend, aided by a private detective (hired to recover the money), try to find her. The detective is killed. The murderer is uncovered as a madman who never even knew about the money. He's put away. Sister and boyfriend are left with the mystery solved and their grief. The story comes from a novel by Robert Bloch, the screen adaptation is by Joseph Stefano.

The film is one of Hitchcock's most popular. It's on television (all one hundred minutes) regularly. The famous set pieces: the shower murder and the death of the detective (Martin Balsam) are almost as famous as Hitch's profile. "Psycho" was shot not by Hitchcock's usual cinematographer Robert Burks, but by a television crew led by cinematographer John L. Russell. With the exception of the shower scene and the detective's death, the film was done quickly, like a TV show. But instead of feeling rushed, "Psycho" has an odd hypnotic tempo and its own sense of time. Because it's in black and white and in the color era, because its story is trashy and wickedly funny, one is more surprised than usual when Hitch stops to bask in detail instead of rushing forward, the way one would expect a film of this sort to move.

After Marion Crane (Janet Leigh) has stolen the forty thousand dollars and started to drive to Sam Loomis (John Gavin), she stops to trade her car for another at a used car lot, the better to mask her trail. When the deal is struck, she goes into the ladies room to privately count out the cash. The traditional, and effective, way to play that is not to show it. After all, we know she's going to the bathroom to take out the money, and to see her do it is to slow down the action. Hitch gives us a short, powerful scene, one of the hidden pleasures of the picture. Marion enters, her face trying to be calm. She stands at the wash basin, her image reflected in the mirror. We see two Marions at a forty-five degree angle. She opens her purse and takes out a folder with the envelope. Then she takes off the rubber band. Endless detail, each step using actual time, until she counts out the money, seven one-hundred-dollar bills. She counts carefully, slowly. And over it all the music drums away, seemingly to each viewer alone. Marion's nervousness is the foil to Hitchcock's deliberate shooting: Every detail is shown. There are only two cuts in the sequence—to and away from a closer angle on the sheaf of hundred-dollar bills. Marion knows, with the audience, that a suspicious highway patrolman is outside; that the salesman thinks she's odd. By now, thief or not, we want her to get the cash in hand and get out of there. To our relief that's what she does. It's less than a minute and there's no dialogue. It's what Hitchcock meant by tempo. And it's proof once again that he can put you on the edge of your seat and stop your heart, no matter what the scene. The scene is helped enormously by Miss Leigh. Audiences and critics love this film and Tony Perkins's performance so much that they seem to have overlooked the precision of her performance. She has an expressive face that tells us what's in her thoughts without dialogue. We know more about Marion Crane than she seems to know herself. Stefano has written it well and Miss Leigh delivers a fine understated performance.

There is another moment in the film that would probably elude a viewer the first time: When Marion makes the mistake of checking into the Bates Motel on that rainy night, she makes small talk with Norman Bates (Tony Perkins). When she asks if he has an available room, he makes a little joke about having twelve cabins and twelve vacancies, and then reaches up for a key—there are a dozen of them hanging on the board. His hand hesitates—which one to pick? Which room to assign? A moment's pause, his hand uncertain, and then he selects cabin number one. For now, Norman's hesitation is meaningless, just an awkward fellow. Soon enough we learn why he selected cabin number one. That's the room next to his office, with the little peephole in the wall. In that moment's hesitation, Norman Bates has made his decision and Marion Crane is doomed. The camera's on Perkins's back during this. It goes by in a moment, but it's a beautifully layered effect.

Throughout his films actors give fine, detailed performances, in the manner of Tony Perkins selecting that key. And yet Hitchcock never "gave acting lessons," as he put it. He always insisted that it would be insulting for him to presume to tell a professional actor how to act. I suspect a clue to the answer to this paradox is to be found in the tempo and rhythm of his pictures. Hitchcock was never afraid to take his time on screen. Marion Crane counting out the money is only one example. In the same spirit, he let actors take their time and explore the moment. It sounds easy, but film sets do not tend to be places where a leisurely approach to the business at hand is often in evidence. After the murder of Marion, Norman Bates mops up the blood and disposes of the body, using an extraordinary amount of screen time. Unlike the money counting scene, one should not mistake this for actual time. Hitchcock always found a way for detail to pile up, until a viewer first watched, then began to associate and identify with the character. In that regard, "Psycho" breaks the usual rules. First we identify with Marion Crane, and hope she gets away with her crime— nothing unusual in that, audiences have identified with villains and criminals at least since Aeschylus. And in this instance Hitchcock presses all the relevant Hollywood buttons: Yes, she's a thief, but she's in love and with this money—which belongs to a crooked vulgarian anyway—she can be happy. No audience can have trouble identifying with that. By the time she's counting out those hundred-dollar bills, we're rooting for her. Then she's dead. Murdered horribly. It's as if our chair has been yanked out. Our compass is gone. The only character left seems to be Norman Bates himself. Is it possible that the maestro will ask us to identify with this man? And that we will? Yes on both counts. Again, largely through the accumulation of mundane detail and one crucial cheat. As Norman is carefully mopping up the blood and stashing the body in Marion's car, we begin to hope that he can cover up his mother's crime. An audience is of course many people, and in the end each of us can speak only for ourself, but I asked Hitchcock when in the picture did he think we began to root for Norman to get away with it. His answer, as so often was the case, was both circuitous and to the point. "You must assume an audience is viewing our story for the first time. Therefore, the assumption is that Norman Bates is the victim of his love for his mother. It is Mrs. Bates who has killed the young woman. She is dead. What is Norman to do—turn his mother in? No. He is a dutiful son. He protects her. And in the process of doing that, we come to hope he will be successful." The "process" Hitchcock refers to is the mopping up of the blood, and the sinking of the automobile in the swamp. By the time that car disappears down into the muck, Hitch has got us—we're on Norman's side.

In his interview with Truffaut, Hitchcock said this about "Psycho":

"I don't care about the subject matter; I don't care about the acting; but I do care about the pieces of film and the photography and the sound track and all of the technical ingredients that made the audience scream. I feel it's tremendously satisfying for us to be able to use the cinematic art to achieve something of a mass emotion. And with "Psycho" we most definitely achieved this. It wasn't a message that stirred the audiences, nor was it a great performance or their enjoyment of the novel. They were aroused by pure film."

The "purest film" is of course film without dialogue. Hitchcock said many times that film never fully recovered from the introduction of

A studious Hitch, in his late twenties.

With George Sanders in "Rebecca."

At age thirty, on the set of "Blackmail," with Anny Ondra. (opposite, above)

With Ronald Coleman (center) and the director A.E. Dupont, in London, about 1930. (opposite, below)

With Cary Grant while shooting "Notorious"...

...and a reunion three decades later. (above, left and right)

On the set of "Spellbound." (right)

With Gregory Peck on the set of "Spellbound." (opposite, above)

With Norman Lloyd during the production of "Spellbound." (opposite, below)

Hitch and Pat at home in the early forties. The house, on the fairways of Bel Air Country Club, was the only home they ever owned in Los Angeles. (above)

Hitchcock and Alma, with Pat, at home in Bel Air. (right)

Hitchcock and daughter Pat with Robert Cummings on the set of "Saboteur." (opposite, above)

The director, his wife, and their granddaughter T.K. O'Connell at the Los Angeles County Museum of Art's tribute to Hitchcock in 1972. (opposite, below)

The man who never drove behind the wheel. At the MGM main gate during the filming of "North By North West."

sound. Of course, he was hardly alone in this view. In "Psycho," the two murders—Marion Crane in the shower and Arbogast, the detective, on the staircase—are indeed pure cinema. Their effects could only be accomplished on film and both depend primarily on montage to achieve those effects. The shower murder—beginning with the close shot of Norman's eye pressed to the peephole and ending on the close shot of Marion's dead, staring eye a few minutes later—has no equivalent in prose. Hitchcock spent a week shooting it, and thirty-five years preparing. Except for substituting a model's torso for Miss Leigh's, the scene is really a straightforward account of the murder—carefully, exquisitely done, very few tricks. It's the last word on murder scenes. Shocking then (1959) and shocking now, despite the countless knock-offs in the years since.

The second murder, the death of Arbogast, has a little of Hitchcock's fancy stepping. When Arbogast is stabbed, he falls backward, bleeding and trying to keep his balance as he tumbles down the stairs. This was accomplished with a process shot. First the staircase and the room behind it was shot. Then Martin Balsam was placed in a chair on a dolly going down the stairs. The chair was lowered—and here's the trick within the trick—at the speed of a stabbed man falling backward. The second piece of film was printed on the first (that's the process) and the result is in the movie. Hitchcock loved that kind of hocus-pocus. I suspect the control he could exert was the real attraction.

"The Birds" like "Marnie," the film that followed it, is among Hitchcock's most perplexing. When "The Birds" is working, mostly its last half, it generates as much power as any film. It begins like a Rock Hudson-Doris Day comedy. A rich playgirl—the sort that the movies used to call a madcap heiress—is playing a trick on a solid lawyer. She pretends to be a sales clerk in a bird shop (yes, that's right, a bird shop). The heiress is Tippi Hedren and the lawyer Rod Taylor. But the laugh's on Tippi, Rod knew all along she was a spoiled rich girl, and he was having her on. The film goes along in this style for about thirty minutes. There are two clues to what is to come: first, the obligatory syrupy sound track is not there. There is no music, only the occasional screech of birds, high and safely overhead. Second, as Hitchcock well knew, anyone going to the film had a pretty good idea of what was to come, and it wasn't Rock and Doris. To begin this way, in the style of popular romances, is very daring, and if Hitchcock had had a better grip on this section, the film might be even more enveloping than it finally becomes. The script, by Evan Hunter, is up to the demands of the two styles, the problem in my view is Miss Hedren's performance in the early scenes. It's full of empty gestures and what acting teachers call "indication." When she gets an idea, one can practically see a little light bulb above her head, like an old Sunday comic strip. She improves when the film turns darker, or perhaps by then acting problems seem trivial in the face of all the havoc. Whatever the reason, Hitchcock seems off his game in these early scenes. In all of Hitchcock's films the accumulation of domestic detail and the accurate portrayal of the psychology of everyday life is vital. First, it allows us to believe the world we're watching is a real place, and most importantly, that belief serves as a foundation for the dazzling set pieces that are at the heart of Hitchcock's greatness. If the acting is unlikely, or the *mise-en-scène* false, or if the effect of the film is to feel that it is commenting on itself, then the power is vitiated. It is a testament to the power of the central driving force of the film—the birds themselves—that these concerns become moot. When the birds attack, the believability of one performance or another, or the wisdom of starting the film like a romantic comedy, is swept aside.

There are other miscalculations in the early section in addition to the problematic performance. When Melanie Daniels (Miss Hedren's character) first arrives in Bodega Bay, a tiny fishing village up the coast from San Francisco, she gets directions from the man who operates the post office and general store. He has a Vermont accent and in fact seems to be playing a stock company taciturn Yankee. He does it very well. But he and Hitch are about three thousand miles off course.

The final irony of the misfires of the first act is that the errors are of execution, of form. When Hitchcock noticed, that is, when he peered down from his mountain top, he heard people accusing him of valuing form over content. Here he got the content right—the idea of a romantic comedy turning darker than the heart can imagine, is a rich one. And in fact, the difficult parts of "The Birds" to execute—that is the birds themselves—is done with a technical mastery that has rarely been equalled. When the birds attack the schoolchildren, when the birds come roaring down the chimney and into the living room, like the Eumenides come again, no viewer is looking for strings attached to the wings, no one sits watching for tricks. The execution of the magic is complete; questions of form and content are swept aside in the face of such destruction—not of property, or even of individuals, but rather of all worlds—romance, small town life, the idea of life itself, is turned on its ear. Miss Hedren's acting in these difficult scenes is quite serviceable. None of it makes any sense—at least, no more sense than flocks of birds turning on schoolchildren.

After the continuity of the script of "The Short Night" was done, that is, after each beat of the movie had been discussed and outlined, and I was ready to start writing the dialogue, Hitchcock asked if I thought it might be a help to visit the locations of the story. That is, walk around the streets in London, see the prison, then go to Finland and have a look at where it was all to take place. Ten years earlier when he had first started thinking about making this film, he had made such a trip and found it useful. Would I like to do the same now? Perhaps I smiled too much or not enough or something, because a few days later Hitchcock didn't think it was such a great idea. "I think there's too much snow in Finland at the present time," he announced. "You won't be able to see the ground." Now I can't imagine actually arguing with Hitchcock. The man couldn't stand any unpleasantness, any dispute. He had to have complete control. Everything must appear calm. There must always be in his life, as Truffaut has remarked about his films, "inner fire and cool surfaces." It was an article of faith with this man that there wouldn't be any unruly behavior or, God forbid, a scene. He'd managed to save all his scenes for his scenes. I proposed reducing the scope of the trip. I didn't need to see midtown New York, and I could probably manage to avoid London, but I'd never been to Finland, and seeing it, snow or no snow, would probably help the script. It wasn't a fight, but it was tense. He looked as if he had an upset stomach and I had given it to him. It's clear he doesn't like my compromise, but he seems resigned. But then he doesn't want to have lunch. He'll just have something at his desk. Then he goes home early and doesn't come in the next day. Enough. If this is the price of some airplane tickets, it's much too high. I try to call him to say it's better than I stay in Los Angeles after all. He's asleep. He's indisposed, and he doesn't call back, nor does he come into the studio the next day. I can't believe it, the man has taken to his bed. So I send a note out to his house with Tony, his driver, who promises he'll put it directly into Hitch's hand. Still no response. He stays home one more day and then comes in and seems fine. He says nothing about the flap, but he seems pleased with himself and wants to have lunch and to know what films I've run in his absence. We never mention travel plans again.

When senility's icy fingers were on his throat and it was clear that no more movies were going to be made, and the truth of that irrevocable sentence was felt by Hitchcock, his drinking, which had been on the edge of being a problem for some time, got seriously worse. He carried an extra hundred pounds around most of his life, a great buffer zone between himself and the world, but now that gut was no longer fueled by Romanee-Conti and Château d'Yquem, but by brandy and a hell of a lot of it. "Claret for boys, whiskey for men, and brandy for heroes," according to Dr. Johnson, and Hitch went for the heroic. He kept it in a brown paper bag stashed in the bathroom of his office. He would laboriously make his way from desk to loo, belt down a bit, and then return.

One morning, at about eleven, he announced as if it were truly an unusual thought, "Let's have a little drink." I nodded and he rolled his eyes in the direction of the bathroom. My job was to say something like "Oh yes, I think I know where it is," as if the subject of Hitch's drinking had only a tiny place on the periphery of my mind. I got the bottle, he opened a desk drawer where two glasses sat, and poured two large brandies. As I stared at mine, wishing for a potted palm, he wrapped his lips around his glass with an urgent bite, bent his head back until his throat and several chins seemed flat, and poured the brandy down into his throat in one continuous gulp.

On a morning when he had made many trips to his brandy bottle, sitting in his office with Peggy Robertson and Bob Boyle, the art director who had worked with Hitch on and off for forty years, Hitchcock asked me to review a section of the script for him. I did, or tried to. As I described a particularly graceful camera move that he had outlined a few months earlier, he stopped and said sharply, "No, no. Don't move the camera." Then he was quiet, while I, nonplussed, just stared until he added, "The camera must never move." Boyle, a graceful man, said, "Hitch, I'm a little tired this morning. Do you think we could take a break?"

"Yes, yes . . . a break," Hitchcock muttered. Boyle and I helped him back to his desk where he sat looking numb and beyond the help of those who would help him. Adrift in senility and depression, he was dismantling his life, putting it away. And indeed, after that, the camera didn't move.

III

Hitchcock loved to tell stories, great, elaborate, complicated rough drafts for movies he would never make. Some of them were about real people and events, but the best and most droll were elaborate fictions that lived best as spoken stories. He told the same ones over and over. They were a performance and that meant they couldn't be interrupted.

He kept his listener attentive by letting his story unfold slowly, with several false climaxes. As he spoke, he managed to both look at his listener and look away, as if into his memory. The listener's task was to wait out the pauses until he chose to go on. It was like a duel. The stories were often like shaggy dog stories, interesting but not heading anywhere special. The point of the false climax was to keep a listener alert. If you laughed, or gasped, or whatever, at a false climax (which was followed by a long pause, suggesting the tale was told), you looked like a fraud, laughing out of politesse. He'd move on anyway, to a slightly more intense false climax. It occurred to me, after hearing many of these stories, that the form is similar to many of his best scenarios. "Vertigo" is an example—the apparent death of Kim Novak is a false climax—unexpected and disconcerting. The shower scene and the death of Janet Leigh in "Psycho" is another.

One of his regulars was about Derby Day at Epsom Downs:

"There weren't proper toilets there, you know, for people who didn't have boxes. Enterprising children would dig holes in the ground and put little tents up and offer people the right to relieve themselves."

His listener smiled politely (well aware there was more to be told) and waited, until he began a little chant that he claimed to remember. He said it was sung by twelve-year-old girls. "Accommodations, one penny, accommodations, one penny . . ." He sang it in a sort of cockney singsong that was very sweet and seemed to come from far away. When his audience was convinced that he was off on a treacly, sentimental memory lane, his voice turned gruffer. "Of course, then there was a rougher sort of boy who did it too. 'Piddle and a poop, one penny. Piddle and a poop, one penny.'" He smiled as if remembering and added, "Of course, when the food was bad, they did quite well." He liked the story, and it would usually set him off on another, also about the Derby.

"You know, tradesman can be quite single-minded of purpose. There were two of them had come down to the Derby to sell refreshments. So far as I know, they were not connected with the children who sold the accommodations. On the way to the Derby, one of the tradesmen noticed that the other had forgotten the cheddar cheese, one of the items they had come to sell. Well, the injured party wouldn't shut up about the cheese. No matter what happened—they saw the Queen, the race was run, crowds of swells were about, and a profit was made. But the man wouldn't stop going on about the cheese. His associate, the forgetful one, was humiliated. 'It went well enough, don't you see,' he said, trying to smooth things over.

"'No thanks to you.'

"'But we've made our profit. Look here now, here's six quid. It's been a very good day. We've sold all the sausage. We've never done that before. Six quid and all the sausage gone. A very good day.'

"'Six quid when it should have been seven, if you hadn't forgotten the cheddar. People want their cheese. We're meant to supply it. You can't be coming to the Derby without the cheese.'

"'But we've done so well.'

"'No thanks to you.'"

Then Hitchcock would pause for a bit, as if he were considering all sides of the cheese question, and add, "You know, for years to come the first one will refer to the entire weekend as 'the time you forgot the cheese.'"

He tells the story almost exactly as he's told it before, to me a few times, and to others many times. The ritual of it seems to soothe him.

Because Hitchcock was at the center of the movie business for so long, many of his stories were about the famous. I believe he really loved stories about urchins and sausage vendors; but he also had in his repertoire more glamorous tales. Anyone who worked with him probably heard this one more than once:

Hitch and Alma were in New York City with Cary Grant and Ingrid Bergman, doing publicity for "Notorious." That would make the year 1945 or 1946. They ran into Grant's pal, Howard Hughes, who, according to Hitchcock, offered to fly them back to Los Angeles in his private plane. "Well, as soon as we had canceled our commercial reservations, in anticipation of the adventure of a private aeroplane, Mr. Hughes began delaying our trip. He would say, 'Meet me at Idlewild Field at such and such a time, on this day or that.' We'd all say, 'Fine. Thank you very much.' Then he'd call back the next day and say the trip had been delayed. Something about a valve in the engine. He did that several times. Such and such a time, such and such a day, then trouble with the valve. It got so Ingrid would say, 'No valve?' I would nod, and we'd tell the St. Regis 'one more night, please.' Alma gave up and took the train back to Los Angeles. Four days after he first said we could leave, the rest of us finally did take off. I do not recall what sort of aeroplane Mr. Hughes had at the time; however, it was quite comfortable as I recall. He did the flying himself, you know. I believe there was a captain aboard, but Hughes kept throwing him out of the cockpit. Well, we thought we were as good as home, but then he began to make stops. In Chicago, I believe, for a change of clothes. Then in St. Louis to go to a nightclub. The problem was, as difficult as it was to get commercial passage from New York to Los Angeles, it was all but impossible from anywhere else. So there we were, dropping in on some cabaret in Denver, or a restaurant in Nevada. It took almost two days to fly from New York to Los Angeles. Eventually, however, we did arrive."

Hitchcock amused himself and his listeners by telling stories that seemed casual, but then contained some unexpected bombshell or revelation. In his screening room one afternoon we were talking about Garbo. Hitch seemed to agree with the traditional view that she was quite beautiful and an extraordinary actress. He thought about her for a moment, and then said that when he and Selznick were preparing

"The Paradine Case," in 1946, he had wanted to cast Garbo but Selznick felt that Alida Valli was perfect for the leading role. Garbo proved hard to get, so Selznick prevailed, but not without some trouble. At the time Valli was in Europe, and in the aftermath of the war, a visa was difficult. Hitchcock casually said that Selznick went to William O. (Wild Bill) Donovan, then head of the OSS, later of the CIA, and the law firm of Donovan, Leisure, Newton and Irvine. According to Hitch, Selznick bribed him with fifty thousand dollars in currency, hard cash, to smooth the way and bring Miss Valli into the country in time to shoot the film. Hitch was quick to add he didn't see the cash exchange hands, but he didn't doubt it happened.

Hitchcock enjoyed formulating his operating principles into pithy stories and aphorisms. Some of them are widely known and frequently quoted. "Some movies are slices of life, mine are slices of cake," and "The better the villain, the better the picture," are examples. One finds these and others in slightly different form in critical articles and they often turn up as other people's thoughts.

"I am from the Man Comes Through a Door How? school of dramaturgy. Suppose a man comes into a room, just walks in. Another chap is there. Then the small talk. 'How are you?' 'I'm fine.' That sort of thing. The second man says to the new arrival, 'Please put the doorknob back,' and we see that throughout the small talk the visitor's had the doorknob in his hand. First we laugh, then we begin to wonder why the man was so distracted that he didn't notice he'd taken the doorknob with him. So you see, maybe it's not all small talk between these two. And we're into our scene."

On cutting: Hitchcock always seemed to know when to cut and when not to. Making that decision is of course at the heart of film making, and it was one of Hitch's favorite subjects. "In a large and elaborate set, you must not use it only as a background. The size of the image (within that set) must be a purposeful thing. If you've shown a bit of the action up close, then at the emotional turning point, you cut wide. Then you can show off all your fine scenery, because you've got real dramatic purpose to it. In 'The Paradine Case' we built an enormous courtroom set. We were on it for forty minutes of the film , a considerable part of our schedule. But not until Gregory Peck is humiliated and walks out, do we cut high and long to show his exit. That's the first time we see the entire room. We see Peck's character change and at the same time we see the size of the forces he's up against. In my view, it was worth the wait."

The traditional way to show that courtroom scene would be a wide establishing shot, taking in the whole set, then maybe a few closer shots of Gregory Peck, the judge, the jury, and the lawyers, then the wide shot again, and then back to the close shot of Gregory Peck. That sort of thing appalled Hitchcock. He called it "just photographing people," or "talking heads." It's the way most television and a lot of films are shot. Although Hitchcock would never have said it, it's one of the reasons his are better than the rest.

The difference between shock and suspense: This is one of his most widely quoted theories. He was known to deliver it in a shorter form to anyone remotely interested. Here's the longer and, I believe, most complete version.

"Suppose we have a group of men sitting around a vast round table covered in green felt. They are, as you may have surmised, playing poker. Then a bomb goes off, exploding in their midst. That is shock. Now suppose we have the same men at the same table playing the very same game of poker. But this time, before the game begins, we cut to a shot beneath the table and see a time bomb, its clock ticking. Now we cut back to the table as a hand is dealt. The clock continues to tick. One of the players folds his hand, throwing down his cards quickly and gets up from the table to leave the room. He knows something the others do not. The ticking grows louder and the audience knows it too. That is suspense."

MacGuffins: The most famous Hitchcock theory of all: "Well, the name comes from a story about two men on a train. One says, 'What's that up on the baggage rack?'

"'Oh,' the second man answers. 'That's my MacGuffin.'

"'Well, what's a MacGuffin?'

"'It's an apparatus for trapping lions in the Scottish Highlands,' the first one says.

" 'But there aren't any lions in the Scottish Highlands,' the second one answers.

"'Well, then, that's no MacGuffin.'" Then Hitchcock would smile benignly, enormously pleased with himself. He really liked that story. The point is, a MacGuffin is something that's nothing. In a film or story, it's the pretext for the plot. The jewels, or the secret documents, or whatever it is that keeps the plot moving. It provides a means for the characters to get to the subtext, that is, the concerns beneath the surface that drive them.

Hitch was always amused when writers or producers argued about the exact nature of a MacGuffin. So long as it was likely, Hitch wouldn't fight over it. In "Notorious" the MacGuffin is Uranium-235. There was objection to that when the script was in preparation. "It could have been industrial diamonds . . . I wouldn't have cared. So long as it was theatrical. The important thing was that it be desperately important to Cary Grant. That's the point of it. People who argue about the MacGuffin do so because they are incapable of analyzing character." I told him that it had been my experience that many producers wanted to change any dollar amount that appeared in a script.

"What do you mean?" he asked, clearly interested in a story that included scripts and money.

"Well," I said, "if you have one character say to another 'I'll bet you fifty bucks,' the producer will say 'Make it seventy-five.'"

"Oh, yes," Hitch answered, smiling. "And if there's a ransom amount they're forever adjusting it. They're comfortable discussing figures. It's all meaningless. I always agree with them, make the change. It puts them at their ease."

.   .   .

One That Got Away: Occasionally he would have ideas for films, or chunks of films, but no real story to hang them on. One beginning that amused him took place at the Metropolitan Opera House in New York. A performance of "Lucia" was in progress. When the soprano was at the height of the mad scene—he said he always imagined Callas doing it—and impossibly high notes are ringing through the great house, a shot is fired, its sound muffled by Callas' voice. But it goes wrong and the man shot—he's seated in a box—pitches forward and tumbles into the seats below. People scream, the orchestra stops playing, and the stage manager whisks the diva into the wings. We cut backstage to her dressing room. She's pale and frightened. Her dresser and various assistants cater to her until she says to them all, "Please . . . thank you . . . but I must lie down. Thank you. Please go now." Her attendants bow and depart. When she's alone, she picks up her telephone, dials, and then says, "Well, it's done. You almost botched it, but he's dead." That's as far as he got.

Hitchcock was fascinated by the Patty Hearst affair. He had followed the trial closely. When we were working together, Miss Hearst was about to be paroled, and planning to marry. "First she says she fell in love with her captors. Imagine! Now she wants to marry her bodyguard. Is it the gun, do you suppose, or the set of keys?" Hitch couldn't get enough of it. Miss Hearst's parents were separated at that point and he kept brooding on which parent the girl would go to before her marriage. He kept mulling the question, over and over.

Trials of every sort interested him, but particularly British murder trials. He claimed that when he was younger he could recite vast sections of the trial transcripts of the more celebrated cases. He did in fact recall from memory the floor plan of the Old Bailey, including a detailed description of the prisoner's staircase in and out of the dock. "The accused had a special staircase that led from the holding cells up into the courtroom, right into the dock, up through a trapdoor. The stairs were stone. Quite old; dirty and cold. If you were found not guilty, the bailiff opened the dock and you stepped into the courtroom, free. If it was guilty, then it was back down the stairs. It was a terrible thing to have to walk back down." Police and courtroom procedures figure in his films again and again. "The Wrong Man" (1957), a film about a miscarriage of justice in New York, uses only the actual words from the arrests and the trial. The notion of "getting it right" in a literal as well as a poetic sense obsessed him. There's been endless speculation about the biographical sources of Hitchcock's movie themes. Such things are, of course, finally mysterious; but he did seem to me a man absolutely intent on correcting the Universe. If not the physical one, then the metaphysical one on the screen. If God couldn't get it right the first time around, Hitch was going to have a go at it and see what he could do. In his quest, he seemed armed with a vast and precise store of general knowledge. He'd met or known almost everyone of artistic consequence over the last sixty years. He was widely read and his eye missed very little. Yet, several times in the six months I worked with him, he would turn to me and ask what some word or another meant. Whether it was actual ignorance, senility, or some obscure test, it's hard to know. The words were mostly simple, commonplace. Synonym was one; euphemism, another.

IV

When Hitch was feeling good, when he was not in pain, he'd throw himself into the business of preproduction. He'd set Bob Boyle to storyboarding sequences—that is, making detailed, shot by shot drawings of the camera set-ups and movements, and then he'd review them the same way he'd go over the script with me. His vision of the film accumulated, detail by detail. Simultaneously, he'd start preliminary casting discussions. These talks usually involved Peggy Robertson, Boyle, and me. At various times, Hitchcock had considered all the major players for the two leading roles. We were talking about Robert Redford one day, an actor Hitch admired. "The difficulty with Mr. Redford is, you see, as I understand it, he gets one million dollars a picture." Hitch knew damn well that Redford gets pretty much anything he wants. And the days in which a director, even Alfred Hitchcock, could get him for a million are gone the way of the sweet-tempered usher. But Hitch enjoyed his reputation as a man who was close with a dollar, as well as a patriarch who couldn't be bothered with the latest indignities of inflation. The Redford business was only a game, a red herring. He really preferred Sean Connery, not only because he's a fine actor, but because Hitch knew him to be a gentleman who would always learn his lines, ask only pertinent, intelligent questions, and always be on the set on time. Connery's fees were high, although not as outlandish as Mr. Redford's. I pointed out to Hitchcock that Connery spoke with a brogue and the character was an American, from New York. "Oh, well, you'll think of something. Perhaps he went to school in Glasgow as a boy." For the woman, who in the script is English, he had in mind that Liv Ullmann would be good. Again, an actress whose qualities do not need my stamp of approval, but not exactly British. It was also pointed out to Hitch that she was soon to begin rehearsals for a Broadway musical and the show already had a big advance sale. She was unlikely to be available for at least a year. He seemed miffed that Liv Ullmann would have the temerity to go off and do a musical when he was thinking of casting her, despite her accent, in his movie. "I suppose she'll want a fortune as well," he said, looking at me as if I were Liv Ullmann's agent. "Get me Batliner," he called out. Batliner was a casting director at the studio and would know what Liv Ullmann was up to. While Batliner was hunted down, Hitch went back to musing on Redford's price and the difficulty of selling enough tickets to cover it. This time he said, "Why, you'd have to charge four dollars a ticket." "It's been known to happen, Hitch," I mumbled. He looked at me darkly, clearly blaming the price of movie tickets on me. I figured he'd start blaming me for lousy popcorn when, mercifully, old Batliner was located. "Batliner on two," came the call from the outer office. Hitch grabbed the phone and barked into it, "Bill, I'm considering Sean Connery for my picture. If you will, please investigate his price and his shed-yule." Hitch was silent for a moment, nodding a bit while, presumably, Batliner checked on Connery's availability. Then, almost as an afterthought, he said, "Oh, yes, one more thing, Bill. I'm very interested in Liv Ullmann for the woman's part, opposite Sean . . . yes . . . oh, I see then. Very well." He hung up, glared at me and said, "Batliner says we can't get Liv Ullmann. She's doing a musical in New York. She'll be tied up for months."

Hitchcock's views about actors were notorious. He was often quoted comparing them to cattle. In fact, he could be quite rude about the profession. He once remarked to me that "Henry Fonda turns in the same performance year after year and the critics always call it wonderful." And yet, he counted actors among his friends. He seemed particularly fond of Hume Cronyn and Jessica Tandy. He said when they played "The Gin Game" in Los Angeles, he sent them a case of gin.

He recalled some of his films from the twenties and thirties, in which he put distinguished West End actors on the screen. He said many of them had trouble making the transition from stage realism to the more naturalistic demands of the screen. Of John Gielgud ("Secret Agent"), Michael Redgrave ("The Lady Vanishes"), and Laurence Olivier ("Rebecca"), only Olivier, according to Hitchcock, made the transition without apparent strain. Those performances were the reason Hitch said he was less satisfied with "Secret Agent" than with "Rebecca." Of Gielgud: "It was as if to avoid the excesses of the stage, he became so low-keyed (on screen) that there was no fire at all. Of course, he got the hang of it later." Of "Rebecca" and Olivier, Hitch said, "Very romantic. One understood why Joan Fontaine stayed with him no matter what. He (Olivier) filled the screen quite easily and still remained naturalistic. He was able to move back and forth from the stage to cinema. Of course, they all do it now, but then it was rather unusual."

An actress Hitchcock always seemed to admire was Ingrid Bergman. They spoke on the phone occasionally, and he would mention her name from time to time. One afternoon we were watching "Autumn Sonata" in his screening room. The film is a very rich, but not particularly cinematic, battle between a worldly mother (Bergman) and her quiet, less successful daughter (Liv Ullmann). The whole thing's in Swedish, and clearly not to Hitchcock's taste. He's watching it because of his fondness for Bergman and because, he says, "She'll be nervous about my opinion." For the screenings, he always sat in the same highbacked upholstered chair in the corner, perched on a little pillow. Sometimes he dozed, but he always looked hopeful, no matter what the movie. From the first shots of "Autumn Sonata," it was clear that this was going to be slow going. On Ingrid Bergman's entrance, Hitchcock said, "She looks old, they've shot her badly." She was the age of the character she was playing, mid-sixties. I think he expected her to look as she did in "Notorious." He seemed peeved that she'd got old, as if it were a personal affront. Later in the film, when she came on wearing a strand of pearls, he snorted, "She looks like the Queen." He was quiet for a bit, then during a long, brilliantly acted sequence between mother and daughter, in which they rip away at each other through a long night, Hitch rose and muttered "Keep running, keep running." I turned up the lights for him and when he got to the door, a matter of a few steps, he called for Tony, his driver and then turned back to me, and ignoring the screen, said, "I'm going to the movies!" And out he went.

When he was in the mood, he liked to ask ingenuous questions and make wisecracks to the screen. When he ran the comedy "Movie, Movie" he watched it all the way through, occasionally smiling, but mostly just watching. When it was over—the two parts—the old boxing movie and the Busby Berkeley backstage takeoff, he turned to me and said, "Very nice, but which was which?"

Another time we were watching an unfortunate weeper that involved a lot of plastic surgery. A young bride was the victim of some ghastly accident on her honeymoon. Her husband was led to believe she was dead. But actually. . . . You get the idea. Well, Hollywood has been making versions of that story for sixty-five years and Hitch had seen them all. He dozed through parts, but stayed for the entire picture. When it was over, he delivered himself of a critique of several of the film's ancestors, particularly "A Woman's Face," a Joan Crawford vehicle, and an analysis of the make-up problems involved. "The trick in a thing like that is to genuinely make the face different, but for the actress involved to retain vestiges of her old personality. Perhaps her carriage or her gait, or some little personal habit. If she were to look quite different after her surgery, but still have a similar affect to her old self, it should make the other characters uneasy in a way they don't understand. If it's done well it can be quite eerie. The danger of course is that the other characters will look quite foolish for not seeing the obvious."

I once asked the least sophisticated person I knew—in this case an earnest but none too bright fortyish workman—what he knew about Alfred Hitchcock. He said, "Monster movies," and when I grimaced, he added, "and he's in them." Now this was in Hollywood, so a certain amount of knowledge is assumed, but still, awareness of Hitch's cameo appearances ran deep. When I was an adolescent, being the first to yell out "There he is!" when the famous profile strolled by was a mark of worldliness.

Hitchcock began the appearances that were finally as much a part of his trademark as his cinematic style, with "The Lodger" (1926). He used himself to fill out the extras in a scene in a newsroom. His back is to the camera. He did it, he said, without any purpose larger than a lack of extras. In that same picture he may also appear as part of the crowd next to a fence near the end of the movie. It certainly looks like Hitchcock. I asked him about this second appearance on two separate occasions. Once he said yes, it was he. The other time he said no, it wasn't.

In "Blackmail" (1929) Hitch's cameo was more elaborate. He was a harried passenger in the underground—a gent just trying to read a book while a small boy in the next seat gave him a hard time. "Waltzes From Vienna" (1933), a film Hitch claimed barely to remember, is apparently some sort of Viennese pastry. The thought of Hitchcock making a frothy light comedy about adultery among the sacher tortes makes one's head shake. Anyway, in his cameo Hitch is a cook, wearing a toque, who has climbed up a ladder to peek into what appears to be a bedroom. He has a distinctly lascivious look in his eye. Standing on that ladder, Hitch looks remarkably like the late John Belushi peering in the sorority house window in "Animal House."

In "The Paradine Case" (1947) Hitchcock emerges from a doorway carrying a cello. He's a few steps behind Gregory Peck. The image seems to say, slyly, here are my instruments: Gregory Peck and this cello and I can play them both. He also uses a musical instrument in "Strangers on a Train" (1951). He's seen boarding the train carrying what looks like a double bass. He's also on a train in "Shadow of a Doubt" (1943) where he's seen playing cards.

In "I Confess" (1952) there's an elegant exterior long shot of Hitch crossing a landing at the top of a long flight of wide stairs. He strolls past in the far background, slow and serene. He's silhouetted against a darkening sky—Hitch always liked to show a lot of sky—giving him a casual quality that implies making a movie is just like going for a stroll.

The funniest cameo is in "Lifeboat" (1943). You'll recall the action is set in a drifting lifeboat. Hitch said it was suggested he be a corpse floating past, but dismissed the idea as too outlandish. At the time he claims to have been on a diet. So he had before and after pictures of himself made. The two photos were put into the advertisement for a fictional diet product called Reduco. The whole busines was put into a newspaper, the newspaper was put into the lifeboat and William Bendix reads it. The camera catches the Reduco ad and *voilà*, Hitch is in the boat, alongside Bendix and Tallulah Bankhead. Hitch said he got hundreds of requests from people wanting to buy Reduco. When I expressed some skepticism about that, he changed the subject. He also appeared in a photograph within the film in "Dial M For Murder" (1953). His visage appears on the sidelines of a reunion photo that figures in the plot.

Just walking by was the most frequent way he dropped into his pictures. In "Murder" (1930), "The 39 Steps" (1935), "Vertigo" (1958), and "North by Northwest" (1959) he seems to be passing through, never in a hurry, but appearing to be going someplace more important. Occasionally he adds a little flare to it. In "Young and Innocent" (1937) he's a photographer outside a courtroom. The image seems to imply Hitch is there to record guilt or innocence. In "Notorious" (1946) he's a guest at a party having a drink. In "The Birds" (1963) he's seen emerging from that bird shop walking his own two small dogs. Once in a while he glances up at the central action as if he too were part of the audience, just a little closer to the characters than you are. In "Rebecca" (1940) Hitch is walking past a phone booth in which George Sanders is making a call. For a moment Hitch appears to want to use the phone.

In "The Wrong Man" (1957) Hitch was determined to keep the film as absolutely real as possible. That meant no intrusion by the famous profile. So instead the master's darkened figure appears in a brief prologue standing in the middle distance on a shadowy soundstage. He's shot from a medium high angle and he takes a few steps forward, casting a long shadow and making a pitch for the factual basis of what is to come. "This is Alfred Hitchcock speaking. In the past I have given you many kinds of suspense pictures. But this time I would like you to see a different one. The difference lies in the fact that this is a true story, every word of it. And yet it contains elements that are stranger than all the fiction that has gone into many of the thrillers that I have made before." The effect is somewhere between a ringmaster and a professor.

In his last appearance, in "Family Plot" (1976), his profile is seen in shadow, through a glass door. The words "Registrar of Births and Deaths" appear to be painted on the door—that's a bureaucratic office known only to Hitch. It's hard to read most of it, but the word Death is clear enough.

By the time of his television show, Hitch had combined the appearances with his Master of Ceremonies act. He appeared in a pith helmet once ("Greetings from darkest Hollywood") and in one astonishing routine, if memory serves, in drag, as Queen Victoria.

From the early fifties on, Hitchcock put the cameos near the beginning of the films, "or else the public would only be waiting for me, and not watching the story." It was probably true, but it was also a small vanity. He liked to think about the public, his usual word for the audience, waiting for his appearance. But like everything else with Alfred Hitchcock, it was more complicated than it seemed. His appearance was like a little boast about his body. It was as if he were saying, "Fat? Overweight? Here, I'll show you fat and make you want to see more." Then out would come the profile—that icon of fame and art—running for a bus, coming unexpectedly out of a doorway or carrying a musical instrument.

Toward the end of my tenure with Hitchcock, the American Film Institute was preparing to honor him with their life achievement award. For weeks preceding the bash, Hitch refused to have anything to do with it. He wouldn't talk to the officials of the AFI or to the press. He ignored it all, until the last week or so. As far as he was concerned, they were preparing his obituary and he didn't care to attend the funeral. As he contemplated the dinner, his drinking got much worse. The physical pain seemed to be constant. He had a doctor who came to his house and gave him shots of cortisone to calm the arthritic pain in his knees. With the physical pain, the drunkenness, and the oppressive AFI date looming, Hitch took to spending long, preposterously flirtatious sessions with a young secretary. When she walked past, he would crinkle his nose and give her little private waves. She always blushed.

Finally, a little flash of the old energy popped up. It was about a week before the wretched dinner. The AFI people were frantic. And then, suddenly, Hitch threw himself, or what was left of himself, into it. He gave a long telephone interview to nine reporters around the country. An elaborate phone hookup allowed them all to speak. He was dazzling, fielding questions, spinning out anecdotes and limericks, sounding thirty-five and hungry for publicity. None of the reporters knew he was in physical pain. On about an hour's notice he called for Bob Thomas of the Associated Press, who'd been after an interview. Could Mr. Thomas come for lunch? Right now? Damn right he could. Mr. Thomas hurried over to the studio. Hitch broke out the champagne and the two of them sat down in the dining room for a couple of hours. Again, using the same material, he was dazzling. Thomas got a great story, but when he left, Hitchcock looked exhausted.

With the dinner pressing in on him, very little work is getting done. I'm turning out pages, but Hitch has lost the thread of it. The journalists are marching in and out, the phones are ringing between the studio and the AFI, and he decides he wants to see the script. It's not quite done, there are several important things as yet unresolved, but it's certainly ready for him to read again. He tells me, "Polish it, polish it." And he tells Bob Boyle to start making sketches for the elaborate sequences. "Angles, show me some angles." So I begin polishing like mad, Boyle begins to make preliminary drawings and things are buzzing. He even manages to trundle his way back to my office to see how I'm doing. He wants the script and I give it to him and with it I give my little speech about how excited and pleased I am with the work. He says terrific, glances at it and says, "Let's send it on up to the front office."

"Well, shouldn't you read it first?" I ask.

"Oh, no. We've been over it, and if you say it's ready, then I'm sure it's fine." A deep gulp from me notwithstanding, Hitchcock sends the script to Thom Mount and his superior, Ned Tannen. Unread. This was on Friday and on Monday, Mount calls me and says it's terrific. Now it occurs to me that Mount's assumption is that Hitchcock has read it—after all, it came from him, so it must have his imprimatur. So Mount loves it. It also occurs to me that it's quite possible Mount never read the damn thing either. Maybe no one will ever read it. I thank Mount for the kind words and tell him that I'm excited and pleased too, but still want to do a little more work on it. Business as usual.

On the day of the AFI dinner, Hitchcock received a wire from Frank Capra, who was in Palm Springs. Mr. Capra was sorry he couldn't attend, but wanted both Hitch and Alma to know he was thinking of them. It was a message from one old lion to another. Hitch held it in his hands, read it, reread it, and cried. Not for the sentiment, I don't think, which was certainly genuine, but because he saw it as attesting to his own demise. Everything connected with the dinner had become funereal in his mind. To Hitchcock, this was not a sweet wire from an old colleague, but a condolence letter on the occasion of his own death.

Hitch's remarks for the dinner were to be prepared by Hal Kanter, who in addition to his career as a writer is well known in Hollywood as a wit and after dinner speaker. Mr. Kanter did not undertake this job because he needed the work, but as a service to the AFI and out of respect for Hitch. Hitch didn't make it easy. He kept canceling dates with Kanter and denying any knowledge of the need to make a speech. The remarks as finally delivered were quite droll. Kanter had apparently cobbled the thing together from Hitch's other speeches, and his own screenwriter's ability to get inside another man's voice.

Before the dinner, Universal took several rooms in the hotel where it was all to take place. By one o'clock the studio had arranged for Hitch to be at the hotel safely awaiting the dinner. The rooms were called the hospitality suite. The staff quickly began calling it the hostility suite. The purpose was clear: Keep Hitchcock off the sauce, and make sure he got to the big event. So there they were, Hitchcock, a team of Universal executives, and a few others with several hours to wait. Hitch, of course, said, "Okay, boys, let's order drinks." A Universal executive, with what I'm sure was a straight face, said, "Gee, Hitch, I'm embarrassed to have to tell you this, but this hotel has a really unusual rule. It's the only one in town where they can't serve liquor in the rooms. Some technicality of the law . . ." Hitch just looked at the man and said nothing. About an hour later, there was a knock on the door. A bellboy with an enormous basket of fruit and two prominent bottles of champagne was there. "Congratulations," he announced, "from CBS." (The network televising the dinner.) The Universal man snarled, "Wrong room," and started to shut the door. Hitch, who misses very little, said, "Just a minute. Come right in. Give the boy a tip." And he reached for the champagne. He was about to consume both bottles when the studio man screwed up his courage and said, "That's enough, Hitch, we're working tonight." And he got rid of the bottles. At the dinner the waiters were instructed not to give Mr. Hitchcock any wine. Hitch managed to talk one of them into a glass or two, but for the most part he was sober. The menu, on the other hand, presented a problem. It featured lobster. Hitchcock hadn't eaten shellfish of any sort in fifty years. He claimed it made him ill to look at it. The lobster was taken away and they found him a steak, something he considered edible.

The dinner went well enough, but the terrors and demons of the last few weeks had taken their toll. The man looked awful. It seemed to me, at least, that he was playing the part of the valiant hero at the end of his life. He insisted on walking to his table unassisted. He might have as easily pole-vaulted his way. His arthritic knees were at their worst, despite the endless shots of painkiller that were now being injected directly into the joint. The audience—tout Hollywood—stood to cheer his slow and painful trek from the wings to the table. Spotlights were on him (as I say, it's Hollywood). He made his way, step by agonizing step, his face red and wheezing, his eyes straight ahead. It lasted several brutal minutes. Mercifully, much of it was edited out of the televised version.

Ingrid Berman and Truffaut were among the hosts for the AFI dinner, and they did a fine job of it, direct, genuine and sincere in their admiration for Hitchcock. At the end of the ceremonies, with everyone standing and applauding, Bergman came down to Hitchcock's table to embrace him. With help, he got to his feet, and when she hugged him, he lifted his arms slightly as if to hug her in return. He was not a man given to casual show business hugs and kisses, and the moment was charged with emotion.

One afternoon earlier on when Bergman's name had come up in a routine casting discussion, in one of his breathtaking conversational transitions, he announced "She's been in love with me for thirty years, you know. Mad for me all her life." And he repeated it from time to time, drunk and sober. "Hitch," I said as gently as I could, after he'd said this for the third or fourth time, "why are you telling me this? You know I was a journalist for some years. You do know that, don't you?"

"I don't read it any more . . . not at all . . ." he said, speaking as much to himself and his private ghosts as to me. His mind seemed to be bouncing back and forth through the years. One minute in the here and now, which at the time was the Universal lot, the next, some distant, partly recalled but intensely felt, trauma with the once glorious, heart-stopping Bergman, that may have been real or may have been only in his heart and head. "She threw herself across my bed. She wept, she wept." We sat there for a while, saying nothing. Then, visual to the bitter end and surrendering to the inadequacy of words, he grabbed a piece of white tagboard and a black marking pen, and began to draw himself, making the famous caricature, the line drawing of his profile that appeared on everything from his television show to his matchbooks. He sketched it quickly, his hand trembling, giving the drawing an awkward, palsied look. Then he began stuttering the word "I . . . I . . . I . . ." as if he were making a last desperate attempt to define himself. His face turned red from the effort and for a moment I thought he might be having a coronary, but then he was still. After a moment he offered me the drawing. Later that morning I reminded him I was keeping a journal of our work together. "Shall I read it?" he asked. "If you like," I said. But he never asked again and I never offered.

Today, with the memories of Ingrid Bergman so vivid in his mind, it seems clear that he's been thinking about her a great deal. When they were working together, forty years earlier, she was in her prime and one of the most beautiful women in the world. She was in a celebrated bohemian period and was considered a scandalous woman. It's not improbable to think they might have had a love affair if he had wanted it, or known how to ask her. And perhaps they did, but I doubt it. Now in his old age he develops crushes on receptionists, gives them money, and asks them to do God knows what. Maybe some hagiographer yet to come will find the stained sheets of fact and memory amidst his papers. But for now, only the sad, half-remembered dreams of maybes and should haves. To make great films, that's one thing; to make yourself happy, that's quite another.

Hitchcock enjoyed talking about honors—he had been awarded the Legion d'honneur and wore a ribbon in his lapel. His ribbon was what he termed "of a lesser grade." He was offered the higher grade and the more familiar rosette, but it meant, he claimed, appearing at the Cannes Festival to get it. The idea of negotiating for honors amused him. As for a knighthood, he told me that during the Macmillan government he was sounded out about accepting an honorary one, but had turned it down. "One would be in the midst of a lot of actors, and besides, they're really only good for impressing shopgirls."

The possibility of a knighthood, I suspect, played a larger part in Hitchcock's inner life than he acknowledged—either to himself or to others. He had been an American citizen since 1955, and he certainly enjoyed acting the charade of Englishman abroad. But he kept his eye on the Queen's honors list and liked to speculate about who might be knighted and who would be passed over. I don't mean to suggest that a knighthood gnawed at him, but it did seem to be on his mind and what went on in that very private zone was so mysterious that any signs from the interior were of interest. Hitch knew what the trade was. Leaving England for the United States was not just a matter of giving up steak and kidney pie. Moving to Hollywood had permitted him to change his films from very fine to unparalleled. "North by Northwest," after all, could only have been made in Hollywood, and not by a visitor.

But at the end of his life, after the AFI dinner, in his last months, the Queen offered, and he accepted, a knighthood. For a few months before he died, he was Sir Alfred after all. The script we had cooked up together was called "The Short Night," a title I didn't care for and one he always promised to consider changing. Puns always made Hitch laugh, his or anyone else's. When I had tried to persuade him to drop the title "The Short Night," I proposed calling the picture "Pursuit." He was interested, but wouldn't commit himself, so to bolster my case, I told him we should actually call it "Pursuito" like "Vertigo" or "Psycho." He nodded and said, "Call it "Prosciutto" and change the locale to Italy." He always managed to put off changing the title. Now with his knighthood he was able to call himself the short knight. My guess is the appeal of the pun was a big part of the attraction.

After his knighthood, I stopped by to see him and call him Sir Alfred. I arrived at the bungalow and found his staff standing about stunned, some of them in tears. "They're shutting it down. They've fired him," one of the secretaries said. And they believed that. The fact was, he'd gone up to what he always called "the front office" and what everybody else at Universal called The Black Tower, to say, in effect, I just can't do it anymore. The studio took him at his word and jumped at the chance to close down, or at least reduce, his costly operation. A few days later, a studio functionary called to say the offices were to be vacated. The staff was furious at him for not making an announcement to them himself, and more importantly, not helping them look to their futures. His own sense of himself was so wrapped up in being a film maker, that when he wasn't one anymore, he just closed up his shop and released his staff. The people around him had trouble seeing past his recent cruelties and drunken behavior; they saw venality where there was only human frailty. They left angry and hurt, and when they were gone, he came back, supposedly to clear out his personal effects.

He sat in his office while furniture movers and truckers came in and out of the bungalow to pack up and move twenty years accumulation of files, books, old films, equipment—the detritus of his business. He might have sent the clerical staff and various deputies on their way, but he himself stayed on and called for Nino the barber to shave him and trim his hair. He sat in the center of the office, draped in a barber's cloth, ignoring the swirl of workmen. He would nod to them occasionally, but mostly he sat Buddha-like at the eye of the storm while Nino carefully, lovingly, trimmed his sideburns.

Then when he'd had his fill of it, he left, saying goodbye to those few who remained to help him, calling friends to say that henceforth he could be reached at home; and out he went. He stayed at home for a few days and then he just started coming back to the studio, as if nothing had changed. He'd kept the few offices at the front of the bungalow, now oddly barren. He'd found a new secretary and resumed his rituals, unencumbered by the fiction of being a film maker, or the trappings of power and authority. There was only one phone line left, and when it would ring, the bell would echo, oddly, off the walls. He was like some crypto English-Chekovian figure, playing out the last days of his private, imagined Raj.

Now that he was Sir Alfred, there was one final blast of publicity. A TV crew was there, reporters were calling again. He was in publicity heaven, a place he adored, and he was full of talk of the future. For a moment or two he almost meant it. "Do you think we could redo the script, so that I could shoot it on a stage? Keep the location work to second unit, so I wouldn't have to be away from Alma? Think about it, Da-vid."

A few months later I was on the other side of town walking across the Paramount lot, going I don't remember where. The Santa Ana winds—hot, dry, wicked winds off the desert—were blowing across the lot, when a mob of actors dressed as fifties teenagers, shooting the umpteenth episode of "Happy Days," ran past, laughing and shouting. Then a friend I hadn't seen in a while stopped me and said she'd just heard on the radio that Hitch was dead. He'd died at home, in his sleep, his family nearby.

He had the last laugh, though. At his funeral—formal, Catholic, correct—his coffin was not present. He had managed to arrange a cremation. He didn't want to be there exposed, unable to shift the focus when he felt like it.

In his study, at home in Bel Air.

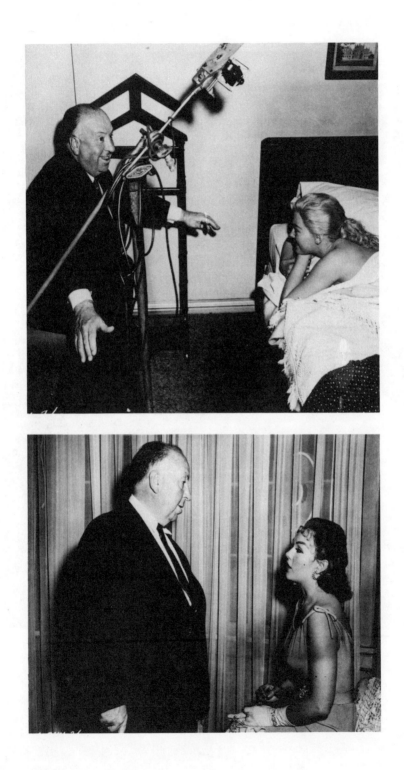

A casual glance at Kim
Novak as Madeleine Elster
in "Vertigo." (opposite,
above)

With Kim Novak as Judy
Barton in "Vertigo."
(opposite, below)

Hitch and Janet Leigh
discuss her performance, on
the set of "Psycho." (left)

With Tony Perkins and
Janet Leigh at the Bates
Motel. (below)

Listening to the machine that made "The Birds" squawk... and auditioning the cast.

Requesting loyalty from the crew, on the set of "The Birds."

With Rod Taylor and
the remains of
Suzanne Pleshette on
the set of "The Birds."

Bird watching on
Bodega Bay.

On location at Bodega Bay.

With Tippi Hedren and Rod Taylor while filming "The Birds."

In London during the filming of "Frenzy." (above)

Hitchcock in his office at Universal in March 1979. (below) Los Angeles
Times photo.

With the crew of "The Birds" at Bodega Bay. (opposite, below)

That infamous profile which he drew for me.

"Alfred Hitchcock's The Short Night"

The Screenplay

Hitchcock was fond of quoting the theories and experiments of Lev Kuleshov and V. I. Pudovkin, two early Russian film makers and theorists. An account of their work appears in Pudovkin's book *Film Technique and Film Acting,* and is well known to film students. In the experiments that so fascinated Hitch, Kuleshov had taken footage of the stage actor Mosjukhin and juxtaposed it with other shots—a bowl of soup, a coffin with a woman in it, and a little girl playing with a toy bear. The shots of the actor were close-ups in which he had no apparent expression, they were selected for their neutrality. When the results were shown to an audience, people said in the first shot, with the soup, the actor was pensive. In the second shot, with the coffin, he was expressing sorrow. And in the third shot, with the child, he was amused. Well, Hitch absolutely adored it. What better news? The actor was a prop and an entire performance could be constructed in the cutting room. Hitch's memory of the experiments were a little different than Pudovkin's account. Hitch remembered the plate of soup as a cake and that the audience thought the actor was hungry. The child with the toy he remembered as a beautiful woman which resulted in a lascivious look from the actor. The point of course is that actors are interchangeable, and that montage and context are all.

I bring this up to introduce the script of "Alfred Hitchcock's The Short Night." The title had his name in it—no matter how awkward the locution—as in "Alfred Hitchcock's Family Plot." I think it's impossible to read the script without sensing Hitch as you turn the pages, just as Kuleshov and Pudovkin's Russians sensed hunger or sorrow. If one were told that in some great lapse of common sense Fellini was about to shoot this script, it would read differently. Context is all.

"Alfred Hitchcock's The Short Night"

1   **EXT. LONDON – ARTILLERY ROAD – 6:45 P.M.**

A drizzly London evening in the fall.

Wormwood Scrubs Prison and Hammersmith Hospital sit side by side. Artillery Road, hardly more than a service lane runs between them.

A Humber Hawk sits on the prison side facing Du Cane Road, the main drag that runs past the front of both prison and hospital.

CAMERA is outside the car looking at Brennan, who sits in the front holding a bouquet of chrysanthemums. He's in his early thirties, a little paunchy and very Irish. He's listening to a voice we can't quite make out. It could be the car radio, but Brennan's ear is cocked slightly toward the mums.

CAMERA pans off the flowers, toward the prison wall, over the cobblestones and up the rough red bricks toward the top. As CAMERA pans, the voice starts to become clearer.

As CAMERA goes over the top of the wall and starts down the other side, we realize we're going into the prison, toward the source of the voice.

MAN'S VOICE

(becoming audible; urgent)

. . . I'm here . . . I'm here . . . hurry on now . . . can you hear? I said I'm here . . .

2   EXT. PRISON YARD—NIGHT

Gavin Brand stands huddled against the wall speaking into a walkie-talkie. He's 39, tall and lean, dressed in prison garb, an intense, aristocratic, imperious man who at the moment is taking a very great risk.

> BRAND
>
> Do you read me? . . . I'm here, damn it, I'm here.
> Now move!

3   ARTILLERY ROAD

Brennan, still in the car, speaks into the flowers.

> BRENNAN
>
> *(soothingly)*
> I'm here. You'll be fine . . . you'll be fine . . . stay
> calm.

He starts to get out of the car, when his eyes widen in surprise. He stops talking and looks ahead.

4   HIS POINT OF VIEW—A CAR

It parks on the other side of the road, near the hospital. A Young Couple sit in front. The headlights go off and the couple embrace.

5   RESUME SCENE

> BRENNAN
>
> *(into the mums)*
> Damn . . .

> BRAND (v.o.)
>
> What is it? What's the matter?

BRENNAN

It's a bloody lovers' lane.

6   **PRISON SIDE OF THE WALL**

Brand is huddled against the rough bricks.

BRAND

What? What are you saying? Just hurry up, man.

BRENNAN (v.o.)

Won't take but a second.

7   **ARTILLERY ROAD**

Brennan flashes his headlights into the lovers' car.

The couple, who are in a feverish clinch, look up to see who's bothering them.

Brennan grins at them, lasciviously.

The lovers pull apart embarrassed. The young woman averts her eyes as her boyfriend starts his engine. He pulls forward past Brennan, giving him a dirty look.

Mums in hand, Brennan gets out of his car and hurries around to open the boot.

8   **PRISON SIDE OF WALL**

BRAND

(more urgent)

For Christ sake, man, they'll be back from the cinema. What are you doing?

9   **ARTILLERY ROAD**

Brennan has the boot open, about to remove a rope ladder.

> BRAND (v.o.)
>
> God damn it, what are you doing there? It's all
> going to be over . . . It's too late . . .

Headlights illuminate the boot as Brennan is removing the ladder.
He drops it quickly and turns to see an old Morris approaching.

He closes the boot and reaches into the mums, turning off the
walkie-talkie, silencing Brand's voice.

The Morris stops adjacent to Brennan. An Elderly Couple are in
the car. The woman leans across her husband and speaks to
Brennan.

> ELDERLY WOMAN
>
> Excuse me young man, we're looking for the
> hospital.

> ELDERLY MAN
>
> Hammersmith Hospital. It's on Du Cane—

> BRENNAN
>
> Yes . . . Yes. This is it. Straight on and turn to the
> left. Visitors' entrance is to the left.

> ELDERLY MAN
> *(to his wife)*
>
> What did he say?

> ELDERLY WOMAN
> *(loudly)*
>
> He said it's to the left for the visitors' entrance.

10   **OTHER SIDE OF WALL**

BRAND

What's wrong? What is it? Answer me damn you, answer. What is it?

11   **ARTILLERY ROAD**

ELDERLY MAN

Where should we park?

ELDERLY WOMAN

My husband wants to know . . .

BRENNAN

On the street. Park on the street. You just go up and turn to the left. Hurry or you'll miss visiting hours. They're very strict.

ELDERLY WOMAN
(re Brennan's flowers)

Mums?

BRENNAN

Yes. Hurry along now.

ELDERLY WOMAN
(holds up a bouquet)

Me too. For our daughter-in-law. Her liver's shot to hell.

BRENNAN

Lovely. Hurry along.

ELDERLY WOMAN

Thank you.

ELDERLY WOMAN (Cont'd)

(loudly, to her husband)
It's to the left. We park on the street.

The Morris pulls away, slowly.

Brennan opens the boot again, grabs the rope ladder and flips
on the walkie-talkie. When it clicks on, a torrent of abuse comes
out.

BRAND (v.o.)

(midsentence; almost in tears)
. . . not going back. Where the bloody hell are you?
I can see the first of them coming back. You've
bollixed it. You bloody Irish ass. I'm not going
back. I'm not. I'm not going back.

BRENNAN

We're there. We're there.

He drops the mums on the ground, and tries to find a spot to
throw from. He steps back into the road, then moves forward
again and climbs up onto the back of his car.

The mums are on the ground with Brand's pleas coming out.

BRAND (v.o.)

You drunken ass. You bloody Irish fool. You've
killed me. You've done it. It's on your head.

Brennan winds up and tosses the ladder, hard and high.

12   PRISON SIDE OF THE WALL

As the ladder comes floating over the wall.

> BRAND
> *(sees the ladder)*

Oh god.

He lunges for it and starts to climb frantically, hungrily.

13 ARTILLERY ROAD

Brennan waits and watches. He can hear the thump, thump of Brand's feet against the wall.

> BRENNAN
> *(now he's scared)*

Is it you, then?

There's the start of activity and lights going on at the far end of Artillery Road, on the hospital side.

> BRENNAN

Oh, god.
> *(calling)*

It's the hospital. The shift's changing. Hurry the hell up.

Brand's face appears at the top of the wall. He stares down for an instant to see if it's really Brennan.

> BRENNAN

We lost time. The shift is changing.

Brand swings his body up over the top of the wall. He looks up the road to the hospital activity.

14 THE HOSPITAL

Workers come out and head toward their parking lot.

15   RESUME SCENE

Brand tries to hurry down the ladder. He manages the top few rungs, and then falls, bouncing his head against the wall, tumbling to the ground.

BRENNAN

Oh Christ.

Brand is in a groggy heap on the ground. His forehead is bleeding. Brennan lugs him to the car. The hospital activity continues.

BRAND
(muttering; as he's being dragged)
I won't go back there . . . I won't go. Just shoot me . . . I won't go back.

BRENNAN

Shut up. Nobody's going to shoot you, so you might as well go through with it.

Brennan pushes him into the front seat, slams the door, and goes around to the other side and jumps in.

The car jerks away. The rope ladder and the mums are left behind.

16   INT. CAR – TRAVELING – NIGHT

BRENNAN
(reaches to back seat)
Here's a mac for you. Put it on. The key's in the left pocket.

He hands Brand the mac. Brand clutches his left wrist. He's still groggy from his fall.

BRAND

It's my arm. I think it's broken.

BRENNAN

Just put on the mac.

A siren blasts, filling the car, terrifying both of them.

BRAND

(starting to whine)

You've done it. You wasted so much time. You fool.
You bloody . . .

Headlights fill the car, the siren gets louder as an ambulance
marked "Hammersmith Hospital" roars past them.

Both men shudder with relief.

BRENNAN

Just put on the mac and shut up.

17   EXT. CAR–TRAVELING–NIGHT

It pulls cautiously out of Artillery Road, turns left and drives
past the hospital.

Brennan turns right, goes past the train line toward Westway
and turns on Latimer Road, drives a short way and turns on
Oxford Road. In the traffic, we notice the London buses, and the
English cars.

The car stops abruptly at an intersection, near some drab row
houses.

18   INT. CAR

BRAND

What are you stopping for?

BRENNAN

This is where you get out.

BRAND

(frightened)

We're too close. We're right by the prison.

BRENNAN

Number fifteen. Key's in the left pocket.

19   EXT. STREET CORNER – NIGHT

Brand gets out of the car and walks across the intersection to number 15. As he does, the car drives away, quickly.

CUT TO:

20   INT. BED SITTER – NIGHT

Brand enters cautiously. The main room has a daybed, a few chairs, and a table. Off that there's a small kitchen and a bath. It's very bleak.

Brand takes off the mac, tossing it on a chair, then he rips at his prison shirt, popping the buttons, tearing it off his body.

He moves through the place, inspecting. He opens the closet door, looks into the kitchen and the bath, then glances out the window at the street, two floors below.

When he's satisfied he's alone, he looks at the articles on the bed: civilian clothing, currency of several nations, a passport, maps, cigarettes.

He goes back into the bathroom and stands in front of the mirror and basin. He wets a face cloth and wipes away the gravel in the cuts on his forehead. He uses only his right hand, holding the left close to his body.

Before the cuts are entirely clean, he drops the cloth into the basin and goes back to the main room. He's getting dizzy and has to hold onto the furniture. He plops down in a shabby chair and passes out.

DISSOLVE TO:

21   INT. BED SITTER – NEXT MORNING

Brand, in civilian clothes with his arm in a make-shift sling, is with Brennan. They're reading the morning papers, which are filled with news of the escape.

BRENNAN

(reading a headline)

Look at this one: "Traitor Brand Escapes from
Scrubs Prison. Gavin Brand, the foreign service
officer who spied for the Russians—"

BRAND

I can read.

BRENNAN

Look at your picture. Go on look.

BRAND

I don't care about the newspapers. They get it all
wrong anyway.

BRENNAN

Here now, listen, my flowers have got them baffled.
"The clue of the mysterious mums." They think I'm
a florist.

BRAND

I want to know how I'm going to get out of
England. It's stupid of you to have me so near the
prison.

BRENNAN

(still reading the paper)
It says you got forty-two years because you caused
forty-two deaths.

BRAND

Stupid.

BRENNAN

I got you out of prison. I'll get you out of England.

There's a knock at the door. Brand jumps up. Brennan quiets him.

BRENNAN

(to door)
Yes?

MAN'S VOICE

We're here.

Brennan goes to the door, peers through the peephole.

22   HIS POINT OF VIEW – THROUGH PEEPHOLE

A young couple (Ian and Rosemary), and a middle-aged man
(Doctor) dressed in black with a doctor's bag.

23   RESUME SCENE

BRENNAN

(to Brand)
We'll take care of that arm, now.

He opens the door, and the three visitors enter. The young couple nod at Brennan and stay near the door.

BRENNAN

How'd you do, Doctor.

The doctor doesn't reply. He sits at the table. Brand sits next to him.

BRAND

It's the wrist. I think it's broken.

The doctor says nothing. He feels the bones, checking for a break.

Ian and Rosemary stand back watching and whispering quietly to themselves. He holds her hand, protectively. They're very impressed to be in the room with Brand.

The doctor, with his sleeves now rolled, spreads the morning papers on the table. Brand's picture and the headlines are prominant, and unmistakable.

The doctor has two basins of water and he mixes plaster for a cast. The doctor takes Brand's wrist in his hands and sets the bone, sharply and quickly. It's painful.

BRAND

Jesus! Careful man.

The doctor, still silent, coats the wrist with plaster. Bits of plaster and water drop on the newspapers, spattering the picture of Brand's face.

The cast in place, the doctor stands, wipes his hands, unrolls his sleeves, closes his bag, and gets up to leave. Still saying nothing, he walks to the door, and exits.

BRAND

He's a strange one.

BRENNAN

One of the boyos. This is Ian and Rosemary.
They've played a great part in getting you here.

IAN

How do you do, sir.

Rosemary smiles, shyly. She's about 25. Studious looking. Brand
nods at them.

BRENNAN

We've got a lorry fitted out for you. Ian will drive.
Can you travel now?

BRAND

Just get it.

IAN
(to Brennan)
I'll need help.

BRENNAN

All right. Rosemary'll stay. We'll be back with the
lorry, and then we're off.

Brennan and Ian leave. Brand and Rosemary are left.

ROSEMARY
(a hint of coquettishness)
I'm glad I have you to myself for a moment.

> BRAND
>
> *(looks her up and down)*

Yes.

> ROSEMARY

I'd love to hear about your days in East Berlin. You
did amazing things there for the party. Just
remarkable.

No answer. Brand stares at her.

> ROSEMARY

I see. Quiet as that doctor, is it? He's IRA you
know. "One of the boyos." Shall I make tea? I'm
sure there's tea.

She walks toward the kitchen. Brand gives her a moment, then
follows.

24   KITCHEN

Rosemary's at the sink. He's behind her. Watching. She can sense
his eyes on her back and it makes her uncomfortable.

> ROSEMARY
>
> *(starting to chatter, nervously)*

Ian and I will be driving you. They've made a little
bed for you in the lorry. It's not going to be very
comfortable, I'm afraid. It's really sort of a drawer.
You'll be cramped, but hidden. Ian and I will be
the perfect young couple on holiday in our van.

The kettle whistles. Rosemary pours the water for the tea.

> ROSEMARY

There. We'll just let that steep a little. Now perhaps
you'll tell me about Berlin.

BRAND

Rosemary. For remembrance.

ROSEMARY

Yes. That's right. Rosemary for remembrance.

He draws her to him and kisses her. She doesn't kiss back, but
she doesn't push him away, either.

ROSEMARY

Please . . . Don't . . . They'll be back very soon.

BRAND

They left you here for a bit. To be with me.

ROSEMARY

No, no. Ian needed help. The van's in a garage. We
keep it out of sight. It takes two to get the door
open. Two men. You know I respect you so much.
We all do.

BRAND

Um-huh.

ROSEMARY

We really do.

BRAND

You know how long I've been in prison.

ROSEMARY

You'll be seeing your wife soon. They've made all
the arrangements. She'll be so happy . . .

He strokes her breasts.

ROSEMARY

(starting to get scared)

Don't. Please don't do that. They'll be back any
time now.

BRAND

There's plenty of time. It's all arranged.

The more nervous she gets, the more bold he becomes.

BRAND

So soft . . . It's been five years since I felt anything
so soft.

ROSEMARY

Don't do that . . . Please stop . . . I'll yell out . . .
really I will. I don't care . . . Stop . . . Please . . .
Don't do that.

He holds her mouth with his uninjured hand, squeezing her
cheeks, so she can't speak. Her voice is muffled and distorted,
but growing more urgent.

BRAND

Stop babbling.

He distorts her face further, then pushes his mouth at hers,
kissing her and running his hands along her body.

She reaches back behind her for the cup of tea, fumbles around
for it as he continues to grope and paw at her. She finds the cup
and swings it forward, splashing the hot tea on him. He jumps
back, but it only angers him more.

BRAND

Stupid cow. You'll do as I say.

He slaps her. She yells out, and he slaps her again. Once he starts he can't seem to stop, and he hits her several times. She gasps for breath and scratches at his face. She draws blood on his cheeks.

ROSEMARY

Help me . . . Stop it . . . Help me . . .

BRAND

You bitch. You stupid bitch. Shut up.

He covers her mouth with his injured hand. She bites down on his fingers, sinking her teeth into the flesh. He yells from the pain and then presses his thumbs into her neck, harder and harder, cutting off the flow of blood and oxygen. He squeezes and Rosemary begins to gasp for breath. She flails her arms about, desperate to breathe.

BRAND

Bitch . . . bitch . . . what do you think of that?
What? Tell me. What?

Her arms go limp as she collapses in his arms.

Brand looks at her eyes, puts his hand on her heart, and then realizes she's dead.

BRAND

Oh good god . . . Oh damn you to hell.

He slaps her face—in anger and desperation—but she's dead, limp in his arms. He lets the body fall to the floor, and hurries toward the living room.

25 LIVING ROOM

He puts on the mac, and hurriedly grabs the money, the passport, and the maps.

26   EXT. – HOUSE – DAY

Brand stands in the doorway and glances around.

27   EXT. – STREET – DAY

He strolls up the street, away from CAMERA, past the row
houses. When he comes to the intersection, he turns the corner
and disappears.

An unmarked van approaches from the opposite direction and
parks in front of number 15.

Brennan and Ian get out and walk toward the house.

28   INT. HALLWAY

Ian and Brennan approach the door. Brennan knocks softly. No
answer.

                              BRENNAN
     It's us. Hello . . . it's us.

They exchange nervous looks and Brennan opens the door with
his key.

29   INT. BED SITTER

They enter cautiously.

                                IAN
     Rosemary?

Brennan looks around the living room as Ian goes to the kitchen.
We hear him scream, off camera. Brennan hurries toward the
kitchen.

30   INT. KITCHEN

Rosemary's corpse is sprawled on the floor, her skirt up over her legs and a grotesque look on her face. Ian is kneeling over her.

BRENNAN

Oh my god.

He turns and runs back out of the kitchen.

31   LIVING ROOM

As Brennan races through and out the door into the corridor.

32   DOOR TO STREET

Brennan peers out cautiously. He sees a patrol car cruising, moving toward the van. He stays in the building, shutting the door.

33   INT. BED SITTER

As Brennan reenters. Ian, pale, his teeth chattering, stands in the kitchen doorway. They exchange looks.

IAN

She's gone.

BRENNAN

That makes forty-three then.

CUT TO

34   INT. COURT TENNIS BUILDING—NEW YORK—DAY

Before we see where we are, we hear the thud, thud, thud, of a tennis ball as it bounces off the walls of a court (or real) tennis court.

As the ball comes into focus, we get our first glimpse of the players: Marian, an attractive woman in her late twenties and Joe Bailey, a man of 35, good looking, intense, and a player who won't give an inch to his opponent, no matter how beautiful.

As the quick cuts of Joe and Marian become longer, their comments and their grunts and groans echo through the court and mix with the sound of the ball.

JOE

Faster . . . damn it . . . that a boy, that's the way . . .

MARIAN

Oooh . . . Joe . . . My lord, I can't . . . hah! . . .

35   HIGH COMPREHENSIVE ANGLE—ENTIRE COURT

For the first time we see clearly that the ball is played off all four walls, the low roof of the penthouse (viewing gallery), and the floor.

36   COURT

Joe works very hard at this game, harder than necessary. he runs for every ball, extends every volley. He's in good shape, and determined to have a victory at the expense of a good time.

He jumps high for a ball and drives it past Marian's backhand.

She drops her racket, and panting, exhausted, stops playing.

MARIAN

Joe, that's enough. What do you do to opponents you don't like?

JOE

I wasn't even keeping score.

MARIAN

Hah!

(*flirtatious*)

It's separate showers in this joint—but we could
have a drink together.

Her invitation makes him smile.

JOE

That's even better than breaking your serve.

An elderly Messenger—a club retainer in bellman's uniform—
toddles out onto the court. He holds a tray with a message.

JOE

(*to the messenger*)

Want to play the winner?

MESSENGER

No, sir. They said it was urgent.

Joe glances at the note. His mood changes as he crumples it up.

JOE

(*to Marian*)

I'll have to take a raincheck.

He gives the ball an angry whack. Marian's disappointed, and the
messenger startled, as the ball caroms around the court.

CUT TO:

37   EXT. WEST 52ND STREET–NEW YORK CITY–DAY

The street is noisy and active, clogged with pedestrians and
traffic. Joe threads his way through the crowd, past a large
"Keep New York Clean" sign.

Joe's wearing a velour warm up jacket and no tie. He has a newspaper under his arm.

38 **EXT. ENTRANCE TO 21–DAY**

Joe goes down the steps, under the painted statues of the jockeys and through the main entrance.

39 **INT. 21 MAIN ENTRY**

From a distance, we see Joe talking to the Maitre'd who is offended by Joe's outfit. He gestures toward Joe's throat.

Joe is insistent, and the Maitre'd picks up his phone and speaks. The Maitre'd hangs up and turns his back on Joe.

A Busboy appears, carrying a necktie.

> BUSBOY
>
> Are you the gentleman without a necktie?

> JOE
>
> Guilty.

Joe takes the tie and puts it on at a jaunty angle, tossing one end over his shoulder. He hands the busboy a dollar.

> JOE
>
> The new look.

> MAITRE'D
>
> Yes, sir.

Hold on the snooty Maitre'd as Joe goes toward the dining room.

40 INT. 21 UPSTAIRS DINING ROOM – BEFORE NOON

A Captain leads Joe through the center of the empty dining room, toward a solitary man at a table in the rear. The Captain seats Joe, and withdraws.

During the scene we will hear, but not see the room slowly filling up, off camera.

41 CLOSER ANGLE

The two men sit in profile, facing each other across the table. The man is Paul Zelfand, about 45, professorial with gray hair and horn rim glasses. A Waiter speaks to Joe.

WAITER

Can I get you something, sir?

JOE

(looking at Zelfand)

How about a rational explanation. On the rocks.

WAITER

Sir?

ZELFAND

Mr. Bailey will have a Scotch.

As the waiter leaves, Joe tosses the newspaper on the table. The lead story is about Brand's escape.

ZELFAND

It's even bigger news in Europe.

JOE

I don't care about him. It's all in the past.

ZELFAND

Yes. But the forty-two, those men are still dead.

JOE

I don't need to be reminded who's dead.

ZELFAND

(gently)

We both know who he killed.

JOE

It wouldn't surprise me if you broke him out. Is he joining us for lunch?

ZELFAND

We don't want him. Not officially anyway. The man's been in jail for five years. Anything he knows is out of date.

JOE

And you just like to scratch at old wounds? Why'd you drag me over here?

ZELFAND

If the break was KGB, then Brand's in Moscow. I don't think it was. I think he's trying to get there. I thought you'd want to know his travel plans.

JOE

You going to "terminate" him, or whatever the hell you thugs call it these days? Well, you can find him and bomb him for all I care.

ZELFAND

He poses no active threat to the US so we won't
make a move. British Intelligence, same problem.
That leaves Scotland Yard, and they've already
blown it.
                    (carefully, letting it sink in)
The man who killed your brother will be scot free.

JOE

You're speaking for yourself, aren't you? This
doesn't have anything to do with the CIA?

The waiter returns with Joe's drink. He places it and leaves.

ZELFAND

Please . . . quietly.

JOE
                    (loudly)
Correction. The Red Cross. Or the Health Service.
Or Pepsi Cola.

ZELFAND

Shut up.
                    (puts two photos on the table)
This is Brand's wife. These are his sons. He's
obsessed with his children. All his prison corre-
spondence, his conversations. Everything. Always
his children.

JOE

                    (sarcastic)
And no mention of my brother?

ZELFAND

Joe, you're not the only one who lost somebody.
I knew every one of the forty-two. Every one.

JOE

So you get Brand. You're equipped for it. Not me.

ZELFAND

It's a different world. It's not like when your brother
was with us. I'm taking a risk by talking about
this. I'm speaking to you as a man. Brand has
caused us both immeasurable pain. I know what to
do. And how. But I can't do it.

Joe thinks about that for a moment, looks at the photographs.

ZELFAND

They were in London up to a week ago. Now,
who knows. Wherever they are, Brand will go to
them.

JOE

Find the wife and sons, find the father?

Zelfand nods yes.

JOE

Too risky for you, so I should pull the trigger.
What you want are the good old days when you
could go around the world killing people. Look, I'm
a civilian. It was my brother who bought your line.
You got the wrong Bailey.

ZELFAND

It's the only way to even the score.

JOE

It's anarchy.

ZELFAND

You want him free or dead?

JOE

Why me? Forty-two, I can't be the only one still
angry.

ZELFAND

Stop wasting time. You know you're going to do it.

JOE

What makes you so sure?

ZELFAND

I was at your brother's funeral. I saw your face. If
you get near him, you'll do the job.

JOE

(angrily)
You'll say anything won't you.

ZELFAND

If it'll stop Gavin Brand.

Joe looks at the photos again, tosses them on the table and rises
to leave.

JOE

It's not for me. No.

He leaves.

42 FULL LONG SHOT—ANGLE THAT DELIVERED JOE TO TABLE

The tables are filled now. Active. Joe walks toward CAMERA and out of shot. Zelfand remains seated at the table in background watching him go. Then, without any particular urgency, he gestures to the waiter, who hands him a plate with the check on it. Zelfand throws down a couple of bills and rises to his feet.

43 EXT. SIDEWALK BEFORE 21

A uniformed Doorman is standing before the entrance. CAMERA pans him to the curb to meet a limousine pulling to a stop. The doorman opens the rear door for the well-dressed Man and Woman. They get out, and CAMERA pans them toward the entrance as they go inside. CAMERA holds for a moment, and then Zelfand emerges from the restaurant. He looks off past CAMERA, then moves forward, CAMERA retreating with him, and comes face to face with Joe, standing there on the sidewalk waiting. Zelfand smiles.

> JOE
>
> Don't grin. You look like a cat. I don't like it or you, but I have to live with myself. I'm going to try. Where will I be able to reach you if . . . ?

> ZELFAND
>
> You won't.

> JOE
>
> I mean just in case . . .

> ZELFAND
>
> I mean never. Do you have a gun?

JOE

I told you. I'm a civilian.

ZELFAND

That'll be taken care of.
(hands him an envelope)
Prices in Europe are outrageous. It's on us.

JOE

(spurning the envelope)
No. I want you to owe me everything and me to
owe you nothing.

ZELFAND

I insist.

JOE

I can get very angry.

ZELFAND

(smiling)
I know.

The dialogue, above, is interrupted when: A limousine pulls up
to the curb as CAMERA eases back to shoot over the top of the
car on Joe and Zelfand. The Chauffeur opens his door, pre-
paratory to getting out to open the rear door for his passenger, a
Woman of means. As he does, we hear the thud of a large-caliber
bullet hitting him in the back of the head. He is hurled against
the car door, the door slams shut, his chauffeur's cap goes flying,
his body whirls around to face CAMERA for a moment and we
get a brief glimpse of a destroyed bloody face before the body
slumps down to the pavement out of picture, and CAMERA
zooms in close on the shocked faces of Joe and Zelfand.

44   FLASH CUT

In the entrance to the building across the street, glass doors are closing as a gun with a silencer on it is being withdrawn.

45   CLOSE TWO SHOT—JOE AND ZELFAND

JOE

Jesus Christ! What am I into.

ZELFAND

(with urgency)

Meant for me, not you. An old score. Get moving.

Zelfand hurries back into 21. Joe exits hastily in the opposite direction.

CUT TO:

46   EXT. TOP OF HIGH BUILDING NEAR JFK AIRPORT—
DAY

Atop the building, which is below screen, we see a weathercock with its swaying arrow pointing northeast. The weathercock fills most of the screen, and in the distance we hear then see the Concorde, flying northeast.

47   INT. HEATHROW (LONDON) INTERNATIONAL
TERMINAL BUILDING—NIGHT

CAMERA shoots down from a high angle on a group of uniformed constables and plainclothes Detectives, standing in a loose circle, listening to instructions from a Superior. As the men disperse, CAMERA pans up to a comprehensive shot of the hall. In the distance, we see Joe with a suitcase, approaching a newspaper stall.

48   NEWSPAPER STALL

Joe looks at a stack of Evening Standards. The lead story is Brand's escape, and the manhunt. The Cashier reads a magazine, and ignores Joe.

> CASHIER
> *(a little sharp)*
> They're for sale, you know.

> JOE
> Do you have a good guidebook for London?

> CASHIER
> "London A to Zed."
> *(hands him the book and the paper)*
> Two quid in all.

> JOE
> *(paying)*
> I thought everyone in England was supposed to be polite.

> CASHIER
> Everyone in England's on strike.

She rings up Joe's sale.

CUT TO:

49   EXT. HYDE PARK – NEXT MORNING

Joe wanders, lost. He stops, consults his guidebook, and proceeds.

He stops a Nanny pushing a pram, to ask directions. She points vaguely ahead and Joe moves on, still confused. He starts to go one way, changes his mind and goes the other.

50   NEAR THE ALBERT MEMORIAL

A boy's soccer game is about to start. Two rows of 10-year-olds face each other. One team wears yellow jerseys, the other scarlet. The scarlet team is missing two players.

Joe walks into the shot and approaches the Coach who is speaking to the teams, pleading with them. His voice becomes audible as Joe gets near.

COACH

Come on now lads, we can't play with uneven sides. What good is it if we don't play? Now let's even it up.

YELLOW JERSEY BOY

I'm not playing for them. We wear the yellow, or we don't play!

The others cheer him.

JOE

(to coach)
Excuse me, I wonder if you might . . .

SCARLET JERSEY BOY

We don't want them. We'll beat them the way we are.

His team mates cheer him.

JOE

I wonder if you would direct me. I'm looking for Earl's Court Road.

The boys on both teams giggle when they hear "Earl's Court Road."

JOE

Why's that so funny?

COACH

Quiet lads.
(points to the scarlet jerseys)
These are the Earl's Court Flyers. Or most of them.
Two didn't show and now it's a mess.
(pointing out of the Park)
To the right, Queen's Gate to Cromwell, then right
to Earl's Court. Fifteen minute walk.

JOE

Thank you.
(to the scarlet jerseys)
Stick to your guns lads, don't be turncoats.

The coach gives Joe a dirty look as he leaves.

CUT TO:

51   EXT. BRAND FLAT–EARL'S COURT ROAD–DAY

Row houses that have been converted into apartments. The
Brand flat is the street level and has a front and back yard. A
Constable stands in front. Sightseers in cars and on foot stop to
stare and take photos.

Joe is across the street from the house, among the curious. He's
been here awhile and he seems unsure what to do next.

52   JOE'S POINT OF VIEW

A curtain near the door is drawn aside and a glint of light
reflects off a pair of binoculars.

53   RESUME SCENE

Joe watches the window, concerned, as a Policewoman (Sergeant Letweiler) in blue uniform emerges from the house and speaks to the Constable, who nods and walks toward Joe. Joe watches him approach.

The Constable comes closer and closer to CAMERA. He peers into the lens.

> CONSTABLE
>
> Would you mind coming with me, sir?

> JOE
>
> In there?

The Constable nods yes and leads Joe toward the house. CAMERA moves with them as they cross the street and enter the house.

**54   INT. ENTRYWAY AND HALL LEADING TO
LIVING ROOM**

The Constable leads Joe through the hall. There's a staircase leading to another apartment and a door leading to the Brands'. In the living room, Inspector Wadleigh is with Sergeant Letweiler, the woman officer we saw a moment ago. Wadleigh is Scotland Yard, low key and efficient.

> WADLEIGH
>
> Carry on Constable.
> *(offering his hand to Joe, as the
> Constable leaves)*
> Good morning. Inspector Wadleigh.

JOE

(shaking his hand)
Bailey. Joseph M. Bailey. Now what's this . . . ?

WADLEIGH

Sergeant Letweiler.

Joe doesn't glance at her. He continues to look expectantly at Wadleigh.

WADLEIGH

Sit down, Mr. Bailey.

JOE

I think I'd prefer to stand.

WADLEIGH

Haven't you done quite enough of that out there?
How long was it, Sergeant?

LETWEILER

One hour and five minutes, sir.

JOE

Illegal standing? Sounds like a capital offense to me.

WADLEIGH

You're an American.

JOE

Yes.

WADLEIGH

Americans are always so sarcastic about the law.
Why do you suppose that is? Here on business? Or
pleasure?

Joe removes his wallet and extracts a business card which
Wadleigh reads quickly.

WADLEIGH

Estate planning. Insurance. Business then?

JOE

My firm has an arrangement with Lloyds. I'm here
frequently. Business and pleasure.

WADLEIGH

Passport?

Joe hands him the passport. Wadleigh glances at it, then hands it
and the card to Letweiler, who goes through a door into a
hallway to the telephone. She leaves the door slightly ajar and in
the background, we can see her on the phone.

WADLEIGH

Not many trips abroad for a man who's here
frequently.

JOE

It's a new passport Inspector. That's how we do it.
Every five years. The last one was thoroughly
stamped.

WADLEIGH

I'm sure.

JOE

Is that an example of the investigative powers of
Scotland Yard?

WADLEIGH

No. Just idle curiosity. I take it you're not looking
for Gavin Brand by any chance.

JOE

To sell him insurance? I think he'd be a poor risk.

Joe begins to saunter idly about the room as Letweiler's voice on
the telephone drifts in. Joe's trying to absorb whatever he can.

WADLEIGH

Suppose you tell me what really brings you here,
Mr. Bailey.

JOE

Good God, Inspector, half the press corps of the
western world is out there. And most of Ken-
sington as well.

WADLEIGH

Yes. The reporters stand around gossiping and the
area people take their photographs and move on.
You just stand and stare.

Sergeant Letweiler returns, leaving the door ajar. Through the
now open door we can see a window to the back yard. A
clothesline is visible and on it, a few women's garments and two
scarlet soccer shirts, identical to the ones Joe saw in Hyde Park.
When Joe sees the shirts, it stops him cold.

LETWEILER

Everything checks sir.

WADLEIGH

There you see. Give Mr. Bailey his passport.

55   **JOE'S POINT OF VIEW – THROUGH THE WINDOW**
A middle-aged woman (Mrs. Jenkins) with a laundry basket, takes the laundry—and the red shirts—off the line.

56   **RESUME SCENE**
As Joe watches the shirts disappear. Now he's anxious to get out of the flat.

WADLEIGH

I do hope we haven't inconvenienced you.

JOE

No. Not at all. If it's all right with you, I'll just be running along.

WADLEIGH

Shall we summon a cab for you?

JOE

No, that's not necessary. I'll just be on my way.

WADLEIGH

I'll keep your card if I may.

JOE

Fine. Of course. I'll just let myself out.

Joe hurries to the front hall and heads toward the door, out of the living room.

>   WADLEIGH
>
> That's the fourth insurance salesman. How many
> more can we expect?

57   INT. HALLWAY AND STAIRCASE

Joe is about to exit the house. He sees the staircase leading to the upstairs apartment, and in the opposite direction, the outside door, and beyond it the Constable, his back to Joe. Joe hesitates for a moment then chooses the stairs. He hurries up, two at a time.

58   DOOR AT TOP OF STAIRS

"Jenkins" is written on a card near the bell. Joe rings. He waits for a moment, rings again, and the door opens a bit. The woman Joe saw in the yard opens the door a crack. She's very cautious.

>   MRS. JENKINS
>
> I don't want to talk to no one.

>   JOE
>
> I'm not a reporter.

>   MRS. JENKINS
>
> Fine. That makes two of us who ain't reporters. I
> still don't want to talk to you.

>   JOE
>
>   *(desperate)*
> I'll pay you. I'll give you money.

That offends her enough to open the door a bit to get a look at
Joe.

> MRS. JENKINS
>
> Haven't those people suffered enough? It wasn't her
> that done it, you know. And certainly not the
> boys. You people are vultures.

59 **JOE'S POINT OF VIEW – IN THE APARTMENT**

The garments are in the laundry basket, and the two soccer
shirts are on the table, in a cardboard mailing carton, partially
wrapped in green and white paper. Joe pushes the door open,
and puts his foot in it.

> JOE
>
> Sorry to be the Fuller Brush Man.

> MRS. JENKINS
>
> The what?

60 **INT. JENKINS FLAT**

> JOE
>
> American term.

> MRS. JENKINS
>
> You get out of here. Who invited you in?

Joe moves toward the table and the mailing carton. As he gets
closer he can see an address label on the parcel, tantalizing him.

> JOE
>
> *(trying to calm her and still get to the parcel)*
> I apologize for the intrusion. If I could just have a
> word . . .

MRS. JENKINS

Just where do you think you're going? You stay out
of my house till you're invited in, which will be
never. Oh, you're a right one.

As she speaks, she moves around Joe and back to the table. She
picks up the parcel before Joe can read the address. She swings it
back, about to clobber Joe with it.

As the parcel comes toward him, Joe grabs her wrist.

MRS. JENKINS
(loud)
Oooow! Get your bloody hands off me.

Joe quickly reads the label: Mihkelsson, General Delivery, Main
Post Office, Helsinki, Finland.

JOE

No need to be violent.

He drops her wrist and turns back toward the doorway.

61   DOORWAY

Wadleigh and Letweiler stand in the doorway, watching Joe and
Mrs. Jenkins.

WADLEIGH

Mr. Bailey, I don't believe Mrs. Jenkins has any
need for Estate Planning today.

MRS. JENKINS
(frightened)
Here now. You've brought the police.

WADLEIGH

(soothing)

It's all right.

(to Joe)

Mr. Bailey, are you familiar with the laws of
criminal trespass?

MRS. JENKINS

Out of here. All of you, get out of here. No
criminals and no trespass. All of you out!

JOE

Mrs. Jenkins and I have had a small language
misunderstanding.

MRS. JENKINS

(muttering)

Bloomin' busybody reporters.

WADLEIGH

Mrs. Jenkins, if Mr. Bailey has been disturbing you,
it's your right—

MRS. JENKINS

I don't want no police. I ain't done nothing.

WADLEIGH

It's quite all right.

JOE

(airily, as he passes)

Good-bye Inspector. Sergeant. Sorry to have been a
bother.

62   STAIRCASE – WADLEIGH'S POINT OF VIEW

As Joe bounces down the stairs, out the door, and into the crowd.

63   RESUME SCENE

WADLEIGH

Sergeant. Best to keep an eye on that one.

LETWEILER

Yes, sir.

CUT TO:

64   EXT. HELSINKI – ESTABLISHING – NEXT DAY

The Finnish capital. Busy streets, the central market place and beyond, the harbor with international ship traffic. Bright rising sun.

65   EXT. MAIN POST OFFICE – DAY

The sun overhead. About noon.

66   INT. POST OFFICE

Joe stands near a circular stand-up writing desk not far from the general delivery windows. He's alert, but he looks tired of watching and waiting. The general delivery window does a brisk business, but none of the customers look like Mrs. Brand. Joe glances at the wall clock: 12:50.

He waits, then takes the photo of Mrs. Brand and the children out of his pocket and looks at it for a moment, staring privately.

As he waits, Joe looks around the post office and studies the glass case on the wall behind him, which contains wanted posters. He examines the photos of Finnish thugs and criminals, then looks again at the picture of Mrs. Brand and her children.

The clock now reads 2:30. He's uncomfortable and getting restless.

He continues to watch the line, listening to the Clerk and the Customers converse—all of course in Finnish. The name "Mihkelsson" floats by, and Joe looks up suddenly to see a middle-aged woman (Hilda) accepting and signing for the green-and-white parcel. The woman is definitely not Mrs. Brand. She's Finnish, a little masculine, with short gray hair. She tucks the parcel—beaten up now, with canceled stamps and torn corners—under her arm and starts past Joe, toward the exit.

She leaves the post office, turns to her right and disappears from view.

67   **LONG SHOT—SHOOTING IN, THROUGH THE ENTRANCE**
Joe starts toward CAMERA. He stands in the doorway and looks in the direction the woman took.

68   **JOE'S POINT OF VIEW—STREET OUTSIDE POST OFFICE—DAY**
He sees her moving away with the package under her arm.

69   **CLOSE SHOT—JOE**
Looking off, he quickly starts forward and out of shot.

70   **CLOSE SHOT—PACKAGE—JOE'S MOVING POINT OF VIEW (CHEATED CLOSER)**
CAMERA follows her as she walks. The screen is practically filled with the package under her arm.

71   **HIGH SHOT–MARKET PLACE–HELSINKI HARBOR–
DAY**

The market is filled with noontime activity. Hilda threads her
way through the crowd.

72   **CLOSE SHOT–JOE**

Following.

73   **MARKET PLACE–PACKAGE**

As Hilda stops for a moment at a produce stand. The package
dominates the screen, but we can see Hilda buying tomatoes and
grapes. When the package moves on, it's with two bags of
produce.

74   **JOE**

Watching. Hanging back, but following.

75   **THE PACKAGE**

As Hilda walks idly through the marketplace. Her hand plunges
into one of the produce bags and we see a ripe tomato removed.
Then, after it's out of view for a moment, tomato juice and a few
seeds drip down and spatter across the parcel.

76   **OUTDOOR STAGE**

She stops near the outdoor theater on the esplanade of the
marketplace.

A group of Folk Dancers are performing. We see just their legs
and the bottoms of their costumes.

77   **JOE**

Nearby. Watching.

78   **PACKAGE**

In front of the stage. As Hilda watches the dancers, she puts the parcel and the produce down for a moment to applaud.

79   **JOE**

In the background, also applauding, keeping his eye on the package.

80   **PACKAGE**

Flops down onto the ground. As Hilda gets up to leave, she takes only the produce, accidently leaving the package.

81   **JOE**

Surprised. Unsure what to do as the parcel lies deserted.

82   **PACKAGE**

Masculine hands pick it up and hurry out of the shot.

83   **JOE**

Worried. Watching.

84   **LONG SHOT**

An Usher from the outdoor theatre hands Hilda the package. She's surprised that she lost it, thanks him, and then moves on.

85   **JOE**

Relieved. He continues to follow her.

86 BUS DEPOT

Hilda—with the package—boards a bus marked Savonlinna. She takes a seat by the window, and puts the parcel prominently on the luggage rack above her seat. It can be seen through the window.

87 JOE–LONG SHOT

He hurries across the plaza toward the bus depot.

88 JOE AND BUS DRIVER–LONG SHOT

The Driver stands next to his bus while Joe speaks to him. We can't hear what they say, but the driver raises several fingers, then points to his watch, indicating the hour.

DISSOLVE TO:

89 INT. BUS–TRAVELING–DAY

Close on the parcel in the luggage rack as the bus bounces along the road out of Helsinki into the countryside. CAMERA stays on the parcel, but we can hear the sounds of the passengers, of the motors, and other traffic noises.

90 INT. BUS–TRAVELING–VARIOUS ANGLES OF THE PARCEL–DAY

Revealing the countryside through the bus windows, and in the rear of the bus, keeping his eye on the parcel, Joe. He has an overnight bag with him.

DRIVER (v.o.)

Savonlinna.

The bus comes to a stop and the parcel is removed from the rack. The passengers leave the bus.

91   EXT. SAVONLINNA – DAY

A resort and fishing village a few hours out of Helsinki. The bus stops at the dock. Some of the passengers go into town and others go to the end of the pier to board a ferry that goes across the bay.

Hilda and the parcel head for the boat. Joe follows. CAMERA continues close on the parcel.

92   EXT. FERRY – DAY

Hilda boards the boat and puts the package down next to her. The shot loosens to reveal the other passengers, including Joe.

93   PARCEL

As it bounces up and down with the ferry, moving along the shore line.

94   EXT. FERRY AND FIRST STOP

Shooting from the boat, as it docks at the first stop, a promontory in the bay, about a half mile from Savonlinna.

When the ferry is moored, a few of the passengers, including Hilda, get off.

Joe follows Hilda and the little knot of disembarking passengers. Hilda detaches herself from the group and walks to the other side of the jetty.

95   STAIRS LEADING DOWN TO THE WATER

She steps down off the jetty, and heads for the water, moving out of Joe's sight.

96   JOE

Hurries to the jetty, following her.

97   WATER AT BOTTOM OF STAIRS—JOE'S POINT OF VIEW

A motor launch is waiting. It's piloted by another Finnish woman (Olga) who is about Hilda's age, but stouter and stronger, and a little more mannish. Olga's irritated, apparently because she's been waiting for a long time. She pulls Hilda into the launch. Joe hears the last of their conversation.

> OLGA
>
> You waste time. You dawdle.

> HILDA
>
> I was shopping. I got some grapes.

> OLGA
>
> I don't want grapes. Just hurry.

Olga starts the engine and the launch pulls away.

98   JOE

Watching it move out into the bay. He turns and hurries back across the dock.

99   FISHING SUPPLY AND BOAT RENTAL PLACE—JOE'S POINT OF VIEW

Joe hurries toward it. The boatman is tying flies, to sell to the fishermen.

Joe fumbles through a "Finnish For Travelers" book.

JOE

(laboriously)

Mista voin vuokrata moottori veneen?

The boat man laughs.

BOATMAN

I could do more Englanti a little.

JOE

Good.
(points to a small motor boat)
How much? Real quick. For the day.

BOATMAN

(starting to prepare the boat)
Sixty marks.

JOE

(flipping through the book)
How much in American?

BOATMAN

About seven pounds, English.

JOE

Here's twenty bucks.

The boatman pulls the starting cable, accepts the twenty-dollar bill and helps Joe into the boat.

As Joe heads out into the bay, the boatman stands on the dock examining the twenty-dollar bill.

100   **EXT. BAY – DAY**

Joe moves out into the open water in his rented boat

101   **JOE'S POINT OF VIEW – THE WOMEN'S MOTOR
LAUNCH**

Far ahead of him, but still visible.

102   **JOE**

Trying to make the rented boat go faster.

103   **WOMEN**

As they go around a curve in the bay, momentarily out of sight.

104   **JOE**

Nervous, as he nears the curve.

105   **HIS POINT OF VIEW – AROUND THE CURVE**
Nothing. Open Water.

106   **JOE**

Staring at the void.

                         JOE

   Damn!

                                          CUT TO:

107   **INT. HOTEL LOBBY – SAVONLINNA – DAY**
Joe enters and walks through the lobby toward the registration
desk.

108   **REGISTRATION DESK**

> JOE

English?

> CLERK

Yes. Hello.

> JOE

I'd like a room please. Is it possible to have it on
the water?

> CLERK

Yes, of course. Your name?

> JOE

Bailey. Joseph Bailey.

> CLERK

Oh yes, Mr. Bailey. Did you have a reservation?

> JOE

No, no. Is it a problem?

> CLERK

I thought we had made an error. A package
arrived for you. But I couldn't find your
reservation.

> JOE

A package?

> CLERK

I'll send it up. Sign here, please.

                    JOE

                (as he signs)
Fine. One more thing. Do you have binoculars I
could rent?

                   CLERK

Of course. Are you a bird watcher, Mr. Bailey?

                    JOE

            (hands him the signed card)
Depends on the bird.

The clerk smiles and rings for the bellman.

                                        CUT TO:

109   INT. HOTEL ROOM

Joe stands at the window, binoculars in hand, looking out the
window across the bay.

His bag is open on the bed.

He puts down the binoculars, sits on the bed, and takes out the
photo of Mrs. Brand. He stares at it, studying it, trying to
fathom it.

There's a knock at the door. He puts the picture in his pocket
and goes to the door.

110   DOORWAY

A Bellboy has a large package with Joe's name on it.

                  BELLBOY

For you, sir.

Joe accepts it, tips the bellboy, closes the door, and puts the package on the bed. He takes off the wrapping paper.

It's a wicker picnic hamper and when Joe opens it, he sees it's filled with food, paper plates, napkins, etc. Everything has the 21 logo on it.

The food is very elaborate—cracked crab in steaming dry ice and a bottle of Pouilly fumé.

Joe smiles until he discovers what's beneath the food: a gun, broken down into separate parts: stock, grip, and telescopic sight. And with it, a box of cartridges.

Joe looks at the pieces of the gun, touching them, examining each part.

He takes another look at the photo of Mrs. Brand, savoring it. Then he snaps the gun together.

CUT TO:

111   EXT. THE BAY–DAY
Joe sits in another small boat in the middle of the bay, looking at the islands through his binoculars.

The gun is in his pocket. He checks it from time to time. He drifts and continues to scan the water and the distant islands, including the jetty where the ferry stopped. The gun makes him uneasy.

112   EXT. DOCK–OVERLOOKING THE BAY–DAY
A slightly overweight man in a rumpled suit, who is at once decorous and yet a little seedy, stands on the pier, watching Joe cruise the lake. This is Sergeant Linnankoski of the Savonlinna Police.

113   THE BAY–JOE

Cruising. In the far distance, he gets a quick glimpse of an outboard boat with what appears to be two small boys, as it skims across the water and disappears from view beyond the next curve, a promontory of land. They go by quickly, but it looks as if they're wearing red shirts. Joe moves off in the direction of the dinghy.

114   THE DOCK

Linnankoski can see only Joe and not the boys.

115   THE BAY–JOE

CAMERA travels with the boat as Joe speeds across the lake. He enters a narrow connecting passageway leading to a larger area of water. Joe arrives at the spot where he saw the boys' boat, but now there's nothing.

116   LINNANKOSKI

Nothing left to watch, so he turns and leaves, sauntering back toward the town.

117   JOE

He raises his binoculars and slowly pans from left to right. As he does, we hear a distant outboard motor, to his left, and behind him. As the sound gets closer, he lowers his binoculars and starts to turn his head as CAMERA zooms back into a looser angle revealing the boys speeding in an arc around the stern of Joe's boat, into clear view. The boat is the one that picked Hilda up at the ferry stop, and the boys, Roy and Neal Brand, ages eight and ten are wearing scarlet soccer shirts. They wave at Joe as they pass, and he waves back. Their boat goes out of the shot, and Joe follows it.

118   OBJECTIVE SHOT – THE LAKE

From a safe distance, Joe follows the boys. When the boys reach another curve in the shoreline, their boat momentarily disappears from view. But when Joe goes around the same curve, the boys are in view again. And beyond them, a small island, with a pier and a few outbuildings visible. The boys, about 100 yards from the island's pier, are moving their boat in dizzying circles, each of them taking turns at the tiller. They shriek and yell, obviously having a great time.

119   JOE

He watches the boys for a moment, looks off beyond them at the island with its house, and makes a decision. He turns away from the boys, to the fuel tank of his outboard motor.

120   OUTBOARD MOTOR – CLOSE SHOT

We see Joe's hands opening the gasket at the bottom of the fuel tank, letting the gasoline gush out into the lake. CAMERA pans from Joe's hand to:

121   EXT. THE ISLAND – DAY

Standing on the shore line, Olga is watching Joe. She's holding a laundry basket and she's too far away to know exactly what Joe is doing, but it's clear to her he's doing something. She turns and goes up the path.

122   JOE

Shooting from the prow to the stern, Joe turns toward CAMERA and revs up the motor. The boat moves forward, parallel to the shore for a few yards, sputters and dies.

                        JOE

                (yelling across the water)
    Hello. Hello. S.O.S.

123   **THE BOYS**

Excited by the break in their routine, start shouting back. Neal
is the older one.

                        NEAL

                   (yelling back)
    Hello. Do you speak English?

                        ROY

    What's the matter?

124   **JOE**

                        JOE

    Ran out of fuel. Can you help?

125   **BOYS**

As they head toward Joe. Neal scrambles to the stern, with a
line in his hand.

                        NEAL

    Catch this.

126   **BOTH BOATS**

As the boys near Joe, Neal tosses the line. Joe catches it and ties
it to his prow. The boys speak at once, excited.

                        NEAL

    Can you tie a bowline?

> ROY
>> *(Repeating; enjoying the excitement)*
>
> S.O.S. We can fix it.

> JOE
>
> Thanks, mates.

When Joe has tied his boat to theirs, the boys start to tow him to the island. They call back to him as they do.

> NEAL
>
> Rudder to port, and we'll take her in.

> JOE
>> *(yelling back)*
>
> Aye, aye, Captain.

> Roy
>> *(repeating)*
>
> Aye, aye.

127   JOE

Watching the boys and trying to scan the island as he gets closer.

128   COMPREHENSIVE VIEW OF ISLAND—
STARTING FROM JOE'S POINT OF VIEW—DAY

As Joe is towed closer to the island it starts to come into clear view. Near the pier, there's a sauna and woodshed, with smoke coming from the chimney. Beyond that, a path leading through the woods to several other structures. Those buildings, which can't be seen clearly yet, are a main house, a caretaker's cottage and a storage shed.

129 THE BOATS

Nearing the dock. The boys are excited.

Joe waits, trying to look calm, studying the island. He puts his hand in his pocket, touching the gun.

> NEAL
>
> We'll pull in here. We'll get it fixed.

Joe doesn't answer. He stares at the island's shoreline, as he gets closer.

130 ISLAND

Joe is close enough to see the activity on the shore. It's sylvan, pastoral, and with the activity, like a Brueghel painting.

131 OLGA

With the laundry, near the woodshed.

132 HILDA

Walking on the path from the house, down toward the shore.

133 WOODCHOPPER

A powerful man, who does the heavy chores. He's at the rear of the woodshed, splitting logs. He's bare-chested and wielding a large axe. He chops smoothly and rhythmically. He looks up for a moment, and then continues working.

134 OLGA AND HILDA

Look up at the pier, off camera, and then move away.

135   **THE PIER**

As the boats dock. Both boats are together now, and Joe ties his to the dock with the towline.

> NEAL
>
> I'll be right back
>
> *(to Roy)*
>
> You wait.

> ROY
>
> I want to go, too.

> JOE
>
> You both go. I'll be all right.

The boys scramble off, up the path.

136   **JOE**

He gets out of his boat, stands on the jetty, and looks over the island.

He touches the gun in his pocket and then walks across the jetty and onto the shore.

137   **ISLAND – WITH JOE**

His hand in his pocket, Joe moves along the path. He stops at the sauna and opens the door.

138   **INT. SAUNA – JOE'S POINT OF VIEW**

Empty.

139   **RESUME SCENE**

He continues on toward the main house, up the path, which curves into the trees.

140   **MAIN HOUSE – JOE'S POINT OF VIEW**

The door gets larger as Joe walks toward it.

141   **RESUME SCENE**

Joe nervously grips the gun in his pocket as the door gets bigger and bigger.

142   **WINDOW OF MAIN HOUSE**

A little way from the door. Eyes appear at the window looking out, watching Joe.

143   **JOE**

Feeling the eyes on him. He stops before he gets to the door and turns toward the window. He walks along the side of the house toward the window.

144   **WINDOW**

The eyes are gone as Joe arrives. He looks in.

145   **INT. HOUSE THROUGH WINDOW –**
       JOE'S POINT OF VIEW

It's a bedroom. On the bed, a man's clothes are laid out neatly. He sees them and his hand goes back to his pocket, onto the gun.

146   **FRONT OF HOUSE**

The door opens and Joe turns quickly to see the eyes that a moment ago were at the window. It's Carla Brand, the woman he's come halfway around the world for. He stares for a moment, unsure what to do now that he's found her.

Carla's wary, polite but cautious.

Silence as Joe looks at her for a moment. His self possession apparently crumbling a bit.

He walks toward her, the hand which has been on the gun, comes out of his pocket in greeting.

147   **TWO SHOT–JOE AND CARLA**

JOE

Hello. I've had some boat trouble.

CARLA

(re Joe at the window)
And a little trouble finding the door, too.

JOE

I was admiring your house. You're a pleasant surprise.

CARLA

Why is that?

JOE

I guess I was expecting a fisherman or a fisher-man's wife . . . or a boat mechanic . . . I don't know what I was expecting.

CARLA

That's the surprise, that I'm not a mechanic?

JOE

The surprise is that you're so beautiful.

CARLA

Is that why you're staring at me?

JOE

No, no. I don't mean to be. I'm sorry. I can't seem
to stop myself.

CARLA

(trying to change the subject)
If my sons can't fix your boat, they can tow you
to the ferry. I don't mean to be rude, but it isn't a
good time for visitors.

JOE

You're very lovely.

CARLA

Please stop looking at me like that. It makes me
uncomfortable. It's so intense. You make me feel
. . . naked.

JOE

I apologize. But I have to say the prospect isn't
altogether—

CARLA

I'm curious, do you always talk to strangers like
this?

JOE

No. I think it's that everyone here is a Finn.
You're not.

CARLA

(smiling; intrigued but wary)
You work very hard at being charming, don't
you? I'm sure you can do better than that.

                    JOE

I hope I get the chance to try. Can I at least
admire your house?

Joe begins moving along the house toward the window, admiring it.

148   **FLASH CUT – WOODCHOPPER**
In a clearing beyond the house, chopping with the same steady
rhythm.

149   **JOE AND CARLA**
Joe nears the window.

                    JOE

It's beautifully crafted.

                  CARLA
                  (dryly)
Yes. Just like the Finns.

                    JOE

It's simple, but so carefully made.

When he gets to the window, he tries to see in for another look
at the man's clothing on the bed.

150   **WINDOW**
The blinds are drawn shut.

151   **JOE**

As he turns back to Carla an arrow thuds into his chest. It has a rubber suction cup on the end, but it frightens the hell out of Joe.

152   **ROY AND NEAL**

Neal with a gasoline can and Roy with a toy bow and arrow approach.

> ROY
>
> I didn't mean . . .

153   **ALL FOUR – FRONT OF HOUSE**

> CARLA
>
> *(furious)*
>
> I will not have that kind of behavior. If you can't learn to play with your toys properly . . .

> NEAL
>
> Roy did it.

> JOE
>
> There's no harm done. I'm really all right.

> CARLA
>
> I don't care! I will not have that sort of thing.

> ROY
>
> I said I'm sorry.

Joe laughs. Carla smiles a bit.

> NEAL
>
> What's so funny?

CARLA

It's nothing. There's a lot of apologizing in the air.

Joe smiles at Carla.

JOE

Apologies aren't the only thing in the air.

CARLA

(refusing to acknowledge it)
I think you should leave now.

JOE

I've been through so much with your sons I feel
I know you. but I've been so busy apologizing,
I haven't introduced myself. I'm Joe Bailey.

CARLA

I'm Carla Langstead. And these are my wild
Indians. The little one is Roy. The slightly less
little one is Neal.

JOE

You're good sailor boys. And I thank you for the
rescue.
          (hands them back the arrow)
I'll live.

NEAL

We fixed your boat. You were just out of petrol.
You should always check it before you go out.

JOE

You're right.

ROY

(to Carla)

Does he have to pay for it? We put in two litres.

CARLA

Certainly not.

ROY

Petrol costs money.

JOE

(laughing; takes out his wallet)

Can't argue with that.

CARLA

Oh, no. Please.

NEAL

(looking at the money)

Finnish money? Don't you have any real stuff?

JOE

I guess you haven't been here very long.

CARLA

(avoiding the suggestion)

Long enough for them to have better manners.
Don't pay any attention.

JOE

(hands them assorted currencies and coins)

Here fellows. Some Finnish, some English, and
some American. Not for the gas, but for the
rescue work.

ROY AND NEAL

Thanks!

They busy themselves counting and dividing the money.

JOE

Mrs. Langstead, if I don't do this, I'll hate myself
later, so let me just ask you where Mr. Langstead
is.

CARLA

My husband and I were divorced some time ago.

JOE

I see.

CARLA

I don't discuss it . . . the boys. I'm sure you
understand.

JOE

Then you must let me take you to lunch. All
of you. I'm at a hotel with a name I can't
pronounce. It's the only one in Savonlinna. Come
join me. And then afterward—

CARLA

Oh, no. Mr. Bailey, my life is very complicated.
No. I'm afraid I can't.

She's cut off by the clamor of the children.

ROY AND NEAL

Oh yes. Yes. Please mother, please. Oh please,
please . . .

154   FLASH CUT–OLGA

At the bedroom window. Watching and listening.

155   RESUME SCENE

> JOE

You must let me repay your kindness properly.

> CARLA

It's really impossible.

The boys dance around their mother pleading and tugging at her skirt.

> ROY AND NEAL

I want to go to the mainland. Oh, please, please.

> JOE

I'd have made the invitation more intimate if I thought I could get away with it.

> CARLA

You're very forward, aren't you?

> JOE

Not always. I made it for all three of you, so you couldn't say no.

Carla gives a little smile and shrugs helplessly.

> JOE

Wonderful. Say noon at the hotel.

> NEAL
> *(to Joe)*

Are you going now?

CARLA

Yes he is. You make sure his boat starts.

JOE

I'm glad I met you. I intend to take this as a sign
of encouragement.

CARLA

(smiling despite herself)
Now go! Good-bye.

Joe and the boys walk down the path toward the dock.

156   **FLASH CUT – WOODCHOPPER**

He glances at Joe as he passes.

157   **THE PIER – JOE AND THE BOYS**

ROY

You know what this island is called?

JOE

No. Tell me.

ROY

Squirrel Island. But that's not what we call it. We
call it Danger Island.

JOE

Is this the only way to get onto Danger Island?

NEAL

No. You can come ashore lots of places. We like to
do it on the other side.

ROY

Nobody sees you.

JOE

(easy; casual)

Has anybody else come to visit you here?

ROY

Not yet. But we're waiting for—

NEAL

We're not supposed to tell.

Joe smiles at the information and gets into his boat and starts the motor.

JOE

I'll see you tomorrow fellows. Thanks for the help.

ROY

Can we have anything we want for lunch?

JOE

Anything.

He pulls out into the open water. The boys wave good-bye.

158   CARLA

Standing on the path, a little way from the house, at the point where she can see the jetty, but not be seen. She stands there for a moment watching Joe leave.

She turns and walks back toward the house. CAMERA follows her up the path. She's pensive, preoccupied.

159   INT. KITCHEN OF HOUSE

As Carla enters. Olga and Hilda are waiting for her. They look very serious.

OLGA

Sit down, Mrs. Brand.

During the following: Olga goes to the table, takes a cigarette, lights it, and begins to pace before Carla, who sinks into an easy chair.

CARLA

Before you start in, I tried to say no, but the children wanted it. I couldn't just say—

OLGA

They wanted their favorite red shirts, too. I said no, you said yes. So we took the chance and sent away for the favorite red shirts. Suppose now they decide to burn down the house? Do we give them matches?

CARLA

But what's the harm? A day in Savonlinna. He's lonely and he was trying to be nice.

OLGA

The only situation without harm is the one in which your husband arrives here safely, picks up his wife and children, and travels without incident across the border. That is why you've agreed to come here.

CARLA

Persuaded to come.

OLGA

You are not here to get involved with strange men
on the whim of your children.

HILDA

You were flirting with him.

CARLA

What do you want me to do, throw rocks at him?
Men flirt all the time. Frankly, I enjoyed it. He
was so nervous. What would you know about
flirting anyway.

OLGA

Call it what you like, but you were carrying on
like a school girl.
(imitates; mocks)
"I'm sorry. You're sorry. So sorry."

CARLA

I see what this is about. You're jealous.

OLGA

Not jealous. Cautious.

CARLA

You can't expect two little boys to stay cooped up
on this island or ride in circles on the lake, hour
after hour, day after day.

OLGA

I don't expect anything of them. They are children. But you aren't. You know how valuable
your husband is.

CARLA

Please. Not a political lecture. I can't bear it.

OLGA

No lecture. I don't have to remind you that the continued well-being of your children—

CARLA

That's right, you don't have to remind me.
(*gets to her feet abruptly, runs her hands through her hair*)
What do you want me to do?

OLGA

Write him a little note of regret. Any excuse. Hilda will take it across the lake and deliver it to the hotel.

CARLA

The children . . . I feel so awful.

OLGA

Maybe I can make you feel less awful. Hilda, tell her.

HILDA

I'm sure he was on the bus from Helsinki with me yesterday. And the ferry, too.

OLGA

And he just happened to run out of gas at this island and none of the others.

HILDA

And you saw him look in the window.

OLGA

Mrs. Brand, even as naive as you are, you can't
believe in so many coincidences. If he comes here
again on any pretext, I will deal with him as
harshly as necessary.

Carla says nothing more. She gets up abruptly and goes to the
table, opens a drawer, takes out a writing tablet and pen, and
begins to write a note to Joe. Olga and Hilda watch her.

CUT TO:

160   INT. HOTEL SAUNA – DAY

A large modern sauna, enough room for several people. Joe sits
on the bench trying to enjoy the heat. He's wrapped in a hotel
towel, talking to the Sauna Attendant. They're having a language problem. They talk at the same time.

ATTENDANT

(In Finnnish; getting frustrated)
I want to put the soap on you. That's all. Then I'll
scrub it off. It's good for you. Why are you
making such a fuss? Just lie down on your
stomach.

JOE

I don't speak Finnish . . . Je ne comprends pas . . .
No hablo . . .

161   SAUNA DOOR

As Sergeant Linnankoski, the police officer who was watching
Joe from the dock, enters. He's also wrapped in a towel.

LINNANKOSKI

(precise, accented English)

Perhaps I can be of some assistance here.

162   WIDER SHOT – SAUNA

JOE

You certainly can.

LINNANKOSKI

(to Attendant; in Finnish)

What is the problem?

ATTENDANT

(a torrent of Finnish)

Does he only want half a sauna? He won't let me do my job. I can't spend all day with him.

LINNANKOSKI

(in Finnish)

Yes, yes. I understand. Calm down. It's not your fault.

(to Joe, in English)

He wants to scrub you. It's really very pleasant.

JOE

Tell him it sounds terrific, but right now I'm comfortable. Another time for the deluxe job.

LINNANKOSKI

(in Finnish)

No more today. The gentleman is content.

ATTENDANT

(in Finnish; miffed)
What good is half? Americans!

The attendant gathers up his things and leaves.

JOE

What did he say?

LINNANKOSKI

You are not his favorite customer. And America is
not his favorite nation.

JOE

And you're the perfect diplomat.

LINNANKOSKI

(offers his hand)
Detective Sergeant Linnankoski of the Savonlinna
Police Department.

JOE

(shaking hands)
I'm Joe Bailey. Do you always come here at this
time of day?

LINNANKOSKI

In Finland we don't need a reason to sauna. I
come here sometimes, other places too. This is a
fine facility. The best in Savonlinna I would say.
All electric. Some of the older ones are primitive
with gas pipes. They can be dangerous. I enjoy
this one.

JOE

And it made it possible for us to meet.

LINNANKOSKI

That is a constructive way to look at it.

JOE

Though we were going to meet eventually anyway, no?

LINNANKOSKI

(parrying the remark)
In Savonlinna, everyone meets everyone.

JOE

What do you want, Sergeant?

LINNANKOSKI

Do I want something?

JOE

I think you do.

LINNANKOSKI

You're on a vacation trip here?

JOE

Strictly.

LINNANKOSKI

(a velvet-gloved unmistakable warning)
We abhor trouble of any kind in Finland. That is
why we are a neutral country in a polarized
world. And here in Savonlinna, I like to think

LINNANKOSKI (Cont'd)

that I dedicate myself to seeing that visitors from
other lands not only stay out of trouble themselves, but never inflict it on others.

Joe meets the man's eyes, unflinchingly.

JOE

I find it reassuring, Sergeant, to know that a man
of your purpose and dedication is always so close
at hand.

LINNANKOSKI

I thank the Lord that my superior cannot hear us
now, Mr. Bailey. He does not like me to work
when I am off duty. Of course, as long as you are
here in Savonlinna . . .

JOE

You'll be watching over me, right?

LINNANKOSKI

In spirit, at the very least. Let me call the
attendant back for you. I think you'll enjoy it.
(he raps on the door for the attendant)
Sauna is done simply for pleasure. You should
have some, on your vacation.

The attendant returns.

LINNANKOSKI

(in Finnish)
Give Mr. Bailey the works. He's ready now.
(in English)
Till the next time, Mr. Bailey, if there is one.

JOE

I have a feeling we can bet on it.

Linnankoski turns and leaves.

The attendant pushes Joe down on his stomach—he's not taking any chances this time.

ATTENDANT

(in Finnish)

I'll give you more than you deserve. And you're
lucky to get it.

He begins sloshing Joe with soapy water, and scrubbing him with his brush. He sings a Finnish song as he works.

Joe looks pained.

CUT TO:

163   INT. HOTEL ROOM

Joe sits on the bed alone. He's staring at the photograph of Carla. He looks at it for a very long time.

CUT TO:

164   EXT. LAKE—NEXT DAY

Joe is coasting toward the shore of the island in his rented boat. The jetty and buildings are far to his left. He's coming ashore at an unused part of the island.

165   REVERSE—JOE IN BOAT

Shooting from the shore, as the boat glides the last few feet, through some reeds and rocks. Joe gets out, pulls the boat up on the sand and secures it.

He puts his hand in his pocket, touching the gun, then reaches for something: The wicker hamper from 21.

As he starts into the woods, in the direction of the house. His eyes dart back and forth, searching, He hears something in the distance and stops for a moment. We can hear the faint sound of an outboard motor, going away from the island.

> CARLA'S VOICE
> *(calling)*
> Not too far. Not in the open water.

166   WOODS – TOWARD THE HOUSE

Joe, carrying the hamper and regularly feeling for the gun in his pocket, goes into the woods. He's approaching the house from the rear. He moves as quietly as he can, looking for Brand or any sign of him.

167   WOODS – NEAR A CLEARING

CAMERA moves with Joe as he discovers a path and follows it. The outboard motor in the distance is fainter now. When he comes to the edge of the clearing, he stops close to CAMERA, as he sees something.

168   HIS POINT OF VIEW – NEAR THE CLEARING
        BESIDE THE LAKE

Carla is stretched out in the clearing, an open book in her hands. A picnic lunch is next to her. She's looking off toward the lake.

169   RESUME SCENE

Joe looks out at the lake too.

170 **HIS POINT OF VIEW – THE LAKE**

Far out on the lake, Roy and Neal are fishing, their boat at anchor.

171 **RESUME SCENE – CLEARING WITH LAKE BEYOND**

Joe starts slowly toward Carla. When she senses his presence, she sits up and looks around. And when she sees Joe, she gets very tense.

>   JOE
>
> Hello.

>   CARLA
>
> Didn't you get my message?

>   JOE
>
> I did. I decided if you don't want to come to
> lunch, lunch will come to you.

>   CARLA
>   *(dryly)*
>
> I've eaten, thank you.

>   JOE
>
> But not like this.

He opens the hamper. It's filled with Finnish delicacies—open face sandwiches, paté, etc.

>   CARLA
>
> Where on earth did you get all that?

>   JOE
>
> I had it flown in from 21.

CARLA

(starting to smile)

Well you can fly it back. I canceled lunch because
I didn't want to see you. And I still don't.

JOE

I don't believe you.
(offers her some of the food)
Reindeer sandwich?

CARLA

What?

JOE

I had it made specially. It's a little bit of Donner
and Blitzen on rye.

CARLA

(laughing)

You're very funny.

JOE

Well, if running out of gas didn't do it, maybe
jokes will.

CARLA

No.

JOE

Is it your husband?

CARLA

If you must know, my housekeeper thinks you're
not to be trusted.

JOE

With what?

CARLA

She feels you followed Hilda to Savonlinna from
Helsinki.

JOE

Look Carla, I'm exactly what I seem to be.
            (takes out a business card and hands
                    it to her)
I'm in the insurance business. I don't follow
housekeepers.

CARLA

Fine. I'm glad to believe you. And now, please
leave.

She gets up to go. He takes her hand and pulls her back down.

JOE

Don't.

CARLA

I'd rather you didn't touch me.

JOE

I'd rather I did.

He kisses her. Hard. On the mouth. She bristles and pulls back.

CARLA

You have no right to do that.

JOE

I don't know a lot about love, but Carla, I'm
drawn to you and I can't believe you don't feel
some of the same thing.

CARLA

I don't trust you.

JOE

Trust your feelings.

CARLA

Now you're an amateur psychologist. That's paperback rubbish.

JOE

Shhh . . .

He kisses her again. Even more intensely. She's confused by it,
but despite herself, she begins to respond. The kiss deepens and
they hang on the edge of intense feeling until Carla pulls away.

CARLA

Just go away. I can't be here like this. No.

JOE

(tender; trying to soothe her)
Carla . . . easy . . . I want to be your friend.

CARLA

(not buying it)
This is an awful mistake. I don't want to kiss you
or anybody else. I just want you to let me and my
babies alone.

JOE

I don't believe you.

CARLA

I don't care what you believe. I can see right
through you. You're ridiculous . . . and I want you
out of here. I won't be responsible for what
happens to you.
(getting upset)
I don't care. None of it matters . . . none of it.
Don't touch me . . . get away from here. I want
you out of here. Take your preposterous food and
go away. I know what you are. And it's going to
get you killed and you deserve it . . . you hear
me, you deserve whatever happens to you.
(and tears)
Let me alone . . . oh, everything's upside down.

JOE

What is it? What's upside down?

CARLA

You're working for the British, aren't you?

JOE

I just gave you my business card.

CARLA

Then you're a reporter.

JOE

Why don't you believe I find you attractive. You're
a beautiful woman with two appealing children.
And we're all in some make-believe country.

Carla, this is how people find each other. It might
be paperback psychology, but it's true.

He starts to kiss her again, but she stops him and speaks.

CARLA

You kiss better than you lie. You know who I am,
and who my husband is too. So just stop it. It's
very insulting you know. You kiss me and I'm
supposed to melt and tell you everything. Your
ego is astonishing. I don't want to kiss you. I don't
want to make love with you. I don't even want to
know you.

JOE

Of course I know who you are. Your picture's in
every paper in the world. Does that mean I can't
also find you attractive?

CARLA

(wrought up; near tears)
Look you . . . whatever you are. I have had a very
rough time. Maybe you know who I am, but you
don't know what it's like to try to raise two boys
with their father in . . .
(can't say it)
away . . . like that.

JOE

I want to make things easier for you, not harder.

CARLA

Oh damn you. I don't believe you for a minute.
You know that's what I want. What I need. But

not from you. You're going to go back and put it
all in some magazine.

                    JOE
         (intense; the truth for once and he's able to
                 say it strongly)
I am not a reporter.

                   CARLA
Then whatever you are.

                    JOE
I don't believe you love him. I don't believe it.

He takes her in his arms again and kisses her. She responds,
clutching at him, hungrily. CAMERA moves around their embrace, and pans off them to Roy and Neal, standing at the edge
of the clearing, watching.

                   NEAL
Wow! Hey mom, that's a good one.

Carla jumps back.

                    JOE
I thought you guys were fishing.

                    ROY
We were.
         (holds up a string of fish)
Look.

Carla grabs the boys and pulls them to her. She's shaking.

                    ROY
You kissed him, huh?

The boys start making smooching sounds, giggling and enjoying themselves.

CARLA

Come on. We'll go home now.
(to Joe)
Go away. If you have any feeling for me at all—
no matter what your plan was—if you have any
human feeling at all, go away.

She turns and walks out of the shot, with her sons. Joe watches her go.

When he's alone, he looks down at the wicker hamper for a moment, then kicks it viciously breaking it, spilling the contents.

CUT TO:

172   BOAT

As Joe is leaving the island. He's pensive, lost in thought, unaware he's being watched.

173   OLGA

Standing on the shore, watching Joe leave.

CUT TO:

174   INT. HOTEL ROOM—DAY

Joe sits on his bed examining his pistol. He breaks it down and then snaps it together again. He stares at it for a moment and then walks to the window and looks out at the buildings below, and the lake beyond.

175   HIS POINT OF VIEW – POLICE STATION

Carla, grim faced, with Roy and Neal in tow, walks up to the Patrolman in front of the police station. He points toward the station and Carla and the boys go inside.

176   RESUME SCENE

Joe hurries back to his bed, lifts up a corner of the mattress, and stashes the gun there.

He grabs his jacket and hurries out of the hotel room.

                                                        CUT TO:

177   INT. POLICE STATION – WAITING AREA

Roy and Neal are sitting on a bench opposite the Desk Sergeant. They're waiting as patiently as they can.

                         ROY
                  (to the Sergeant)
           Can I put your handcuffs on my brother?

                    DESK SERGEANT
                     (all business)
No.

                         ROY
Then can I put them on you?

                    DESK SERGEANT
Shh.

As the Sergeant scowls, CAMERA pans off the boys toward an office door marked "Detective Sergeant Linnankoski." The top half of the door is pebbled glass. We can see silhouettes, and hear voices inside.

178   INT. OFFICE

Carla is talking with Linnankoski who is accompanied by an Aide.

Linnankoski hold's Joe's business card. He looks at it, turns it over, runs his fingers over the surface.

> CARLA
>
> He seems to confine most of his boating to wherever on the lake my boys happen to be. I wouldn't want anything to spoil my vacation. You understand.

> LINNANKOSKI
>
> And you want me to prevent this American, this Mr. Bailey, from coming near your children?

> CARLA
>
> I wouldn't expect that, Sergeant. But I wondered whether you have means to look into his background. To verify what he's told me about himself.

> LINNANKOSKI
>
> *(still looking at Joe's card)*
>
> This is a very fine business card. Engraved. We don't have anything nearly so elegant here in Savonlinna. He's told you the truth about himself.

> CARLA
>
> You know?

> LINNANKOSKI
>
> I can even add a few personal details. He's thirty-eight. He is divorced—from his first and only wife. Five years ago. He has no police record and

he is indeed in the insurance business. So I
suspect your children are safe unless you're afraid
they could be talked into buying policies they
can't afford.

                    CARLA

How do you know all that?

                LINNANKOSKI

Mrs. Langstead, Finland is a neutral country.
We've found it easy to cultivate the appearance of
disinterest bordering on ignorance. It's a cloak
behind which we hide an obsessive nosiness.

                    CARLA

But surely you don't investigate every tourist, do
you?

                LINNANKOSKI

We have a certain selectivity.

                    CARLA
                (smiling; rising)
Thank you, Sergeant.

                LINNANKOSKI

It's my pleasure.

                                        CUT TO:

179   **EXT. POLICE STATION**

Joe is pacing in front of the station, waiting, worried about
what's going on inside. The patroman in front keeps his eye
on Joe.

                                        CUT TO:

180   INT. LINNANKOSKI'S OFFICE

He's with his aide.

> LINNANKOSKI
>
> It's just fine. He'll follow her until she leads him
> to her husband.

> AIDE
>
> Should we follow her then?

> LINNANKOSKI
>
> Oh no. Then Brand will never show up. No we
> just hang back and everything will fall into our
> lap.

CUT TO:

181   EXT. POLICE STATION – DAY

Carla and the boys exit the police station. She's smiling.

When Joe sees the look on her face, he's relieved. He walks over
to her.

> JOE
>
> If I offer lunch a third time, you have to say yes.

> CARLA
>
> Well, you seem to be everywhere.

> JOE
>
> It's a small town.
> *(to the boys)*
> Hi fellows. Been fishing?

ROY

We were in the jail.

CARLA

Not quite. I came here to check on you. I guess you've been honest with me.

JOE

You're a very cynical woman, Carla. I think you would have preferred a lie.

CARLA

In some ways it would have made things easier. I could have just cut you out of my life. Nice and simple.

JOE

Boys, how would you like to take the ferry back by yourself?

ROY AND NEAL
(excited)

Yeah!

CARLA

No, no. It's not possible.

JOE

I'll get you home later. I know those waters pretty well by now.
(hands the boys some money)
This is for the ferry. And you can buy some ice cream or whatever passes for it around here.

ROY

Can we Mother?

NEAL

Is it all right?

CARLA

It's a terrible idea. But go ahead.

As they're talking, Linnankoski and his aide exit the police station.

182   **LINNANKOSKI AND AIDE**

They watch as Roy and Neal run off in one direction and Joe and Carla go in the other.

LINNANKOSKI

Fine. Let's hope they become great friends.

CUT TO:

183   **EXT. STREET–SAVONLINNA–DAY**

Joe and Carla walk through the town, talking. They're both a little uneasy. Carla more so. Joe takes her hand. She pulls it back.

CARLA

I'll enjoy this if you don't make it difficult. I don't do this very often, so be patient.

JOE

I don't want to be patient. It takes too long.

CARLA

(laughs)

You can always make me laugh. How do you do that? I don't laugh very much.

They turn off the street, onto a back road.

184   **BACK ROAD**

CARLA

(nervous again)

Where are we going?

JOE

Good God Carla, we're going for a walk. And then we're going to stop for lunch. Do you want to clear that with the police? Or with Hansel and Gretel back on your island?

CARLA

How do you know about them?

JOE

I've been on your little island twice, and each time those two whatever they are, kept peering at me.

Joe takes her hand again and grips it more tightly.

CARLA

Please stop. You're hurting me. There's so much feeling in you. You either make me laugh, or you try to hurt me. It's always so extreme. Please let go of my hand.

JOE

Don't be coy. It doesn't suit you. We're both in a
hurry and we both know it. I'm drawn to you
Carla, and it makes me dizzy.

CARLA

It's so complicated . . . everything is so
complicated.

JOE

It's simple. You know what you feel.

CARLA

I feel frightened.

JOE

It's passion. That's what you feel, and you're afraid
of it. I'm flattered.

CARLA

No, no, no.

JOE

Why not? Because it's inconvenient? It's always
inconvenient, Carla.

They step off the road toward an adjacent field.

185   FIELD

High grass, moving gently in the breeze.

JOE

Grab it, Carla.

CARLA

I don't want it.

JOE

We felt the same thing back there. On your
island. Didn't we? In the woods.

CARLA
(shaking)

No. It's not true.

JOE

It is. Look at you. You're trembling. It is.

CARLA

Why are you chasing me like this? What do you
want? You know who I am. You know I can't
give you anything.

186   BEHIND A TREE – NEAR ROAD

Joe stops and turns Carla around to face him.

JOE

You're the one. You came to the police to ask
about me. To find me. It's you. You're chasing me.

CARLA

It's not true. You're confusing me.

JOE

Only because you want to be.

CARLA

Oh, I don't care, I don't care.

They embrace and kiss, standing by the tree, oblivious to every-thing but each other. We hear the sound of a great many small bells, behind them, approaching, off screen.

They turn to see a swarm of happy, laughing Bicyclists, dozens of them, almost upon them and approaching swiftly. The cy-clists laugh at the lovers as they go by, bells clanging wildly.

CUT TO:

187   EXT. GARDEN RESTAURANT – DAY

A romantic setting, with tables set far apart, under individual arbors of trees and ferns.

An Elderly Waiter bearing a tray with demitasses moves across the lawn arriving at the secluded table where Joe and Carla sit side by side on a love seat. The remnants of their lunch is before them. They look happy, contented to be here and with one another.

JOE

You know we're going to make love. You know that, don't you?

CARLA

I don't know that.

JOE

Coy again?

CARLA

No. It's just—

JOE

We are. I know.

CARLA

Well, we're not going to do it here.

JOE

Well, okay. But before your ex-husband shows up.

CARLA

Ex?

JOE

Do I have to disappear when he gets here?

CARLA

Joe . . . don't . . .

JOE

How long do we have together? Until he arrives?

CARLA

I don't know. It makes me sad to talk about it.

JOE

I can't believe you love him. I just don't believe it.

CARLA

Don't keep asking about him. Don't you know
when you do that, I get so scared.

JOE

I hate him.

CARLA

Stop. When you talk like that I don't believe
anything you say.

JOE

You're wrong. I hate him. And that's the truest
thing I've ever said to you. I hate him because he
has some hold on you. And for what he's done.

CARLA

I don't care what he's done. My feelings about him
have nothing to do with the past. The future's
scary enough for me.

JOE

I want to tell you something about me. My
brother was a spy. He lost his life. Twenty-seven.
It was terrible. When he started to work for the
government, I tried to talk him out of it. He
wasn't even much of a patriot. It was the excitement. He was working on a Ph.D. He ran off for
the adventure of it.

CARLA

Yes. Yes. I don't think Gavin did any of it for the
reasons they said. Money or politics. Oh, maybe a
little. But mostly for adventure, and to feel powerful that all these countries depend on him. It's so
stupid.

JOE

Spying and espionage. Everybody suffers from it.
The gains are vague and abstract. And the losses
are all personal.

CARLA

Oh, I've had enough losses. No more.

JOE

Did you know what he was when you married
him?

CARLA

He was in the Foreign Service. It was very
attractive. I think the trouble started after we
moved to Berlin. But I never knew for sure.

Joe leans toward her and kisses her gently.

JOE

You don't love him, do you?

CARLA

Love? Love is for other people. I'm married to
him. We have children. I want them with their
father.

JOE

Anywhere?

CARLA

You mustn't make me talk about this. I wouldn't
want my boys involved in anything like this. Ever.
There are pressures on me. Great pressures. I've
made a decision to go with my husband. To try. I
can't tell you any more about it. I've already said
too much.

JOE

I don't want to cause you pain Carla, but I must
know.

CARLA

(a smile; changing the subject)
I liked it more when you told me how we're going
to make love.

He kisses her again. More deeply.

JOE

There's only one answer to our dilemma.

CARLA

What's that? As if I didn't know.

He puts his hand under her skirt, roughly and suddenly. She
jumps back, shocked; knocking over a cup of coffee.

CARLA

Stop that! Now look what you've . . .
(sees something off screen and stiffens)

188   OLGA – CARLA'S POINT OF VIEW

Olga is standing by the table. She puts the spilled coffee cup
upright.

OLGA

You're making a mess.

189   RESUME SCENE – WIDER ANGLE INCLUDING OLGA

CARLA

Why are you here?

OLGA

I think the question is why are *you* here?

JOE

Stop treating her like a child. We're here because
we want to be.

Olga sits at the table, joining them.

OLGA

I won't treat you like a child if you don't act like
one. Did you enjoy your lunch?

CARLA

It was lovely.

OLGA

And now it's over.
(to Joe)
Mr. Bailey, if you will excuse us.

Olga rises. Carla does likewise.

JOE

(to Carla)
You don't have to go.

CARLA

Yes I do. Good-bye.

Joe rises as Olga leads Carla away.

190   WIDER ANGLE – RESTAURANT

As Carla is led through the restaurant, Joe calls to her.

JOE

Will I see you again?

Before she can answer, and during the preceding, we hear the approaching sound of bells again. As the sound gets louder, Carla says something to Joe, but her words are lost in the clanging of the bells.

191   ROAD ADJACENT TO RESTAURANT

The swarm of cyclists, bells ringing, moves along next to the restaurant, till they fill the screen.

CUT TO:

192   EXT. SAVONLINNA DOCK – DAY

Olga stands on the dock, near the ferry slip, talking to Three Men we haven't seen before: two Russians and a Finn. We can't hear what they say, but after a moment or two of their private conference, they all look at their watches and nod.

Olga turns away from them and marches across the pier. CAMERA follows her to:

193   CARLA

Sitting on the waiting bench by herself.

194   OLGA AND CARLA

CARLA

(as Olga approaches)
I know what you're going to say.

OLGA

I don't think you do.

195   **THE FERRY**

Nearing the slip, about to dock to let off and take on passengers.

CUT TO:

196   **FERRY – MOVING**

Olga and Carla stand on the deck, away from the other passengers, talking privately.

> CARLA
>
> I've been to the police. I inquired about Mr.
> Bailey. That's why I came here today. To find out.
> He's exactly—

> OLGA
>
> The police here are good for giving directions and
> traffic tickets. It may interest you that your Mr.
> Bailey was related to an American agent.

> CARLA
>
> Yes. His brother. I know. He told me. He's exactly
> what he says he is.

> OLGA
>
> You are a fool, aren't you? Your new boyfriend is
> here to murder your husband. Do you understand
> that? Can you get the stars out of your eyes long
> enough to understand that?

> CARLA
>
> I don't believe you.

OLGA

(gently)

Carla, don't be foolish. I've tried to be nice to
you.

(puts a hand on Carla's arm)

To offer you friendship. Affection.

Carla looks at the hand on her arm, appalled.

CARLA

I don't want that.

OLGA

(withdrawing her hand; coldly)

If anything should happen to your husband, I
could never persuade my superiors that you and
the American were not acting in collusion.

CARLA

(frightened)

Is my husband here? Now?

OLGA

He arrives tonight. Get the children ready. You
leave in the morning. The train leaves Helsinki at
noon. By four o'clock you will be in the Soviet
Union.

The ferry is approaching the first stop. In the distance we can
see Hilda in the motorlaunch waiting.

CUT TO:

197   INT. JOE'S HOTEL ROOM—NIGHT

Shooting toward the door of the darkened bedroom. We hear
the sound of the key in the lock. The door bursts open as Joe

enters. He snaps on the lights and walks to the bed, CAMERA panning with him. He seizes the mattress, raises it, looks down.

198   **UNDER THE MATTRESS**

The gun and the shells are gone.

199   **JOE**

Drops the mattress back in place, surprised and angry.

JOE

Linnankoski. Son of a bitch!

CUT TO:

200   **INT. CARLA'S HOUSE – ISLAND – NIGHT**

She sits in the main room of the house, saying nothing as Hilda putters about with suitcases, packing the boys' clothes and toys.

HILDA

(as she packs)

They certainly do get things dirty, don't they?

(holds up a shirt)

We just won't be able to wash it all. You can have it done there.

Carla says nothing, lost in her own thoughts.

HILDA

(nattering on)

They're all excited. I didn't think they'd ever get to sleep. They don't even know their father, do they?

Carla, still ignoring Hilda, hears something and walks to the window to look out across the water.

201   OUT WINDOW – CARLA'S POINT OF VIEW

She can hear the faint sound of a boat's motor. She scans the horizon, but can see nothing. Only the water and the faint sound of the motor.

202   RESUME SCENE

> CARLA
>
> *(at window)*

He's coming.

> HILDA

He certainly is. Well. I'll leave these bags here. We'll be back in the morning. I'm glad you're going to see your husband. I know you'll have a nice night.

Hilda leaves.

Carla is left alone, looking out at the horizon, listening to the sound of the approaching boat, still faint, still far away.

CUT TO:

203   EXT. FAR SIDE OF ISLAND – NIGHT

In the bright moonlight, Joe is nearing the shore at a remote point on the island. He cuts the engine of his motorboat, tilts the propeller shaft out of the water and glides silently through the reeds, in a hidden cove, until the boat bumps against the rocks. He gets out, beaches the boat and stands on the shore, about to move into the woods in the direction of the house. The sound of the approaching motor continues, fainter on this side of the island.

204   **CARLA**

Appears on the beach, silhouetted in the moonlight.

CARLA

I knew you'd be here.

205   **JOE AND CARLA**

He takes her in his arms.

CARLA

He's coming.

JOE

I know.

CARLA

They said that's why you're here. For him.

JOE

For you. I've come for you.

CARLA

And for him? To kill him?

JOE

I'll leave now if you want me to. Is that what you
want?

CARLA
(softly; can hardly say it)

No.

JOE

If he were dead, then I'd have you to myself.

CARLA

Yes, yes.

JOE

Then it'll be both of us who pull the trigger.
Together.

Carla embraces him. In the far distance, on the other side of the island, the sound of the approaching motor can be heard.

206   CARLA'S FACE

As she kisses Joe and at the same time listens for the motor.

CUT TO:

207   INT. HOUSE – NIGHT

The children's suitcases, all packed, are where Hilda left them.

Joe stands waiting as Carla goes to the window and pulls all the drapes shut, so the approaching boat can't be seen, and the sound of the motor is muffled.

When the drapes are drawn, Carla turns to face Joe, who stands across the room from her. They're alone, her husband and the rest of the world shut out.

208   CARLA

She begins to unbutton her blouse. It's sensual and clearly sexual, but direct, without coyness.

209   JOE

Watches her, transfixed. Then he begins to open his shirt.

210   **WIDER–BOTH OF THEM**

Neither moves toward the other, nor do they take their eyes off one another. Joe starts to walk toward her.

CARLA
(whispering)
Wait. . . I want to feel you looking at me.

They look at one another for a long moment.

211   **CLOSE–JOE'S FACE**

Gazing at her. Transfixed.

212   **CLOSE–CARLA'S FACE**

Radiant. Flushed.

213   **JOE'S EYES**

Hungry and searching.

214   **CARLA'S EYES**

Langorous and finally ready.

215   **JOE AND CARLA**

As they step into each other's arms. They drop gently to the floor, entwined in an embrace and a deep, lingering kiss.

CUT TO:

216   **EXT. THE HORIZON–NIGHT**

In the moonlight. The sound has become a power launch, in the distance.

217   **EXT. LAKE – NIGHT**

The power launch comes into view, approaching the island.

218   **POWER LAUNCH**

Gavin Brand sits patiently in the prow, his eyes scanning the island as he gets nearer to it. The boat is operated by the woodchopper who sits in the stern.

Brand favors his injured wrist. The cast is still in place, but it's soiled now. Brand looks tired, but he's feeling victorious, and that gives him renewed energy.

219   **EXT. THE DOCK – NIGHT**

Olga and Hilda wait for the launch.

220   **LAUNCH**

As it pulls along side the pier. Brand gets out and walks toward Olga and Hilda, as the woodchopper tends to the boat.

221   **DOCK**

Olga is about to make a welcoming speech. Brand looks past her, obviously looking for his wife and children.

OLGA

Mr. Brand, welcome. Seeing you—

BRAND

(ignoring the speech)

Where are they?

OLGA

Come this way. I have difficult information for you.

The three of them start up the path toward the house.

222   **WOODCHOPPER**

Securing the boat.

CUT TO:

223   **PATH TO THE HOUSE**

In the distance we see Brand, Olga, and Hilda walk toward the house. Olga talks to Brand as they walk. Her manner is urgent and direct. We can't hear what she says, but Brand's expression turns from pleased and expectant to grim.

CUT TO:

224   **INT. HOUSE**

Joe and Carla are still on the floor, in each other's arms, in a gentle mood of *après-amour*. They hear Brand approaching.

CARLA

(quietly)

He's here. Hurry. Go.

JOE

No. I came to see him.

CARLA

Then it is why you came. For him. Not for me.

JOE

I came for you both. Now I want to see him.

CARLA

(urgent)

He'll know you're here by now. He'll have a gun.

Joe looks around the room for a weapon.

225   SHELF

A hunting knife, in the midst of the children's things, is sitting on the shelf.

226   JOE AND CARLA

Joe starts to reach up for the knife and then stops.

JOE

Get it. I want you to hand it to me.

CARLA

I can't. Hurry. He's coming.

JOE

Get it.

Carla reaches for the knife. She's fully aware of what it means to hand this weapon to Joe. She's scared, but she offers him the knife. He takes it from her, kisses her quickly, and leaves.

CUT TO:

227   EXT. HOUSE

As Brand, with Olga and Hilda approaches.

BRAND

I'll do it by myself.

OLGA

But we can—

BRAND

By myself.

Olga and Hilda stop and Brand walks up to the door of the house.

CUT TO:

228   INT. HOUSE

Carla has dressed hurriedly, and she's still a little unbuttoned as
her husband enters.

CARLA

Hello, Gavin.

Brand doesn't answer, he looks around the room, still standing
in the doorway. Finally:

BRAND

Where are the boys?

CARLA

Asleep. How are you, Gavin?

BRAND
(terse)

Out of prison.

CARLA

Yes. I—

BRAND

It smells like a brothel in here.

He turns and leaves. Carla watches him go, shaking.

CUT TO:

229   EXT. HOUSE – NIGHT

Brand steps outside, a gun in his hand, looking for a sign of Joe.
He goes around to the rear of the house and looks into the
woods. He sees only darkness.

He turns and goes back toward the front of the house.

230   PATH TO DOCK

Brand walks away from the house toward the water. He moves cautiously.

231   WOODSHED AND SAUNA – NIGHT

Brand stops in front of the sauna.

He walks around it, noticing the pipes leading from the sauna into the ground. When he's circled the woodshed and the sauna, he opens the sauna door.

232   INT. SAUNA – HIS POINT OF VIEW

Empty.

233   RESUME SCENE

He continues on toward the dock.

234   JOE

He steps out of the darkness near the water, the knife in his hand. He's a good distance from Brand, watching him, staring at his back. He seems transfixed. He slaps the blade against his palm. He hesitates, summoning the courage to kill.

235   BRAND

Continues toward the water, unaware Joe is watching him, until he senses Joe's presence and the sound of the knife blade slapping. He turns quickly and without any hesitation, fires the gun.

236   DARKNESS – WHERE JOE WAS

Gone now. Nothing.

237   **BRAND**

Hurries toward the spot. He looks around frantically, searching.

238   **WATER'S EDGE – NIGHT**

Brand's eyes scan the water of the bay, passing across the marsh grass and tall reeds near the pier, and stopping at the two boats tied at the dock, his power launch and the island's dinghy. All is deserted. The woodchopper is gone and there's no sign of Joe.

Then he looks back at the marsh.

239   **TALL REEDS**

The tips of three of them seem to have moved.

240   **BRAND**

He moves away from the boats back toward the reeds. He stands and watches them. There's no movement. Brand studies them for a moment, then takes a revolver out of his pocket and fires into the reeds.

241   **TALL REEDS**

The tips move again.

242   **BRAND**

Watches the surface of the water as it shimmers from the gun shot. He puts the gun on the dry ground and wades into the water, toward the three reeds.

He dives beneath the surface.

243   THE REEDS – VARIOUS ANGLES

The tips of the reeds move, first one way, then the other. CAMERA skims across the top, suggesting a skirmish beneath the surface.

The tips move back and forth, illuminated by the moonlight.

Finally: Brand rises up out of the water in the midst of the reeds. He wades to the shore and looks around still unsatisfied.

244   THE SHORE – BRAND

CAMERA moves with him as he picks up his gun and walks back to the pier, toward the boat.

245   POWER LAUNCH

Brand climbs into the boat. He sits and waits. His face is grim. He looks determined to wait until he believes Joe is dead or until Joe shows himself and he can kill him. He holds the gun prominently in his lap.

CUT TO:

246   INT. CARETAKER'S COTTAGE – NIGHT

Olga and Hilda stand in the window, looking out. They're stoic, waiting. Olga glances behind her at a clock. We hear the sound of its ticking.

CUT TO:

247   INT. BOY'S BEDROOM – NIGHT

Roy and Neal are asleep in their beds. They're the only ones who seem to be at peace. CAMERA pans off them to Carla, standing in the doorway, watching her children. She's frightened, but also pensive.

CUT TO:

248   THE DOCK – ALMOST DAWN

Brand is still sitting in the boat. When he sees the first rays of sunlight, he gets out and walks toward the path to the house.

249   EXT. MAIN HOUSE – DAWN

Carla leaves the house and walks down the path to the pier.

250   EXT. PATH BETWEEN HOUSE AND DOCK – DAWN

Brand, walking toward the house, sees Carla approaching. They stand at a distance from each other. As they speak, Brand moves nearer and nearer to Carla.

                    CARLA
Gavin . . . I . . .

                    BRAND
                    (cool)
        Are there clothes for me? Dry ones?

                    CARLA
                    (nods yes)
        Were you out all night?

                    BRAND
I was.

                    CARLA
I'm so sorry. I didn't want that.

Brand's drawing closer to her makes Carla edgy.

                    BRAND
It wasn't exactly the reunion I had in mind.

CARLA

Do you still want me? To go with you?

BRAND

Of course I do. Are the boys asleep?

CARLA

Would you like to wake them?

BRAND

Yes.
            (genuine; from very deep)
I would. Very much.

CARLA

            (sensing the depth of his feeling)
Good. They might . . . Well, they're not used to
you, Gavin. They might not recognize you. Be
careful.

BRAND

I'll try not to scare my own children.

CARLA

I want to talk to you, Gavin. To explain things.

BRAND

Fine. I'd like that.

He puts an arm around her. She stiffens a bit and Brand feels it,
and he removes the arm.

BRAND

You go on down to the boat. I'll be along.

He moves past her toward the house. Hold on Carla's uncertain face for a moment.

CUT TO:

251   NEAR HOUSE – BRAND AND OLGA

Olga has the boys' suitcases.

OLGA

We're almost ready. Where is Mrs. Brand?

BRAND

At the boat.

OLGA

What shall I do?

BRAND

It's up to you. She's no longer my concern.

Brand goes past her, toward the house.

252   INT. HOUSE

Hilda is dozing in an easy chair. She awakens, startled when Brand enters and speaks to her.

BRAND

(shaking her)
I want dry clothes and my children.

HILDA

Oh! Mr. Brand. Can I get you some coffee?

BRAND

Clothes and children.

HILDA

(pointing toward bedroom)
You can change in there. The boys are in the
cottage.

CUT TO:

253   INT. BEDROOM

His clothes are still laid out on the bed. Brand looks at them,
and then begins to take off his wet things.

CUT TO:

254   EXT. THE DOCK – DAY

Olga is walking with Carla, away from the boats toward the
house. We can't hear what they're saying.

255   EXT. PATH NEAR SAUNA AND WOODSHED – DAY

As they approach the sauna we hear their conversation.

OLGA

You change trains at Vainikkala. It's the last stop
on this side. From there you go on to Leningrad. I
would imagine, you'll fly to Moscow from there.

As they pass the sauna, the door opens and Olga suddenly
shoves Carla sideways, into the sauna.

Olga turns and walks back toward the dock, as the sauna door
slams shut.

Hold on the closed door for a moment, then the door opens and
the woodchopper steps out. He walks around the sauna, toward
the rear of the woodshed.

CUT TO:

256   **INT. BOYS' BEDROOM**

Brand, wearing the dry clothes, stands in the doorway looking in at Roy and Neal, asleep in an enormous double bed. He watches them for a moment.

> NEAL
> *(eyes still closed)*

I'm not asleep.

> BRAND
> *(smiling)*

Good morning.

> ROY

I am.

> *(pretends to snore)*

Zzzz.

> BRAND

We're going to go now.

> NEAL

What happened to your arm?

> BRAND

I broke my wrist.

> NEAL

Does it hurt?

> BRAND

No. Not very much.

ROY

How'd you break it?

NEAL

(privately; to his brother)
Shh. You know.

ROY

No I don't. How?

BRAND

I'll tell you all about it later. I'm very glad to see
you both. Do you know that?

No reply from Roy and Neal.

BRAND

I'm a little rusty at being a father. But I'll try.

NEAL

It's not hard. You just be one.

BRAND

Right. Come along now, boys. Out of bed. Time to
get dressed.

The boys scramble out of bed.

CUT TO:

257   EXT. PATH FROM HOUSE TO DOCK – DAY

Brand, with Roy and Neal on either side, walks toward the pier.
Hilda is a few feet behind, carrying the boys' bags.

BRAND

We're going to have an exciting day. We're going
on a boat, a train, and a plane. How's that?

NEAL

Okay.

As they pass the sauna, there's no sign of Carla.

ROY

Where's mummy?

BRAND

She'll be coming later.

258 **EXT. DOCK – DAY**

Olga is waiting in Brand's boat. She has tied a line from Brand's power launch to the dinghy.

Olga reaches out for Roy and Neal. They hesitate.

ROY

Where'd this boat come from?

BRAND

It's mine. Do you like it?

ROY

It's okay.

NEAL
(seeing the rope)
Are we taking our little boat, too?

BRAND

Yes.

NEAL

How's mummy going to come?

BRAND

Another boat's coming for her.

Roy and Neal consider that. They're still standing on the pier, ignoring Olga's outstretched arms.

NEAL

Can we go in our boat?

OLGA

No, no. Just come along.

BRAND

Of course they can. They can go in whatever boat they want.

The boys climb into the little boat.

CUT TO:

259   EXT. DOCK AND LAKE–DAY

As the two boats move away from the pier, sailing in tandem. Brand with Olga and Hilda is in the front boat, and the boys are pulled along behind in the other.

260   CLOSE–ROY AND NEAL

Upset. Uncertain.

261   HIGH ANGLE–BOTH BOATS

The two boats chug out into the open water in tandem.

CUT TO:

262   EXT. DOCK AND MARSH AREA – DAY

Joe rises up from the rushes and the reeds, mud and water rolling off of him. He looks out at the lake.

263   LAKE – JOE'S POINT OF VIEW

The two boats disappear around the bend on their way to the mainland. They're far enough away so Joe can't see who's on board.

264   RESUME SCENE

                    JOE
              (straining to see)
    Damn!

He turns and runs toward the house.

265   PATH

Joe passes the sauna, and continues on up the path.

266   INT. HOUSE

He enters guardedly, going from room to room, searching.

267   BEDROOM

He looks into the empty bedroom. Brand's wet clothes are in a heap on the floor.

                    JOE
    Carla? Carla . . .

                                    CUT TO:

268   EXT. REAR OF SAUNA – DAY

The woodchopper, with a large pipe wrench, is working on two pipes that lead from the ground into the sauna. The pipes are marked in German: *Gaz und Wasser.*

                                                                CUT TO:

269   EXT. FRONT OF HOUSE – DAY

Joe exits, running back toward the dock.

270   EXT. SAUNA

As Joe runs past it. Gas fumes are seeping out from under the door. Joe doesn't notice as he hurries by to continue his search.

271   WOODCHOPPER

Pipe wrench in hand, looking for Joe.

272   JOE

Senses something. He turns.

273   SAUNA – JOE'S POINT OF VIEW

The fumes seeping out from under the door.

274   RESUME SCENE – JOE

He moves toward the sauna door. He's hurrying, but wary. As he passes the woodshed, he picks up the axe that rests there.

275   SAUNA DOOR

Gas seeping out from under the cracks. As Joe gets near the door, instead of stopping, he continues around behind the sauna.

276   **REAR OF SAUNA**

The axe comes smashing into the frame suddenly, hitting the woodchopper on the head.

277   **WOODCHOPPER'S FACE**

As he's knocked out, collapsing to the ground.

278   **JOE**

Axe in hand, rushes back to the front of the sauna.

279   **SAUNA**

Fumes getting heavier. Joe pulls on the door but can't open it.

                              JOE

    Carla . . .

He smashes it open with the axe. As the door falls into splinters, a wave of fumes comes out. Joe gags on it, and then Carla, her face turning blue, and her eyes starting to bulge, flops out and into Joe, knocking them both down.

                              JOE

    Carla, Carla . . .

He shakes her and slaps her face.

                              JOE

    Carla, for God's sake.

She starts to cough and gag.

CARLA

(through the cough)

I . . . can't . . . my babies . . . where are my
children?

JOE

Are you all right?

CARLA

No. I'm terrible. Where are they?

JOE

Shh . . . easy. First you.

CARLA

(edge of hysteria)

No, no. I want them. He took them. He took my
babies. They'll never come back.

JOE

We'll get them.

(soothing)

We'll get them . . . we'll find them.

CUT TO:

280   **EXT. FAR SIDE OF ISLAND–DAY**

Joe and Carla climb into Joe's boat. Carla is a bit calmer now.

CARLA

He'll take them. I'll never see them again.

JOE

We'll find them. The boys are safe. He won't harm
them. Now if we hurry, we can get them back.

CARLA
(crying)
I'll never see them. I know I won't.

Joe starts the boat's engine.

CUT TO:

281   EXT. LAKE–HIGH ANGLE–DAY

Joe and Carla, in Joe's boat, sail out across the lake. They move past the ferry stop and on into the open water toward Savonlinna.

282   JOE AND CARLA–CLOSER

Carla is terrified. Her teeth begin to chatter. Joe puts an arm around her, trying to comfort her. It doesn't do much good.

CUT TO:

283   EXT. SAVONLINNA DOCK–LONG SHOT–DAY

Joe is speaking on a public phone at the dock. He's gesturing urgently, trying to be understood. Carla is with him, waiting anxiously. Joe is still dripping wet from his night in the marshes and passersby stare at him.

284   JOE AND CARLA

He hangs up and turns back to Carla.

JOE

He's at home.
(points off screen)
We'll take one of those.

285   **TAXI STAND – JOE'S POINT OF VIEW**

Several cabs sit awaiting passengers. The Drivers lounge about.

286   **RESUME SCENE**

Joe and Carla hurry from the phone to the line of taxis.

                                                CUT TO:

287   **EXT. CAB – TRAVELING – DAY**

Through the Savonlinna streets.

288   **INT. CAB – TRAVELING – DAY**

JOE

Can you find it?

DRIVER

Yes. Yes.
(keeping an eye on them in his mirror)
It's a long trip. Are you sure you have money?

Joe fishes in his pocket and extracts some Finnish bills. They're soaked of course. He drops the money onto the front seat.

JOE

There.

The driver stares at the wet money for a moment, but says nothing.

                                                CUT TO:

289   **EXT. LINNANKOSKI RESIDENCE – DAY**

Joe and Carla are at the front door arguing with Mrs. Linnankoski. She can't see past Joe and Carla's disreputable state.

Mrs. Linnankoski is a proper Finnish housewife and the front of her house is scrubbed clean.

MRS. LINNANKOSKI

Well I'm sure my husband doesn't have any
business with you.

JOE

Tell him it's Mr. Bailey. It's very important.

CARLA

My children have been taken from me. Do you
understand what that means?

MRS. LINNANKOSKI

Yes, yes. All right. You wait out there.

She closes the door on their faces, and turns back into her house.

290   INT. FRONT HALL

She walks from the door to a staircase leading to the second floor. She mutters to herself as she goes.

291   STAIRCASE

Mrs. Linnankoski climbs at a leisurely pace.

292   OUTSIDE BATHROOM DOOR–SECOND FLOOR

She calls through the door.

MRS. LINNANKOSKI

Aki?

LINNANKOSKI'S VOICE

Yes.

She opens the door part way and speaks to her husband.

293   INT. BATH

Linnankoski is soaking in a huge tub. He's relaxing and reading police reports. Mrs. Linnankoski stands in the doorway.

MRS. LINNANKOSKI

There are two people here for you. One's dripping wet and the other's raving about her children.

LINNANKOSKI

A Mr. Bailey?

MRS. LINNANKOSKI

That's it.

LINNANKOSKI

Tell them I'll be down in a few minutes.

She snorts to herself and withdraws, closing the door behind her.

Linnankoski puts down the papers he was reading, sighs, and pulls the plug.

CUT TO:

294   FRONT HALL

Mrs. Linnankoski comes down off the staircase, walks across the hall to the door.

295   **DOORWAY**

As she opens the door, Joe and Carla are still there. More anxious.

> CARLA
> *(angry)*

Where is he?

> MRS. LINNANKOSKI

He'll be down. You should learn to make appointments in advance. You may come in.

> JOE

How gracious of you.

They follow Mrs. Linnankoski into the house.

296   **FRONT HALL**

Joe and Carla start to walk into the house.

> MRS. LINNANKOSKI

That's far enough.

> JOE

Do you think we might sit down?

> MRS. LINNANKOSKI

No.

She turns and walks back into the living room.

Joe takes off his jacket and wrings out his sleeves, dripping water onto the floor.

CUT TO:

297   THE BATH

Linnankoski is toweling himself off, and preparing to dress. He doesn't waste time, but there's a lot to do. He powders himself, combs his hair, and then starts to put on his clothes.

CUT TO:

298   FRONT HALL

Joe and Carla are agonizing.

CARLA

Do something Joe. They're on the train by now.

Joe walks to the stairs and yells up.

JOE

Come on Linnankoski, hurry the hell up!

299   STAIRS

As Linnankoski comes down.

LINNANKOSKI

I am hurrying.

300   FRONT HALL—ALL THREE

CARLA

He has my children.

LINNANKOSKI

(to Joe)

You're soaking wet.

JOE

I'll dry off. The train's already left.

He grabs Linnankoski and the three of them hurry out.

301 **MRS. LINNANKOSKI**

Peering out at them from the living room.

CUT TO:

302 **INT. LINNANKOSKI'S CAR – TRAVELING – DAY**

Linnankoski drives with Carla and Joe next to him. The car is
going very fast.

> LINNANKOSKI
>
> Our chance is at Vainikkala. The train stops there
> for an hour. They put a Russian diesel on the
> Russian cars.

> JOE
>
> Where's Vainikkala?

> LINNANKOSKI
>
> Seven miles from the border.

He increases the car's speed.

303 **EXT. LINNANKOSKI'S CAR – TRAVELING – A HIGH
ANGLE – DAY**

CAMERA chases the car as it races along the country road
parallel to the empty railroad tracks.

CUT TO:

304 **EXT. FINNISH COUNTRYSIDE – THE TRAIN –
TRAVELING – DAY**

CAMERA travels ahead of the train in a raking angle, on the
steam locomotive which is pulling two brown Finnish coach
cars and behind that, two red carriages each with the crest of
the Soviet Union.

The train travels at a high speed through a wooded area gaining on CAMERA. The train speeds past CAMERA, disappearing around a bend, and into the woods.

CUT TO:

305   **EXT. COUNTRYSIDE – LINNANKOSKI'S CAR – TRAVELING – DAY**

CAMERA pursues the car as it races along the country road next to the railroad tracks. There's no sign of the train, only miles of empty track and deserted road ahead.

CUT TO:

306   **EXT. VAINIKKALA RAILROAD YARD – DAY**

Start close on a sign on the side of the small passenger terminal: Vainikkala.

Then CAMERA reveals the depot, the platform, and the tracks. This is the last stop in Finland and it's very small.

Two diesel engines stand on separate sidings. The smaller one is Finnish, the larger is green with red wheels. There's a red star on its snout and Russian lettering on the side.

In the distance we hear the sound of the steam engine we saw a moment ago.

A Stationmaster emerges from the depot, goes out on the platform and searches in the distance for the approaching train.

CAMERA pans toward the sound of the approaching train. As the sound grows louder we can see steam rising through the trees until the train looms into view, charging toward CAMERA.

As it comes into the station, the brakes hiss and the wheels screech to a halt.

Train Officials get off first, followed by passengers, who go into the station, or join people waiting for them.

Brand descends the steps, cautiously looking about. Neal and Roy are with him, and behind him the two Russian men we saw Olga speak to on the dock.

A railroad Worker leans in between the last Finnish car and the first Russian one. He decouples the cars and signals to the stationmaster, who in turn signals to the engineer.

The Finnish section of the train starts slowly away from the two Russian cars.

CUT TO:

307   EXT. LINNANKOSKI'S CAR–TRAVELING–DAY

CAMERA is moving ahead of the speeding car, but close enough for us to see the three tense faces in front. Suddenly their eyes all widen.

308   THEIR POINT OF VIEW–MOVING

On the narrow road, ahead of Linnankoski's car, is a slow moving horse-drawn cart driven by an Elderly Man.

Coming toward the car on the other land of the narrow road is a car traveling at a high speed.

Linnankoski is going much too fast to slow down for the cart, and must pass it on the left—which he does—and still avoid the oncoming car. He swerves around first one, then the other, making a snake line twist in the road, at a high speed. The speeding car blasts its horn. The elderly man doesn't seem to notice.

309   RESUME SCENE

Joe, pale and angry, opens his mouth about to snarl, then closes it when he sees Linnankoski, tight lipped, staring straight ahead. Carla's eyes remain shut.

310   EXT. LINNANKOSKI'S CAR – OBJECTIVE SHOT – DAY

Speeding toward CAMERA from the far distance. It roars past panning CAMERA and disappears around a bend in the road.

CUT TO:

311   EXT. VAINIKKALA RAILROAD YARD

Start close on the red star on the front of the Russian diesel. Then the diesel backs slowly away from CAMERA toward the waiting Russian coaches behind it.

312   FRONT END OF FIRST RUSSIAN CAR

Close on the coupling device as the diesel backs into it and locks in place.

313   NEAL AND ROY

The boys run to the end of the platform to watch.

314   THE PLATFORM

As the Russian train is ready to go. A Guard at the front of the train calls out in Russian, "All aboard."

Brand, the boys, and the two Russian men reboard the train.

The guard signals to the engineer completing the final boarding and then mounts the train.

315   CLOSE: WHEELS OF RUSSIAN DIESEL

The wheels fill the screen, the diesel horn blasts, and the wheels roll forward.

316   WIDER ANGLE – RUSSIAN TRAIN AND STATION

The train begins to gather speed as it pulls away. As it does, Linnankoski's car comes screeching in to the station.

Linnankoski, Joe, and Carla jump out in time to see the Russian train building up power on the way out of the station.

LINNANKOSKI

Damn . . .

Carla starts to cry. Joe puts an arm around her.

To their left, in the near distance, there's a freight locomotive and tender on a side rail. Linnankoski sees it, and turns and runs toward the depot. Joe and Carla watch him go.

317   **LINNANKOSKI**
CAMERA pans with him as he hurries to the stationmaster. We watch in long shot as Linnankoski shows the stationmaster his badge, and points to the freight engine. We can't hear what they're saying, but the stationmaster resists, indicating that what Linnankoski is asking for is impossible.

318   **JOE AND CARLA**
He tries to comfort her with a protective arm around her shoulder.

319   **LINNANKOSKI AND STATIONMASTER**
Linnankoski seems to have made some headway. He runs across the yard, toward the freight engine. The stationmaster runs after him—partly chasing, and partly helping.

320   **JOE AND CARLA**

JOE

(seeing it)
Come on. I think he's done it.

They run toward the freight engine, too.

321   FREIGHT ENGINE

In long shot we see the stationmaster talking to an Engineer, a
portly, dignified Finn, who seems baffled by it all.

As Joe and Carla enter the shot, Linnankoski grabs the engineer
and starts to board the freight engine. Joe and Carla follow.

The stationmaster runs ahead on the track and pulls the line
switch, causing the freight engine to change its position, to the
same track the Russian diesel is on.

CUT TO:

322   FREIGHT ENGINE – TRAVELING – DAY

Shooting back to the freight engine and tender as it rumbles
along the track. We see Joe, Carla, and Linnankoski with the
engineer all in the cab, looking forward anxiously.

323   REAR OF THE SOVIET TRAIN – THEIR POINT OF
VIEW

The rear door seems to be getting larger as the freight engine
gains on it.

CUT TO:

324   FREIGHT ENGINE

A few yards from the tail end of the Russian train. Joe is about
to jump off the engine, to run for the Russian train. The
engineer says something in Finnish to Linnankoski.

LINNANKOSKI

He says the rear door will be locked. There's
another on the side that will be open.

Joe nods, and jumps off the front end of the moving freight
engine.

325   JOE

Running along the tracks from the freight engine toward the rear of the Russian train.

He goes alongside the rear, grabs hold of the rails on each side of the door, and swings up onto the Russian train, opens the door and boards the train.

326   INT. RUSSIAN TRAIN

Joe looks down the corridor.

327   CLOSER – JOE

He quickly unbolts the rear door of the train. As it slides open, we see the exterior, and the freight engine approaching.

328   FREIGHT ENGINE – JOE'S POINT OF VIEW THRU REAR DOOR

Linnankoski has mounted the engine, Carla is still with the engineer.

329   RESUME SCENE

Joe turns away from the door, to go into the main part of the Russian train.

330   THE TRAIN COMPARTMENTS – JOE'S POINT OF VIEW

Through a glass door, we see two Conductors entering various compartments, asking for tickets, counting their passengers. They're headed toward Joe, and they turn in his direction.

331   CLOSE – JOE

He ducks into the nearest compartment.

332   INT. COMPARTMENT

Filled with Russian Officers. He's facing an army, and all the seats are taken. Joe salutes them all, and then looks out into the corridor.

333   REVERSE ANGLE

Joe's head emerges from the officers' compartment and he looks down the corridor.

334   CORRIDOR–JOE'S POINT OF VIEW

The corridor is divided by a glass door. On the other side of the door, the conductors are going in and out of the compartments.

335   RESUME SCENE–JOE

Moving toward the glass door. Over his shoulder we can see several empty compartments. Joe hesitates at each one, but no Brand and no Roy and Neal. The climax of the shot takes Joe through the glass door, to the more active side of the car.

336   REVERSE–OTHER SIDE OF THE GLASS DOOR

Joe peers into the first compartment on this side of the door. Nothing.

337   CLOSER ANGLE

Joe glances to his right, about to look into the next compartment. Behind him is the empty corridor.

338   WIDER ANGLE–JOE

Turns and is startled to see Brand and the boys. They're as surprised as Joe.

NEAL

Hey!

Brand jumps to his feet.

JOE

(to the boys)
Quick! Get to the far end of the train.

But the boys are too confused to know what to do.

Brand and Joe look at one another for a moment. For an instant, neither of them knows what to do, either.

Then Brand draws a gun from his pocket. He's about to shoot Joe.

NEAL

Where's my mother?

Brand hesitates to shoot in front of his sons, and in the moment of hesitation, Joe smashes him on his injured wrist.

Brand screams from the pain.

JOE

(while Brand screams)
Go to the back of the train. Your mother's there.
Go on.

Still the boys hesitate. They stare at their father and the gun.

BRAND

Stay here. Your mother's fine. She'll be along. This
man's not fine. He's going to be dead.

JOE

Yell to her. She'll hear you. Go on.

Roy begins to call, Neal quickly joins him.

ROY AND NEAL

Mummy . . . Mummy . . . Where are you?

JOE

Go on. The back of the train. You'll see her.

The boys start to go.

BRAND

(*fierce; yelling*)

No!

Brand kicks Joe, smashing him in the groin. It terrifies the boys and they scramble out of the compartment.

When Joe and Brand are left alone, Joe lunges at Brand and they struggle for the gun.

Brand keeps the gun, and holds it to Joe's forehead—the barrel up against his temple.

BRAND

I want to know who you are. Tell me!

Joe knocks the gun into the air. It discharges, sending a bullet into the ceiling of the compartment.

339   CORRIDOR–FLASH CUT

The conductors turn and look in the direction of the CAMERA as other passengers poke their heads out of the various doors. They start toward CAMERA.

340   **RUSSIAN OFFICERS**

Emerge from their compartment and start toward the CAM-ERA. They're talking among themselves, in Russian, trying to find out what all the commotion is about.

341   **CORRIDOR**

As the officers hurry toward Brand's compartment, Roy and Neal run past them, toward the rear of the train. For a moment, the officers stop to watch the boys, baffled.

342   **REAR OF TRAIN**

Roy and Neal stand in the open doorway, looking out.

343   **FREIGHT – THEIR POINT OF VIEW**

The freight is very close, but there's still a gap between the two trains. Linnankoski is out on the engine, and Carla is crawling toward him, and toward her children.

                    CARLA

    Roy . . . Neal . . .

344   **ROY**

Teeters on the edge of the Russian train as the freight engine edges closer, gaining slightly.

345   **SIDE ON SHOT**

Roy is about to attempt the leap.

                    CARLA

    Don't do it! Don't try.

But Roy makes a daring leap anyway, and Linnankoski leans out perilously far to grab his hand, and pull him aboard the freight engine.

346   **RUSSIAN TRAIN**

Shooting from the freight engine as Neal is about to attempt the jump. As he does, a Russian Officer emerges from the train and stops him. The officer grabs Neal and begins yelling at him in Russian.

347   **SIDE ON SHOT**

Neal wrenches himself free and makes the leap, suddenly, and without much warning.

348   **CLOSE – BETWEEN THE TRAINS**

Linnankoski's hand goes toward Neal's. They are fingertips apart.

349   **FRONT OF FREIGHT ENGINE**

It edges even closer.

350   **CLOSE – LINNANKOSKI AND ROY**

Linnankoski grabs Neal's wrist and pulls him aboard.

351   **RUSSIAN TRAIN**

Comes to a halt, wheels screeching.

352   **FREIGHT ENGINE**

It must do the same. As both trains are trying to stop, Carla is hugging her sons. The boys keep grinning.

CUT TO:

353 INT. RUSSIAN TRAIN—CORRIDOR

The conductors, the Russian Officers, and a crowd of passengers, all talking in Russian, crowd toward Brand's compartment.

354 INT. BRAND'S COMPARTMENT

Joe is sitting with the gun pointed at Brand. They're both scared.

> JOE

I've come a long way for this . . .

> BRAND
> *(sweating; negotiating)*

Do you want my wife, or do you want me dead—
you can't have both, you know.

Before Joe can decide or reply, a Russian Officer bursts in, followed by several of his men. The officer speaks English.

> OFFICER

What the hell's going on in here?

> JOE

I want to get off this . . .

> OFFICER
> *(stunned)*

An American?

> JOE

Yes, and I—

BRAND

He's an enemy of the state.

OFFICER

Who the hell cares about that? I don't want any
Americans or any guns on this train.

BRAND

Shoot him, you fool. Shoot him.

OFFICER

I don't want any incidents with Americans or
English.

BRAND

Do you know who I am?

OFFICER

Yes, yes . . . all English spies wind up in Moscow,
and they all make trouble.
(to Joe)
Please. Don't shoot anybody.

JOE

Fine with me.

OFFICER

Just put it down. We don't want any guns. This
isn't New York.

JOE

I'll just be going along now.

Joe gets up and backs out of the compartment.

355   **CORRIDOR**

Joe backs his way through the crowd, toward the rear of the train. He's followed by the conductors, the Russian officer, and Brand.

As the group gets nearer the open door, we can see through to the freight train.

356   **FREIGHT TRAIN – RUSSIANS' POINT OF VIEW**

Carla, the boys, and Linnankoski are watching. Very tense. When Linnankoski sees Joe's gun, he too gets worried.

357   **JOE**

Gun still drawn, backs down onto the tracks to walk back to the freight train.

358   **BRAND AND RUSSIAN SOLDIER**

The soldier surreptitiously hands Brand a revolver. Brand points it at Joe, about to shoot him.

359   **FREIGHT ENGINE – BRAND'S POINT OF VIEW**

He sees his sons. He realizes he's about to shoot Joe in front of them and in his moment's hesitation, the Russian officer sees the gun, and knocks it to the floor.

OFFICER

Just let him go.

360   **WIDER ANGLE – BOTH TRAINS**

Joe climbs up onto the freight engine.

The conductor on the Russian train calls to the front, to the engine.

361   RUSSIAN TRAIN

Starts moving again, toward the Soviet Union.

362   BRAND

Stands in the doorway at the rear of the last car, looking back at the freight engine and his family.

363   FREIGHT ENGINE

Joe, with Carla and the boys and Linnankosi, watches the Russian train move away from them.

364   BRAND – THEIR POINT OF VIEW

Getting smaller and smaller as the train recedes in the distance.

365   FREIGHT ENGINE

Joe puts his arm around Carla, who is holding her sons near. Carla hugs the boys.

> NEAL

Mom?

> CARLA

What, darling?

> NEAL

Can we do it again?

Joe starts to laugh. He hugs Carla and the boys as the Russian train disappears in the distance.

THE END

"Alfred Hitchcock's The Short Night"

A Commentary on the Screenplay

Reading film scripts isn't always the easiest of activities. A script is by its nature the bare bones of a film, or as the screenwriter Bo Goldman has said, "the essence" of a film. Some scripts read more easily than others. In this one, I suspect the business with the trains at the end, is difficult to follow. I hope the characters and their main actions are a little clearer.

As you can see, "The Short Night" is about love and spies, a favorite area for Hitchcock. Its antecedents in his films are "The Lady Vanishes," "The 39 Steps," and "North by Northwest." The last, one of Hitch's most enduring and entertaining films, was written by Ernest Lehman, who preceded me on "The Short Night."

No rational screenwriter will defend or agree with the auteur theory of filmmaking—it holds that the director is the author of the film, the way the painter or the novelist is the author of the picture or book. I honestly don't know what's more tedious—defending the theory or attacking it. But Hitch made his own rules, and he is one director who passes the auteur test. No matter who the scriptwriter was, no matter who the cinematographer, art director, or composer—you can usually identify a Hitchcock picture. Not quite like being a painter or a novelist, but pretty damn close. That's not to say that others haven't had a hand in these pictures. Hitch was the first to give credit and acknowledgment to professional collaborators, but make no mistake, the others could be replaced.

It is style, the mark of the auteur, that would take the script from Bo Goldman's "essence" to a full-blown Hitchcock film. One recognizes a Hitchcock film by certain literary conventions—there's usually an innocent man caught up in circumstances he doesn't fully comprehend. There's often a beautiful woman, usually a blonde, who is cool and aloof—for a while. Those particular qualities, which are essentially literary, or narrative, or a version of them, are in this script. What isn't in the script, what Hitchcock would add, is the essentially cinematic quality that allows us to identify Hitchcock films by their look and feel. It's the ominous quality of the camera's attention to things, the way it picks out details and frames people and objects in a way that makes one uneasy. There's often a sense, conveyed principally by the camera, that something strange is going on in ordinary circumstances. Now lesser directors can do that by making it "mysterious"—the dark and foggy night on the moors. Hitchcock did it in routine and normal-appearing domestic circumstances. Watch Anthony Perkins offer Janet Leigh a sandwich with those stuffed birds on the wall behind him in "Psycho," or Cary Grant try to get back to his office while all these people insist his name is Kaplan in "North by Northwest," or James Stewart just driving around San Francisco in "Vertigo." All of it is a matter of style, which is of course what the auteur theory is actually about, and Hitchcock's style is unmistakable. Just as action is character in the narrative, style is content in the filming itself. You can see some of it in a script—there's a view of character, but the rest can only be supplied by production.

Nonetheless, the script can tell us a lot about what was on Hitchcock's mind at the end of his life. The draft you've read was very near a finished one. There are a number of scenes that either need more work or that Hitchcock was not quite satisfied with, or that I wanted to reconsider. What follows is a guide and commentary to the script with particular attention to Hitchcock's view of it.

The Lehman draft began in New York, with its focus on Joe Bailey, the hero of the story. In addition to starting with the prison break and Brand's murder of the young woman, I've tried to heat up the love story and add more humor.

For a while the opening of this version of the script was different. It began with an unidentified man sawing prison bars with a hacksaw blade. The blade was bare—that is, it had no handle, not even tape, and the prisoner's hands were bloody. Hitch liked the idea of opening on the bloody hands of a guilty man. It's a good example of his collaborative techniques. It was his idea. Despite the strength of the image, it felt to me like a Warner Brothers Big House picture, circa 1946. I preferred the softer, more mysterious opening that is now in the script. Hitch might have been right, it's hard to say. Part of the reason he went along with my view was, no doubt, the beautiful camera move in Scene 1, which was wholly his idea. I think his thoughts in abandoning his idea to mine, must have been something on the order of "Well, I've hired this fellow, no point in squelching him. Maybe he's right. Let's try it." Also in Scene 1, a specific car is called for, a Humber Hawk. Most scripts don't specify such detail. Hitch was quite certain what he wanted. I had to ask Universal's research library to get me a picture of one. Humber Hawks turn out to be cute enough, but I still didn't see why he wanted that specific car. His answer, which illustrated a Hitchcock working maxim: "It's a timeless-looking sedan, don't you see. A little out of date, but still roughly contemporary. Bear in mind it's the first thing we see. Americans won't recognize it at all, it will be foreign to them. Mustn't let them (the audience) get too comfortable right at the start."

An additional objective for Hitchcock in this opening sequence, roughly scenes 1–15, was to establish that Brand, based on the English spy George Blake, is desperate as well as mean-spirited, a guarded man who trusts no one, and that Brennan is a looser sort who doesn't seem to have planned this escape with the precision Brand would have hoped for. Brennan's character is revealed in Scene 13. He's been talking to a man he believes to be Brand—we know it is, we've seen him. But Brennan has just tossed the ladder over the wall. Who knows who's climbing over? At the last second, it dawns on Brennan that for all he knows, it could be the entire Cold Stream Guards coming over that wall. Hitch insisted that the line be almost neutral: "Is it you, then?" The fear would be on the actor's face. "They're quite good at that, you know."

"Who is that, Hitch?"

"Actors, of course. They play sudden fear quite well. Some of them anyway."

"Why do you think that is?" I asked ingenuously. It probably sounded like the interview question that it was, because he just smiled enigmatically. I figured he was just going to ignore the question and move on to the next script beat. And miss a chance to make a quotable reply? Not at all. He was smiling because he was composing a clever answer. "Fear is the emotion actors are most used to. They're always afraid, you know. Of being hired, or of not being hired. They play it quite well. That and eroticism. Most of them anyway." If there was a chance that his answer would be quoted or might find its way into print, Hitch would make sure he sounded the way he wanted to. Droll and wise. Publicizing himself was as much in his marrow as making movies.

Scene 23, in which the mysterious silent doctor sets Brand's broken bone, is an example of "pure cinema." The medical work is done on the morning headlines. The bits of plaster drop on Brand's picture and the story of his escape. There's no prose equivalent as powerful as that effect. Part of its typically Hitchcockian strength derives from the fact that the scene is apparently about a particular process, setting a broken bone, when in fact its real significance to the story comes from an apparently ancillary meaning, the newspaper headlines being covered over with bits of plaster. Add to that the reactions of the various characters, particularly the silent doctor, and the scene positively shimmers. I asked if he wanted me to put in an insert shot of the newspaper. "No, just say that it's there. We won't make a fuss over of it. It will appear to be about the doctor that way."

In Scene 24, in which Brand makes his clumsy pass at Rosemary, and winds up killing her, the death might remind a viewer of "Dial M for Murder," where Grace Kelly reaches behind her for scissors with which she stabs the intruder. That's a danger in writing a Hitchcock script, you constantly find yourself semiconsciously borrowing from other Hitchcock scripts. It's not the sort of question Hitch would have enjoyed. Too bookish, I think, for him. I knew most of his films and I hoped I had internalized the information, absorbed a sense of the famous shots and elaborate set pieces, as well as the overall content of the pictures. If in fact those films were a part of me, then I could just write, trying to think about the particulars of the situation at hand, and never, ever, their cinematic antecedents. I don't mean to suggest that I never asked about other movies, but I usually tried to keep such questions narrow and specific.

"Is the cup too much like the scissors in "Dial M?""

"Only if we shoot it the same way. The tea's on the counter, we'll only see it from the front of the girl. Not like "Dial M" at all."

The trouble with questions of this sort, was that he could get testy, if we were talking about another of his films in reference to "The Short Night." If the question or statement was purely speculative, he could chew on it for days. But bring up another of his movies in reference to the work at hand, and he could grow short. I don't mean to overstate this. There were times when he would grow effusive at the opportunity to talk about another of his films in relation to the script at hand. Hitchcock did what a lot of Hollywood veterans do, which is to discuss a classic as if it were Kleenex. "A similar thing happened in a little picture we made at Paramount, a few years back." Then the little picture turns out to be "Vertigo." When Hitchcock said something like that it meant he felt like stalling or not working. If he cut off a mention of another film, it meant "Let's get on with it, I'm in a productive, working mood."

The death of Rosemary, in Scene 24 always struck me as second-rate, and we were casting about for a more theatrical or at least more surprising method. How to kill someone is the sort of thing that could engage Hitchcock indefinitely. As you can see, Rosemary's death is tepid theatrically, and it is one of the unresolved story points in the script. During discussions of the point Hitch allowed as how "I can kill a man, you know, with a swift press of the thumb." As he said it, he wiggled his thumbs and grinned.

. . .

In Scene 34, the first of the New York sequence, Joe Bailey, the hero of the story, is playing court tennis. You might ask, what is that? It's a version of tennis that predates by a few hundred years the game we all know. We got to it from the belief that Joe should be introduced doing something active—squash, basketball, tennis perhaps. That sort of thing. I confess to being ready to settle for any of them except jogging. Hitch said he had wanted to get court tennis into a film for years. It's a game so toney and upper class that it makes squash look like bowling. There are about a dozen courts in the United States. Long after I was through with the script, a friend of mine took me to play at the New York Racquet Club, which has one of the dozen courts. It's a wonderful, elaborate game that I'm sure Hitch never played. It is not for the overweight or the sedentary. It makes a fine, strange introduction to the character. It says he lives a life different from yours.

The restaurant scene, at the 21 Club, 38–45, is a version of a standard melodrama scene: the instructions to the hero. An example of a scene of this sort at its best is the ghost instructing Hamlet. At the least, or at least the most direct, it's the tape recorder that self-destructs on "Mission: Impossible." Hitchcock went back and forth on this version—one minute saying, "Oh, these scenes are predictable, just get on with it." Then on reflection, he'd look for a way to make it more interesting. My notes for the next draft of the scene, call for re-angling it, reversing the dynamic. Joe reads about the escape and confronts Zelfand, demanding to know what the CIA will do. Zelfand says they'll do nothing, that Brand's out of date. That angers Joe, who threatens to do something about it himself. "Don't," Zelfand says. And then when Joe's in Finland, the hamper with the gun in it arrives after all. The idea is to underscore that Joe's not a professional detective, but that he's driven by anger. Zelfand takes advantage of that and manipulates the anger to his own end.

My notes for the next draft of the scene outline the nub of the dynamic between Joe and Zelfand:

JOE

(Angry; Zelfand has him steamed)
What are you going to do about this?

ZELFAND

Nothing.

JOE

Then I will.

ZELFAND

We can't have anything to do with it.

Then the gun arrives in Finland. Bear in mind, this isn't meant to be the dialogue of the scene, just a preliminary draft, or sketch, of it. The important thing is that an innocent man is thrust into circumstances he doesn't fully understand; that he be a passionate amateur among cool professionals. Then, when the audience gets a look at the photo of Mrs. Brand, we'll know that Joe is in for a bumpy ride—politically, emotionally, and romantically.

There's one more Hitchcock touch in this scene that might go unnoticed in a first reading.

The scene takes place in the upstairs dining room at 21, which was one of Hitch's favorite New York restaurants. Just as there are "Vertigo" scenes in Ernie's in San Francisco, another of Hitch's favored places, he uses 21 in New York. The 21 Club is of a piece with court tennis, and that's the main reason it's called for in the script, but it's also so Hitch could spend time in a place he liked. When Joe arrives in the dining room, it's empty. Throughout the action of the scene, the off-camera tables are filling up. That means slowly building the sounds of waiters, diners, and clanking dishes in the background. The standard way to do that is just lay in a sound track of restaurant noises, soft at first, and growing louder. Not a chance. Hitch planned to hire 21's waiters, busboys, and captains, and then add to that two dozen *unseen* extras, to come into the scene. He planned to record it all live. No sound effect tracks. In addition to the scene we've been watching, there's been the parallel action—a wholly different and competing scene—going on, off-camera. The main scene—Joe and Zelfand, might be a stock one, but Hitch would find a way to make at least part of it interesting, even if only to himself.

In Scene 43, outside 21, there's an elegant camera move or two, that shows us Joe has changed his mind and is going to do what Zelfand wants. They talk, interrupted by an attempt on Zelfand's life that results in the death of a passing chauffeur. It's meant to suggest the danger ahead for Joe, and it certainly punctuates the scene. It's from the Lehman script and it's well enough drawn, but I always think scenes like this are nonsense. They say to an audience, this isn't real, it's only a movie. I tried to make the point that bullets flying on 52nd Street can't be ignored. The aftermath of such an occurrence would be enormous. I took a couple of serious whacks at getting it out of the story, but Hitch was quite fond of it. The most I could get him to do was say, "Let me think about it," which, translated from the Hitchcockian, meant "Don't be so literal about everything. It's only a movie."

Scene 48, at the news stall in Heathrow Airport, always made Hitch a little uneasy. I liked it mostly for the joke, but also because it showed the character didn't exactly have a master plan here. The avenger shows up in London and has to buy a guidebook. Hitch agreed that part was amusing. He'd never acknowledge it, but I think making fun of the English offended him. I always suspected he'd find a way to cut the scene. He went with it, at least for the script, out of politeness to me. It was quite odd, but not untypical. He'd much prefer a scene in the script that he wasn't completely at ease with, to a disagreement.

.   .   .

Scene 50, the soccer game in Hyde Park, created absolutely manic swings in Hitchcock. One moment he'd express doubts about the coincidence of Joe happening on the game, and then he'd change his mind and declare it dandy. Whenever he was in doubt about a scene, he would retreat into small particularities. In this case it was the directions from Hyde Park to Earl's Court Road. The scene might be loony, but the directions will be flawless.

Scene 54, Joe being interrogated by Inspector Wadleigh, is another example of Hitch's interest in sound. This one is simpler than the dining room at 21. Joe wanders around the Brand living room and in the background we hear Wadleigh's assistant on the phone, in the hall. A simple enough business you might think, but Hitch mused on it at length. Not what was said, but the musical, antiphonal quality of the voices.

The dramatic crux of the scene, the discovery of the scarlet soccer shirts, gave Hitch a chance to be playful almost farcical. The intention for the scene was to have the shirts appear on a clothesline in the backyard, seen through the window, as it now is in the script. But behind Joe, unseen by him. Then he starts to turn, and we assume he'll see them, but he stops. Then when he does turn, Wadleigh blocks his view. Then as Wadleigh moves away, Joe turns again. Finally, Joe turns unexpectedly, about to say something, and there are the shirts. The scene, in Hitchcock's mind, was extended, drawn out, and teasing. It also allowed him one of his favorite excercises—a scene with more than one action. Just as he liked the idea of very real off-camera sounds, because it filled the scene, he liked a parallel action running concurrently with the main, or apparent action, of the scene. From the moment Joe sees the shirts on the line, we know what he's thinking, regardless of what he says. The two strands of action in the scene are joined.

There's an odd moment in Scene 58—Joe speaking to Mrs. Jenkins, the woman with the shirts, that is revealing of Hitchcock's methods. She says:

MRS. JENKINS

Haven't those people suffered enough? It wasn't
her that done it, you know. And certainly not the
boys. You people are vultures.

After writing it, I thought the last sentence, about the vultures, was too
much, that the speech would be stronger if it ended on her thought of
the children.

In a situation like that most directors would say leave it in, it
can always be cut out later. Some might even direct the actress to
pause before saying it, to make it easier to cut later. Defer the decision and use the available technology to deal with it in the cutting
room, when all the evidence is in hand. Not Hitchcock. You decide
now, while the pressure is the least, and you make your decision
based on what the character is like, not on the possible skills of an
actress.

Until we hit on Joe seeing the soccer shirts on the line, there were
several scenes of Joe wandering about in the vicinity of Earl's Court
Road, going in and out of shops—a pastry shop, a sporting equipment
store and the like, making inquiries about the Brands and getting
nowhere. Hitch had a scheme for a while—it must have made sense at
the time—for Joe to have to pay Mrs. Brand's shop bills. The idea, as I
recall, was he would make inquiries about the Brands and the shop-
keepers wouldn't tell him anything until he cleared their debts. That
notion was dropped early on.

After Joe leaves England, chasing the parcel to Finland (Scene 64),
Hitch and I discussed watching the parcel go through the British postal
system—bouncing along a conveyor belt, having its stamps canceled,
being put on an airplane, and then repeating the procedure for the
Finnish postal system. As the parcel moved along, it would get more
and more beat up. Now, please remember, story meetings by their
nature are speculative and wide-ranging. One frequently goes off on
toots and tangents that will never wind up in a script, let alone a

movie. On reflection of the slimmest sort, it ought to be clear that watching post offices in action slows down the story.

The following scene, the establishing shots of Helsinki, might have benefited from something like Scene 46, which is from the Lehman script—the weathercock filling the screen as the Concorde flies northeast toward London. That image was a subtle reference to Lehman and Hitchcock's great film "North by Northwest." Perhaps another weathercock pointing north-northeast as Joe headed for Finland. The two together would underscore the globe-trotting nature of what Joe's doing.

In Finland, Scene 66, Joe, for all his furious activity and travel, should feel a little ridiculous standing in the Helsinki post office looking for a package. The script doesn't make clear enough that the man is filled with self-doubt, that he feels he may well be on a transcontinental fool's errand. Then when he's at low ebb, wondering what he's doing, the package turns up.

Scenes 70*ff* (the parcel being carried through the marketplace) is a sequence largely from the Lehman script. It's a sequence that even the lightly tutored eye will recognize as Alfred Hitchcock. It's fun to watch, certainly, but it's also a lovely cheat. It's as if Hitchcock were saying: If the audience gets hypnotized watching this parcel, they won't stop to think; like the parcel, they'll just be swept along. Also, when Hilda almost loses the damn thing, we know she's not exactly a master criminal.

The parcel also underscores all the movement in the picture. Like the characters, who are on trucks, vans, planes, buses, boats, and trains, the parcel always seems to be going somewhere.

Olga and Hilda, the communist functionaries in charge of Carla and her sons, are, as any reader can clearly see, butch. They are lesbians. Hitchcock has been attacked for being homophobic and it's true that homosexuals are sometimes bad guys in his films, and never good guys.

Since in our time, "the love that dare not speak its name" has become the love that won't shut up, it's pretty clear that "Rope," "Strangers on a Train," "Psycho," and "Frenzy" take a less than charitable view of homosexuality. Given what might be, the homophobia in this script is slight. I admit to some uneasiness about it now. One of the things Hitchcock wanted from me was guidance in what contemporary people thought. He knew that his own view of romance and sexuality might be thought dated and old fashioned. I believed that this story would benefit from an emotional explicitness. Hitch knew he wasn't quite comfortable with that. In fact, some of his greatness was in his ability to get intense sexual longing onto the screen in a way that by the standards of the late seventies (when we were writing the script) was positively quaint. He relied on me to keep the love *au courant*, and he relied on himself to not let me go too far.

Conventional notions of good taste, which were a great part of his personal life, had no place in his art. He wanted to be right without being lewd or unnecessarily shocking. God knows he knew all about aberrant sex, but he was unsure of how to proceed. His body was old, but this—the treatment of sexuality, both hetero and homo—was one of the few areas where his thinking might fairly be termed old fashioned. It worried him, I think, and made this surest of men uneasy.

Scene 110, Joe's hotel room in Savonlinna, is the scene in which a hamper of food from 21 is delivered, and beneath the cracked crab is a gun. All from Zelfand. If the scene in 21 has been re-angled so that Zelfand appeared to refuse any help to Joe, the gun's arrival will come as a greater surprise.

In scenes 128 and 130, Hitchcock and I wrangled endlessly about the activity on the island. He was bewitched by the vision of the island as a Brueghel painting with busy workers and a lot of activity: children playing, animals scampering about, women scrubbing clothes at the water's edge. Since, as you can see, the story depends on the island being secret, there was a contradiction here. I pointed it out to Hitchcock, who nodded and agreed. And then began talking about the Brueghel painting. So I was cast, or perhaps cast myself, in the role of Mr. Plausible working by the rules of logic and not of dreams. That's a no win position if ever there was one, so I finally declared the island reminiscent of an underpopulated Brueghel. I listed the characters and buildings I needed to make the story work—a woodchopper, a sauna, and so forth. Hitch bought it and we moved on.

In scenes 140 and 141, as Joe approaches Carla's house on the island for the first time, the door to the house seems to get larger as Joe walks toward it. The idea is to underscore Joe's nervousness. The door is only getting bigger in Joe's mind, and of course in the viewer's eyes. The device provides a visual correlative for the near panic Joe is feeling. Hitchcock had used tricks of this sort on several occasions. One example is at the end of "Spellbound" when Leo G. Carroll holds a gun on Ingrid Bergman. The gun is a large-scale prop, the idea being to show the weapon as it appears to the victim. At least two conditions have to be met before this sort of thing can work and not feel arbitrarily expressionistic: The prop or piece of scenery must remain realistic and credible, even though its scale has been pushed; and secondly, the character reacting to the device, in this case Joe, must be at a point of great personal tension, so that we are disposed to believe his eyes are playing tricks. Film makers try this sort of thing all the time. Very few can pull it off.

Scene 151, in which Neal and Roy fire an arrow with a rubber suction cup at Joe, was the occasion for Hitch's remark, "Let's pile on the menace." He kept making the sound of a suction cup hitting Joe. It was like talking with an arthritic, overweight, nine-year-old boy.

Scenes 153*ff,* is the first serious meeting between Joe and Carla. For it to work for Joe, he has to insinuate himself into Carla's life. His only tool is charm. He knows he mustn't move too quickly, but yet he has to be bold. When Carla says, "There's a lot of apologizing in the air," Joe answers, "Apologies aren't the only thing in the air." That's Hitchcock's kind of dialogue. It's sexual and the intent is clear, but it's also decorous. The audience and Carla have the same choice— they can respond in kind, or they can pretend not to get it, as Carla does.

Traditional film scripts are divided into three acts. There's no literal curtain, of course, but the act breaks are usually thought to come at those points in the script where the die is cast—that is, the emotional or the melodramatic curve is joined. So in "The Short Night" the first act is over when Joe actually meets Carla on the island. Up to this point, his intentions have been clear. At least to himself. But now he's met the woman herself and he's no longer quite so certain about what he wants or even what he feels. That emotional confusion should propel the script into Act 2. The second act is over at about Scene 279—Carla has been nearly killed and her children taken. The action for the characters is clear: Find her children and keep them from being taken to Moscow. In this script the third act is more traditional, more melodramatic, than the first two. That never bothered Hitchcock. He always felt that if you wish to appeal to a wide general audience, you must allow them a certain amount of narrative comfort. Roughly interpreted that means: No matter what personal crises the characters go through in the first two acts, in the third act, the good guys win and the bad guys lose. He never so far as I know, ever varied from that.

The three-act form is something that by necessity of my work I tend to take more seriously than Hitch ever did. When I made reference to the acts, Hitch asked why I thought there should be three, and not two or four. Before I could frame a suitably judicious answer, he said, "I believe it's the number. Three. It's the number of bears, wishes, and coins in the fountain." Then in a sweet, slightly shaky tenor, he sang a few bars: "Tha-ree co-ins in the foun-ta-in, which one will the foun-ta-in bless?"

.　　.　　.

The scenes in the sauna, 160*ff,* are a good example of one of Hitch's dicta: "If you're in Holland, use windmills." Well, we're in Finland, so we use saunas. This scene prepares us for the use of a sauna in the attempted murder of Carla. It was "Foreign Correspondent," which took place in Holland and did indeed use windmills—you'll recall they turned in reverse as a signal. In "Secret Agent," which takes place in Switzerland, there's an important sequence in a chocolate factory.

"Blackmail" (1929) has a chase through the British Museum. It's quite realistic, and like the chases and action sequences in other monuments and historic places, such as the Statue of Liberty in "Saboteur" (1942) and Mount Rushmore in "North by Northwest" (1959) it was all done in a studio. For "Blackmail," Hitchcock used a technique called the Shüfftan Process, an early German special effects system that was a precursor of the mattes Hitchcock used to such good effect later.

At the end of the first sauna sequence, the sauna attendant sings a bit of a Finnish song as he scrubs Joe's back. A routine request went to Universal's music department for some examples of Finnish folk songs, so Hitch might get a sense of them. Enough Finnish work songs, folk songs, and children's songs were sent over to make the movie a musical. It was partly because the request came from Hitch. If Alfred Hitchcock said jump, there were plenty of people to say, "How high?" But it was also because the people in the music department, technicians all, knew how much Hitch respected their technique. I do believe after watching the man in semi-action, that the thing he respected most in the world was professional competence. I think Hitch was at his most content discussing abstruse technical matters with Bob Boyle or Albert Whitlock, Universal's great matte artist, a man who could simulate a huge costly set with a painting on glass. Whitlock's work, which is legendary in the movie business, is for the most part beyond the comprehension of anyone but other matte artists. Hitch reveled in the fact that he, alone among directors and producers, knew almost as much about it as Whitlock himself. Also, Whitlock's work involved saving serious amounts of money. Technical expertise and cost cutting were a powerful combination for Hitch. But it didn't have to be anything as lofty as Whitlock or Boyle's work to engage Hitchcock. If a janitor could mop the floor quickly and efficiently and make it clean, Hitch would respect him. But let the man leave a dusty corner and Hitch would think him a fool.

One of the things I had hoped to do to the script was add another Joe-Carla scene before Scene 171, the first overt love scene. Hitchcock agreed that it was abrupt this way. A scene between Joe's arrival on the island and 171 would make the arc of his character clearer. The goal was to help the audience feel Joe's ardor developing and to watch his plans become confused with his romantic longings. After Joe meets Carla we should be unsure of just how sincere he is. In that sense, our uncertainty is like Carla's. The truth is Joe is uncertain too. He says he's drawn to her—but it was his plan to say that. The irony of the story is that it finally becomes truer than he intended it to be. The emotions keep shifting and that emotional confusion is part of what drives the story forward. Hitchcock agreed, but we never settled on the specific content of the scene, nor could we find a place for it that didn't slow down the action.

In 171 Joe makes a joke about reindeer sandwiches ("a little bit of Donner and Blitzen on rye"). Hitch asked if the joke wasn't a little too New York? I think by that he actually meant too Jewish, but was too delicate to say so. Hitch was certainly capable of jokes that slighted one group or another, but I never, ever heard anything from him that could be construed as serious ethnic, racial, or religious bigotry. My answer to the "too New York" question was, "Yes, Joe is reaching here; he's working very hard to amuse Carla, and after all, Joe is from New York." Maybe the argument was persuasive—or more likely, he couldn't bear to give up a laugh—so we kept it. Protecting jokes was serious business for Hitchcock. Remember, for all the absolutely legitimate talk of Hitchcock's moral vision, on a day-to-day basis the man was in show business. He was not about to give up a laugh unless it was absolutely necessary.

For this scene to work, we should know, before Joe does, that he's actually falling in love. If we don't feel real libido, what Joe's doing will turn us off to him. It's a very dangerous scene—all sympathy for the hero could dissolve here. It's another reason for one more Joe-Carla scene before this one—to prepare us and to prepare Joe for the lovemaking.

Later in this scene, when Carla stops the kisses and says, "You kiss better than you lie," the scene becomes hers. This is where an actress gets to strut her stuff. One of the reasons Hitchcock so often got good performances was (in addition to hiring good actors), he always tried to give them something complex to play. The last part of the scene is Carla, a troubled, frightened and lonely woman, trying to decide which to believe, her heart or her head. Joe gets his turn again at the end of the scene. Carla tells him to leave her alone and she walks away. Joe watches her go. This is a good example of why it can be so difficult to read scripts. Joe's face must tell us his dilemma. Maybe he should go—perhaps that would be the honorable thing to do. Yet, he's drawn to her, and there's the matter of his original intention—to kill Brand. His face must tell us that he's wrestling with the problem. Finally his frustration boils over and he kicks the hamper of food, spilling it. It's a hard scene, but a good actor can make it all clear, or at least as clear as these sentences, without saying a word.

The little scene in the police station, 177, amused Hitch enormously. When I showed him the draft of it, he laughed and said, "Well, at least the critics will enjoy it." I made some remark about the French and the *nouvelle vague* critics. Hitch considered that and said, "Oh, yes. The nouvelle vagrants." He giggled at his joke. He loved puns, especially his own, and if a pun could cut across more than one language, so much the better.

It was hard to know if Hitchcock, in his late seventies, was still actively fascinated by handcuffs or bondage, or just felt obligated to his myth to keep saying he was taken with the idea of being taken.

In Scene 186, as Joe and Carla kiss, first we hear bells, and then a swarm of bicyclists rides by, laughing and happy. A similar image occurs in scenes 190 and 191, when the cyclists reappear. One might make some tortured case for the bells ringing in romance or danger, but it's both more and less than a particular symbol. It's dreamlike, almost abstract, and its power is undeniable. Logical objections fall away in the face of the thing itself, which if I may say so, is not a bad overall summation of Hitchcock's films.

In every script there is a line or two that sums up the meaning of the story. It's rarely the ones that the authors put there intentionally for the purpose of declaring meaning. In Scene 187, while Joe and Carla are dining in the little cafe, Joe says of the brother whose death he has set out to avenge "When he started to work for the government, I tried to talk him out of it. . . . It was the excitement. . . . He ran off for the adventure of it."

Carla says it was similar for her husband, and ". . . to feel powerful that all these countries depend on him."

"Spying and espionage," Joe replies. "Everybody suffers from it. The gains are vague and abstract. And the losses are all personal."

If there is a psychological-political-cultural meaning in this melodrama, this is it. It leads also to a larger literary question: Just whose view is this? I know it to be Hitchcock's view, at least at the end of his life. But I wrote the dialogue. I believe it, but I probably wouldn't have written it had I not been reasonably certain Hitchcock agreed. Ernest Lehman in the preceding draft did not say it, but it's my judgment, based on his script, that he too would agree. The business of making scripts is a complex one under any circumstances, and when one is working under the direction of a cultural icon, a walking—well, sort of walking—myth, it's doubly complicated. Would I have written that if I believed it, but thought Hitch did not? I might have—and then tried to convince him to adopt the view. Then again, maybe I wouldn't have.

Scenes 201*ff*: This section, and the idea of the lovemaking occurring as Brand approaches, was the part of the script that concerned Hitchcock the most. The idea of slow and languorous lovemaking when time is so limited was at the heart of his interest. It seemed, to me, to parallel his own work. He knew he was very sick, and at the end of his life. But to rush? Of course not. All the more reason to savor. "The journey, not the destination," was said by and about another man, but it seemed to me designed for Hitchcock, in his movies certainly and in his life, at least at the end of it. He loved to toy with and examine the idea of that little boat with Gavin Brand coming over the horizon. The love was real and the husband was real; but the sound of the boat was not. It was real in the sense that it was meant to be an actual boat, but the sound of the engine was only in Carla's head. Hitchcock's sense of the motor's sound was similar to the expressionistic use of sound in "Blackmail" (1929), Hitch's and Britain's first talkie. Hitchcock used sound in that picture not just for dialogue, but as a device to penetrate and reveal character. A woman has stabbed a man, and when she sits at the breakfast table with her family, the word "knife" pops up in casual conversation. It's the only word she can hear. "Knife" bounces in and out of her brain and fills the sound track. Fifty years later, Hitch was still playing about with the possibilities of sound.

Scene 205, in which Joe and Carla face the reality of her arriving husband, is the scene in which Joe's view of what he wants and what he's willing to do, begins its final shift. It's crucial to our understanding of the characters that we realize he's now acting out of love, and not trickery. Joe and Carla decide to kill Brand together. That theme is completed in Scene 226 when Joe asks Carla to give him the knife, so that both their hands will be on it.

The major love scene, 207*ff*, played as Brand approaches, was pure Hitchcock. He insisted that the lovers defer pleasure and thereby, according to Hitchcock, "intensify it."

In 234 Joe hesitates to kill Brand. Brand, however, doesn't hesitate to try to kill Joe. That made Joe, in Hitch's eyes, a contemporary man. Joe has doubts about his actions. He isn't certain. As we talked it over, Hitch agreed that was right for the character and so long as he finally did act—the traditional obligation of the hero—it was okay for Joe to hesitate and have doubts. He did say a few times, "Things have changed." I don't think it bothered him, or made him feel out of date, just amused him.

Scenes 238–243, with Joe under water, beneath the reeds, was, with the prison break and the boat approaching, the last of Hitchcock's favorite scenes. The shots of the reeds, moving slightly and suggesting an unseen battle beneath the surface, was the purest Hitchcock.

Only the cinema could create an effect like the tips of those reeds moving, filling us with fear. And an audience would recognize the power. Consider: Things have been so arranged that the tiniest movement of reeds in the water will fill us with fear and make urgent our need to know what's happened to the hero.

By 248, when dawn breaks, and Brand is still sitting in the boat, the short night is over, and we know that with the sun, someone may soon be dead. But before that, in scenes 250 and 256, we take a moment to humanize the villain. Hitch always said, "The better the villain, the better the picture." He meant give the bastard as much human pain as possible. In "Notorious," it's the Nazi Claude Rains having to admit to his mother that he's married to an American spy. Here it's Gavin Brand wanting to see his sons. The man's been in prison for five years. He's frightened and full of complex longings. Of course one feels for him, bad guy or not.

In scenes 268–278, the attempted murder of Carla in the sauna was never quite satisfactory. The general idea is right, but the notion of a gas line in that rickety little sauna on that tiny island is wrong. Hitch liked the pipes marked in German, *Gaz und Wasser.* I tried to persuade him to switch it to smoke. The woodchopper would block the flue and start the wood fire. The smoke would do the job. Hitch wasn't convinced, but I think, given more time, I could have persuaded him, or perhaps thought of something else.

In Scene 279, Carla is alive—barely—and her children are gone, on their way to Moscow and Joe and Carla must recapture them. Nobody ever said Alfred Hitchcock didn't know how to get at an audience's collective heartstrings.

The tension is now built and running high; What to do? Throw in some jokes of course, when and where they're least expected. In 288*ff*, first we have Joe and Carla, both soaked, having trouble with a cab driver who doesn't believe these two can pay the fare; then there's Mrs. Linnankoski, a proper Finnish matron who doesn't want water dripped in her living room. She takes her sweet time in telling her husband that Joe and Carla are at the door. Linnankoski himself is in the bath. He too takes his time. It's funny and it pokes at bourgeois pretensions, which hold neatness above all things.

Scenes 315*ff*, dealing with the train in the little Finnish border station at Vainikkala, are strictly movie scenes. Hitch liked this stuff and God knows audiences do. Train sequences are at best soothingly predictable. This one is worth doing, not for the shots of those wheels churning, but for the action on the train itself.

Just before Joe boards the Russian train, 324, he gets a chance to show his traditional hero's genes, as he jumps off one train and jumps on another. He might have had self-doubts earlier, but now the chips are down, and we're at the movies. By 332 he's on a train filled with Russian soldiers and he's heading into the Soviet Union. It might stretch credibility just a wee bit, but it's entertaining.

The confrontation in 338 between Brand and Joe is the kind of hokum that always interested Hitchcock. Now the scene is about Brand's behavior in front of his sons. It was established earlier that Joe might hestitate to shoot but that Brand would not. So the tension level is high. I don't mean to suggest that Hitch didn't like the hokum—it's a commerical movie and he never forgot that. He wanted to make it the best hokum he could. He knew audiences are comforted by sequences like this one; they've seen other versions of trains chasing trains. So if he gave them a rousing good action sequence, that was his opportunity to make it psychologically interesting as well.

In Scene 354, when the Russian officer comes to break up the fight between Joe and Brand, we quickly see that the officer's a bureaucrat, not an idealogue. That sort of thing delighted Hitchcock. The officer's worried about his promotions and not getting into trouble. Besides, Hitch knew the line about New York would get a laugh from audiences everywhere in the world.

Throughout the script the only people who care about communism and capitalism and their differences are chowderheads. Sensible people care about themselves and one another. Hitch was quite fond of the idea of making Olga and Hilda, the two women keepers, the only ones interested in politics. Joe wants to avenge his brother and, later, to be with Carla. Carla only wants a life for her children. Politics are of no use to her. Even Gavin Brand, the communist spy, cares about his own problems, not the problems of nations. Hitch, in the late winter of his life, didn't care about politics, only passion. He never said it to me, at least not in words, but I think he thought of the political content of the story as a great, cosmic MacGuffin; the idealogues were the dullards, those who fought for love were vital and worth our concern.

A happy ending? Maybe. But the last image is those two little boys watching their father disappear into the Soviet Union while their mother embraces Joe. Fade out.

The Films of
Alfred Hitchcock

A Filmography

Silent Films

THE PLEASURE GARDEN (1925)

74 minutes
Production: Michael Balcon
(Gainsborough), Eric Pommer
(Emelka)
Screenplay: Eliot Stannard, based
on the novel by Oliver Sandys
Director of Photography: Baron
Ventimiglia
Continuity: Alma Reville
Studio: Emelka, at Munich
Distributors: Wardour & F.; USA,
Aywon Independent
Principal Actors:
Virginia Valli (Patsy Brand)
Carmelita Geraghty (Jill Cheyne)
Miles Mander (Levet)
John Stuart (Hugh Fielding)
Nita Naldi (Native girl)

THE MOUNTAIN EAGLE (1926)

72 minutes
U.S. Title: "Fear o' God"
Production: Michael Balcon,
Gainsborough, Emelka
Screenplay: Eliot Stannard
Director of Photography: Baron
Ventimiglia
Studio: Emelka, at Munich
Location Work: Austrian Tyrol
Distributors: Wardour & F.; USA,
Artlee; Independent Distributors
Principal Actors:
Bernard Goetzke (Pettigrew)
Nita Naldi (Beatrice)
Malcolm Keen (Fear o' God)
John Hamilton (Edward
Pettigrew).

THE LODGER (1926)

85 minutes
U.S. Title: "The Phantom Fiend"
Production: Michael Balcon,
Gainsborough
Screenplay: Alfred Hitchcock and
Eliot Stannard, based on the
novel by Mrs. Belloc-Lowndes
Director of Photography: Baron
Ventimiglia
Sets: C. Wilfred Arnold and
Bertram Evans

Editing and Subtitles: Ivor
  Montagu
Assistant Director: Alma Reville
Photographed at Islington Studios
Distributor: Wardour & F.; USA,
  Amer-Anglo Corp.
Principal Actors:
Ivor Novello (the lodger)
June (Daisy Bunting)
Marie Ault (Mrs. Bunting)
Arthur Chesney (Mr. Bunting)
Malcolm Keen (Joe Betts)

DOWNHILL (1927)

80 minutes
U.S. Title: "When Boys Leave
  Home"
Production: Michael Balcon,
  Gainsborough, G.B.
Screenplay: Eliot Stannard, based
  on the play by Ivor Novello and
  Constance Collier (written
  under the pseudonym David
  Lestrange)
Director of Photography: Claude
  McDonnell
Editor: Ivor Montagu
Photographed at Islington Studios
Distributors: Wardour & F.; USA,
  World Wide Distributors
Principal Actors:
Ivor Novello (Roddy Berwick)
Ben Webster (Doctor Dowson)
Robin Irvine (Tim Wakely)
Sybil Rhoda (Sybil Wakely)
Lillian Braithwaite (Lady Berwick)

Isabel Jeans (Julia)
Ian Hunter (Archie)

EASY VIRTUE (1927)

73 minutes
Production: Michael Balcon,
  Gainsborough
Screenplay: Eliot Stannard, based
  on the play by Noel Coward
Director of Photography: Claude
  McDonnell
Editor: Ivor Montagu
Photographed at Islington Studios
Distributors: Wardour & F.; USA,
  World Wide Distributors
Principal Actors:
Isabel Jeans (Larita Filton)
Franklin Dyall (M. Filton)
Eric Bransby Williams (Claude
  Robson)
Ian Hunter (plaintiff's counsel)
Robin Irvine (John Whittaker)
Violet Farebrother (Mrs.
  Whittaker)
and Benita Hume

THE RING (1927)

116 minutes
Production: John Maxwell, British
  International Pictures, G.B.
Screenplay: Alfred Hitchcock
Director of Photography: Jack Cox
Sets: C. Wilfred Arnold
Continuity: Alma Reville
Photographed at Elstree Studios
Distributors: Wardour & F.

Principal Actors:
Carl Brisson (Jack Sander)
Lillian Hall-Davis (Nelly)
Ian Hunter (Bob Corby)
Forrester Harvey (Harry)
and Harry Terry, Tom Helmore

THE FARMER'S WIFE (1927)

67 minutes
Production: John Maxwell, British
 International Pictures
Screenplay: Alfred Hitchcock,
 based on the play by Eden
 Philpotts
Director of Photography: Jack Cox
Sets: C. Wilford Arnold
Editor: Alfred Booth
Photographed at Elstree Studios
Distributors: Wardour & F.; USA,
 Ufa Eastman Division
Principal Actors: Jameson Thomas
 (Samuel Sweetland)
Maud Gill (Thirza Tapper)
Gordon Harker (Churdles Ash)
Lillian Hall-Davis (Arminta
 Dench)

CHAMPAGNE (1928)

104 minutes
Production: John Maxwell, British
 International Pictures
Screenplay: Eliot Stannard
Director of Photography: Jack Cox
Sets: C. Wilford Arnold
Photographed at Elstree Studios
Distributor: Wardour & F.

Principal Actors:
Betty Balfour (Betty)
Gordon Harker (her father)
Ferdinand Von Alten (the
 passenger)
Jean Bradin (Betty's fiancé)

THE MANXMAN (1929)

106 minutes
Production: John Maxwell, British
 International Pictures
Screenplay: Eliot Stannard, based
 on the novel by Sir Hall Caine
Director of Photography: Jack Cox
Sets: C. Wilford Arnold
Editor: Emile de Ruelle
Photographed at Elstree Studios
Location Work: Cornwall
Distributors: Wardour & F.; USA,
 Ufa Eastman Division
Principal Actors:
Carl Brisson (Peter Quillam)
Malcolm Keen (Philip Christian)
Anny Ondra (Kate)
Randle Ayrton (her father)

Sound Films

BLACKMAIL (1929)

86 minutes
Production: John Maxwell, British
 International Pictures
Screenplay: Alfred Hitchcock, Benn
 W. Levy, and Charles Bennett,

based on the play by Charles Bennett
Director of Photography: Jack Cox
Sets: Wilfred C. Arnold and Norman Arnold
Music: Campbell and Connely, finished and arranged by Hubert Bath and Henry Stafford, performed by the British Symphony Orchestra under the direction of John Reynders
Editor: Emile de Ruelle
Photographed at Elstree Studios
Distributors: Wardour & F.; USA, Sono Art World Wide Pictures
Principal Actors:
Anny Ondra (Alice White)
Sara Allgood (Mrs. White)
John Longden (Detective Frank Webber)
Charles Paton (Mr. White)
Donald Calthrop (Tracy)
Cyril Ritchard (the artist Crewe)

JUNO AND THE PAYCOCK (1929)

85 minutes
Production: John Maxwell, British International Pictures
Screenplay: Alfred Hitchcock and Alma Reville, based on the play by Sean O'Casey
Director of Photography: Jack Cox
Sets: Norman Arnold
Editor: Emile de Ruelle

Photographed at Elstree Studios
Distributors: Wardour & F.; USA, British International by Capt. Harold Auten
Principal Actors:
Sara Allgood (Juno)
Edward Chapman (Captain Boyle)
Sidney Morgan (Joxer)
Marie O'Neill (Mrs. Madigan)

MURDER (1929)

92 minutes
Production: John Maxwell, British International Pictures
Screenplay: Alma Reville, based on the novel and play *Enter Sir John* by Clemence Dane (pseudonym of Winifred Ashton) and Helen Simpson
Director of Photography: Jack Cox
Sets: John Mead
Editors: René Harrison and Emile de Ruelle
Photographed at Elstree Studios
Distributor: Wardour & F.; USA, British International
Principal Actors:
Herbert Marshall (Sir John Menier)
Nora Baring (Diana Baring)
Phyllis Konstam (Dulcie Markham)
Edward Chapman (Ted Markham)
Miles Mander (Gordon Druce)
Esme Percy (Handel Fane)
Donald Calthrop (Ion Stewart)

THE SKIN GAME (1931)

85 minutes
Production: John Maxwell, British
  International Pictures
Screenplay: Alfred Hitchcock,
  based on the play by John
  Galsworthy
Dialogue: Alma Reville
Director of Photography: Jack Cox
  and Charles Martin
Art Director: J. B. Maxwell
Editor: René Harrison and
  A. Gobett
Photographed at Elstree Studios
Distributors: Wardour & F.; USA,
  British International
Principal Actors:
Edmund Gwenn (Mr. Hornblower)
Jill Esmond (Jill)
John Longden (Charles)
C.V. France (Mr. Hillcrest)
Helen Haye (Mrs. Hillcrest)
Phyllis Konstam (Chloe)
Frank Lawton (Rolfe)
and Herbert Ross, Edward
  Chapman, R.E. Jeffrey, George
  Bancroft

RICH AND STRANGE (1932)

83 minutes
U.S. Title: "East of Shanghai"
Production: John Maxwell, British
  International Pictures, G.B.
Screenplay: Alma Reville and Val
  Valentine, based on a story by
  Dale Collins

Directors of Photography: Jack Cox
  and Charles Martin
Sets: C. Wilfred Arnold
Music: Hal Dolphe
Editors: Winifred Cooper and René
  Harrison
Photographed at Elstree Studios
Location Work: Marseilles, Port
  Said, Colombo, Suez
Distributors: Wardour & F.; USA,
  Powers Pictures
Principal Actors:
Henry Kendall (Freddy Hill)
Joan Barry (Emily Hill)
Betty Amann (The Princess)
Percy Marmont (Gordon)
Elsie Randolph (the old lady)

NUMBER SEVENTEEN (1932)

63 minutes
Production: John Maxwell, British
  International Pictures, G.B.
Screenplay: Alfred Hitchcock,
  Alma Reville, and Rodney
  Ackland, based on the play
  and novel by J. Jefferson
  Farjeon
Director of Photography: Jack Cox
Photographed at Elstree Studios
Distributor: Wardour & F.
Principal Actors:
Léon M. Lion (Ben)
Anne Grey (the young girl)
John Stuart (the detective)
and Donald Calthrop, Barry Jones

WALTZES FROM VIENNA (1933)

80 minutes
U.S. Title: Strauss' Great Waltz"
Production: Tom Arnold, Gaumont-British
Screenplay: Alma Reville and Guy Bolton, based on the play by Guy Bolton
Sets: Alfred Junge and Peter Proud
Music: Johann Strauss the elder and Johann Strauss the younger
Photographed at Lime Grove Studios
Distributors: G.F.D.; USA, Tom Arnold
Principal Actors:
Jessie Matthews (Rasi)
Esmond Knight (Johann Strauss the younger)
Frank Vosper (the prince)
Fay Compton (the countess)
Edmund Gwenn (Johann Strauss the elder)
Robert Hale (Ebezeder)
Hindle Edgar (Leopold)

THE MAN WHO KNEW TOO MUCH (1934)

74 minutes
Production: Michael Balcon, Gaumont-British Pictures, G.B.
Associate Producer: Ivor Montagu
Screenplay: A. R. Rawlinson and Edwin Greenwood, based on a story by Charles Bennett and D. B. Wyndham-Lewis

Additional Dialogue: Emlyn Williams
Director of Photography: Curt Courant
Sets: Alfred Junge and Peter Proud
Music: Arthur Benjamin, conducted by Louis Levy; "Storm Cloud Cantata" music by Arthur Benjamin and D. B. Wyndham-Lewis
Editor: H. St. C. Stewart
Photographed at Lime Grove Studios
Distributors: G.F.D.
Principal Actors:
Leslie Banks (Bob Lawrence)
Edna Best (Jill Lawrence)
Peter Lorre (Abbot)
Frank Vosper (Ramon Levine, the assassin)
Hugh Wakefield (Clive)
Nova Pilbeam (Betty Lawrence)
Pierre Fresnay (Louis Bernard)
Cicely Oates (Nurse Agnes)

THE 39 STEPS (1935)

87 minutes
Production: Michael Balcon, Gaumont-British
Associate Producer: Ivor Montagu
Screenplay and Adaptation: Charles Bennett, based on the novel by John Buchan
Dialogue: Ian Hay
Director of Photography: Bernard Knowles
Sets: Otto Werndorff and Albert Jullion

Costumes: J. Strassner
Music: Louis Levy
Continuity: Alma Reville
Editor: Derek N. Twist
Photographed at Lime Grove Studios
Distributors: G.F.D.
Principal Actors:
Madeleine Carroll (Pamela)
Robert Donat (Richard Hannay)
Lucie Mannheim (Annabella
 Smith)
Godfrey Tearle (Professor Jordan)
Peggy Ashcroft (Mrs. Crofter)
John Laurie (Crofter, the farmer)
Helen Haye (Mrs. Jordan)
Frank Cellier (the sheriff)
Wylie Watson (Mr. Memory)

SECRET AGENT (1936)

86 minutes
Production: Michael Balcon and
 Ivor Montagu, Gaumont-British
Screenplay: Charles Bennett, from
 the play by Campbell Dixon,
 based on the Ashenden stories
 by W. Somerset Maugham
Adaptation: Alma Reville
Dialogue: Ian Hay and Jesse
 Lasky, Jr.
Director of Photography: Bernard
 Knowles
Sets: Otto Werndorff and Albert
 Jullion
Music: Louis Levy
Editor: Charles Frend
Costumes: J. Strassner

Photographed at Lime Grove Studios
Distributors: G.F.D.; USA, G.B.
 Productions
Principal Actors:
Madeleine Carroll (Elsa
 Carrington)
John Gielgud (Edgar Brody/
 Richard Ashenden)
Peter Lorre (the general)
Robert Young (Robert Marvin)
Lilli Palmer (the maid)

SABOTAGE (1936)

76 minutes
U.S. Title: "A Woman Alone"
Production: Michael Balcon and
 Ivor Montague, Shepherd,
 Gaumont-British Pictures
Screenplay: Charles Bennett, based
 on the novel *The Secret Agent* by
 Joseph Conrad
Dialogue: Ian Hay, Helen Simpson,
 and E. V. H. Emmett
Director of Photography: Bernard
 Knowles
Sets: Otto Werndorff and Albert
 Jullion
Music: Louis Levy
Editor: Charles Frend
Costumes: J. Strassner
Photographed at Lime Grove Studios
Cartoon: Sequence of "Who Killed
 Cock Robin?" a Silly Symphony,
 Walt Disney
Distributors: G.F.D.; USA, G.B.
 Productions

Principal Actors:
Sylvia Sidney (Sylvia Verloc)
Oscar Homolka (Verloc, her
  husband)
Desmond Tester (Sylvia's brother)
John Loder (Ted, the Detective)
William Dewhurst (Mr. Chatman)
Martita Hunt (his daughter)
and Peter Bull, Joyce Barbour

YOUNG AND INNOCENT
(1937)

84 minutes
U.S. Title: "The Girl Was Young"
Production: Edward Black,
  Gainsborough, Gaumont-British
Screenplay: Charles Bennett,
  Edwin Greenwood, Anthony
  Armstrong, based on the novel
  A Shilling For Candles by
  Josephine Tey
Dialogue: Gerald Savory
Director of Photography: Bernard
  Knowles
Sets: Alfred Junge
Music: Louis Levy
Editor: Charles Frend
*Photographed at Lime Grove and
  Pinewood Studios*
Distributors: G.F.D.; USA, G.B.
  Productions
Principal Actors:
Derrick de Marney (Robert
  Tisdall)
Nova Pilbeam (Erica)
Percy Marmont (Colonel
  Burgoyne)

Edward Rigby (Old Will)
Mary Clare (Erica's aunt)
John Longden (Inspector Kent)
George Curzon (Guy)
Basil Radford (Uncle Basil)
Pamela Carme (Christine)

THE LADY VANISHES (1938)

97 minutes
Production: Edward Black,
  Gainsborough Pictures, G.B.
Screenplay: Sidney Gilliat and
  Frank Launder, based on the
  novel *The Wheel Spins* by Ethel
  Lina White
Director of Photography: Jack Cox
Sets: Alex Vetchinsky, Maurice
  Cater, and Albert Jullion
Music: Louis Levy
Editor: R.E. Dearing
Continuity: Alma Reville
Photographed at Lime Grove Studios
Distributors: MGM; USA, G.B.
  Productions
Principal Actors:
Margaret Lockwood (Iris
  Henderson)
Michael Redgrave (Gilbert)
Paul Lukas (Dr. Hartz)
Dame May Whitty (Miss Froy)
Googie Withers (Blanche)
Cecil Parker (Mr. Todhunter)
Linden Travers (Mrs. Todhunter)
Mary Clare (the baroness)
Naunton Wayne (Caldicott)
Basil Radford (Charters)

JAMAICA INN (1939)

98 minutes

Production: Erich Pommer and Charles Laughton, Mayflowers Productions, G.B.

Production Manager: Hugh Perceval

Screenplay: Sydney Gilliat and Joan Harrison, based on the novel by Daphne du Maurier

Additional Dialogue: J. B. Priestley

Directors of Photography: Harry Stradling and Bernard Knowles

Special Effects: Harry Watt

Sets: Tom N. Moraham

Costumes: Molly McArthur

Music: Eric Fenby

Editor: Robert Hamer

Photographed at Elstree Studios

Distributors: Associated British; USA, Paramount

Principal Actors:

Charles Laughton (Sir Humphrey Pengallan)

Maureen O'Hara (Mary, his niece)

Leslie Banks (Joss Merlyn)

Marie Ney (Patience, his wife)

Emyln Williams (Harry)

Robert Newton (Jem Traherne)

REBECCA (1940)

130 minutes

Production: David O. Selznick, Selznick International

Screenplay: Robert E. Sherwood and Joan Harrison, based on the novel by Daphne du Maurier

Adaptation: Philip MacDonald and Michael Hogan

Director of Photography: George Barnes

Art Director: Lyle Wheeler

Music: Franz Waxman

Editor: Hal C. Kern

Distributor: United Artists

Principal Actors:

Laurence Olivier (Maxim de Winter)

Joan Fontaine (Mrs. de Winter)

George Sanders (Jack Favell)

Judith Anderson (Mrs. Danvers)

Nigel Bruce (Major Giles Lacey)

C. Aubrey Smith (Colonel Julyan)

Gladys Cooper (Beatrice)

Florence Bates (Mrs. van Hopper)

Leo G. Carroll (doctor)

and Reginald Denny

FOREIGN CORRESPONDENT (1940)

120 minutes

Production: Walter Wanger, United Artists

Screenplay: Charles Bennett and Joan Harrison

Dialogue: James Hilton and Robert Benchley

Director of Photography: Rudolph Maté

Special Effects: Lee Zavitz

Art Directors: William Cameron Menzies and Alexander Golitzen

Editors: Otto Lovering and Dorothy Spencer

Music: Alfred Newman

Photographed at United Artists Studio (Goldwyn)

Distributor: United Artists

Principal Actors:

Joel McCrea (Johnny Jones)
Laraine Day (Carol Fisher)
Herbert Marshall (Stephen Fisher)
George Sanders (Herbert ffolliott)
Albert Basserman (Van Meer)
Robert Benchley (Stebbins)
Eduardo Cianelli (Krug)
Edmund Gwenn (Rowley)
Harry Davenport (Mr. Powers)

MR. AND MRS. SMITH (1941)

95 minutes

Production: Harry E. Edington, RKO

Story and Screenplay: Norman Krasna

Director of Photography: Harry Stradling

Special Effects: Vernon L. Walker

Art Directors: Van Nest Polglase and L. P. Williams

Editor: William Hamilton

Music: Roy Webb

Principal Actors:

Carole Lombard (Ann Krausheimer Smith)
Robert Montgomery (David Smith)
Gene Raymond (Jeff Custer)
Jack Carson (Chuck Benson)
Philip Merivale (Mr. Custer)

Lucille Watson (Mrs. Custer)
William Tracy (Sammy)

SUSPICION (1941)

99 minutes

Production: RKO

Screenplay: Samson Raphaelson, Joan Harrison, and Alma Reville, based on the novel *Before the Fact* by Francis Iles

Director of Photography: Harry Stradling

Special Effects: Vernon L. Walker

Art Director: Van Nest Polglase

Assistant: Carroll Clark

Editor: William Hamilton

Music: Franz Waxman

Principal Actors:

Cary Grant (Johnny Aysgarth)
Joan Fontaine (Lina McLaidlaw)
Sir Cedric Hardwicke (General McLaidlaw)
Nigel Bruce (Beaky Thwaite)
Dame May Whitty (Mrs. McLaidlaw)
Isabel Jeans (Mrs. Newsham)
and Leo G. Carroll, Heather Angel

SABOTEUR (1942)

108 minutes

Production: Frank Lloyd and Jack H. Skirball, Universal

Screenplay: Peter Viertel, Joan Harrison, and Dorothy Parker

Director of Photography: Joseph Valentine

Art Director: Jack Otterson
Editor: Otto Ludwig
Music: Charles Previn and Frank Skinner
Principal Actors:
Robert Cummings (Barry Kane)
Priscilla Lane (Patricia Martin)
Otto Kruger (Charles Tobin)
Alan Baxter (Mr. Freedman)
Alma Kruger (Mrs. Van Sutton)
Norman Lloyd (Fry)
and Ian Wolfe

SHADOW OF A DOUBT (1943)

108 minutes
Production: Jack H. Skirball, Universal
Screenplay: Thornton Wilder, Alma Reville, and Sally Benson, based on a story by Gordon McDonnell
Director of Photography: Joseph Valentine
Sets: John B. Goodman, Robert Boyle, A. Gausman, and L. R. Robinson
Editor: Milton Carruth
Music: Dimitri Tiomkin, conducted by Charles Previn
Costumes: Adrian, Vera West
Location Work: Santa Rosa, California
Principal Actors:
Joseph Cotten (Uncle Charlie)
Teresa Wright (Charlie Newton, his niece)
MacDonald Carey (Jack Graham)

Patricia Collinge (Emma Newton)
Henry Travers (Joseph Newton)
Hume Cronyn (Herbie Hawkins)
Wallace Ford (Fred Saunders)
Edna May Wonacutt (Ann Newton)
Charles Bates (Roger Newton)

LIFEBOAT (1943)

66 minutes
Production: Kenneth MacGowan, 20th Century-Fox
Screenplay: Jo Swerling, based on a story by John Steinbeck
Director of Photography: Glen MacWilliams
Special Effects: Fred Sersen
Art Directors: James Basevi and Maurice Ransford
Editor: Dorothy Spencer
Music: Hugo Friedhofer
Costumes: Rene Hubert
Studio: 20th Century-Fox
Actors:
Tallulah Bankhead (Constance Porter)
William Bendix (Gus Smith)
Walter Slezak (Willie)
Mary Anderson (Alice MacKenzie)
John Hodiak (John Kovac)
Henry Hull (Charles S. Rittenhouse)
Heather Angel (Mrs. Higgins)
Hume Cronyn (Stanley Garett)
Canada Lee (George Spencer)

SPELLBOUND (1945)

111 minutes

Production: David O. Selznick, Selznick International

Screenplay: Ben Hecht, based on the novel *The House of Dr. Edwardes* by Francis Beeding

Director of Photography: George Barnes

Special Photographic Effects: Jack Cosgrove

Art Director: James Basevi

Editors: William Ziegler and Hal C. Kern

Music: Miklos Rozsa

Costumes: Howard Greer

Dream Sequence: Salvador Dali

Psychiatric Consultant: May E. Romm, M.D.

Distributor: United Artists

Principal Actors:

Ingrid Bergman (Doctor Constance Petersen),

Gregory Peck (John Ballantine)

Jean Acker (the directress)

Rhonda Fleming (Mary Carmichel)

John Emery (Dr. Fleurot)

Leo G. Carroll (Dr. Murchison)

Norman Lloyd (Garmes)

Michael Chekhov (Dr. Alex Brulov)

and Bill Goodwin, Art Baker, Wallace Ford, Regis Toomey

NOTORIOUS (1946)

101 minutes

Production: Alfred Hitchcock, RKO

Associate Producer: Barbara Keon

Screenplay: Ben Hecht, based on a theme by Alfred Hitchcock

Director of Photography: Ted Tetzlaff

Special Effects: Vernon L. Walker and Paul Eagler

Art Directors: Albert S. D'Agostino, Carrol Clark

Sets: Darrell Silvera and Claude Carpenter

Editor: Theron Warth

Costumes: Edith Head

Music: Roy Webb, conducted by Constantin Bakaleinikoff

Principal Actors:

Ingrid Bergman (Alicia Huberman)

Cary Grant (T. R. Devlin)

Claude Rains (Alexander Sebastian)

Louis Calhern (Paul Prescott)

Leopoldine Konstantin (Mrs. Sebastian)

and Ivan Triesault, Sir Charles Mendl, Maroni Olson

THE PARADINE CASE (1947)

125 minutes

Production: David O. Selznick, Selznick International

Screenplay: David O. Selznick, based on the novel by Robert Hichens

Director of Photography: Lee Garmes

Art Directors: Joseph MacMillian Johnson and Thomas Morahan

Editors: Hal C. Kern and John
  Faure
Music: Franz Waxman
Costumes: Travis Banton
Distributor: United Artists
Principal Actors:
Gregory Peck (Anthony Keane)
Anne Todd (Gay Keane)
Charles Laughton (Judge Horfield)
Alida Valli (Mrs. Paradine)
Ethel Barrymore (Lady Sophie
  Horfield)
Charles Coburn (Sir Simon
  Flaquer, the lawyer)
Louis Jourdan (Andre Latour)
Joan Tetzel (Judy Flaquer)
Leo G. Carroll (Sir Joseph Farrell)
and John Williams, Isobel Elsom

ROPE (1948)

80 minutes
Production: Sidney Bernstein and
  Alfred Hitchcock, Transatlantic
  Pictures, Warner Brothers
Screenplay: Arthur Laurents, based
  on the play by Patrick Hamilton
Adaptation: Hume Cronyn
Directors of Photography: Joseph
  Valentine and William V. Skall
Color: Technicolor
Art Director: Perry Ferguson
Music: Leo F. Forbstein, based on
  "Mouvement Perpetuel #1" by
  Francis Poulenc
Editor: William H. Ziegler
Costumes: Adrian

Principal Actors:
James Stewart (Rupert Cadell)
John Dall (Shaw Brandon)
Farley Granger (Philip)
Joan Chandler (Janet Walker)
Sir Cedric Hardwicke (Mr. Kentley)
Constance Collier (Mrs. Atwater)
Edith Evanson (Mrs. Wilson, the
  housekeeper)
Douglas Dick (Kenneth Lawrence)
Dick Hogan (David Kentley)

UNDER CAPRICORN (1949)

Production: Sidney Bernstein and
  Alfred Hitchcock, Transatlantic
  Pictures, Warner Brothers, G.B.
Screenplay: James Bridie, based on
  the novel by Helen Simpson
Adaptation: Hume Cronyn
Director of Photography: Jack
  Cardiff
Art Director: Tom Morahan
Editor: A. S. Bates
Music: Richard Addinsell,
  conducted by Louis Levy
Costumes: Roger Furse
Continuity: Peggy Singer
  (Robertson)
Color: Technicolor
*Photographed at MGM, British
  (Elstree)*
Distributor: Warner Brothers
Principal Actors:
Ingrid Bergman (Lady Henrietta
  Flusky)
Joseph Cotten (Sam Flusky)

Michael Wilding (Charles Adare)
Margaret Leighton (Milly)
Jack Watting (Winter, Flusky's
secretary)
Cecil Parker (Sir Richard, the tutor)
Dennis O'Dea (Corrigan, the
attorney general)

STAGE FRIGHT (1950)

110 minutes
Production: Alfred Hitchcock,
Warner Brothers, G.B.
Screenplay: Whitfield Cook, based
on "Man Running" and
"Outrun the Constable" by
Selwyn Jepson
Adaptation: Alma Reville
Director of Photography: Wilkie
Cooper
Art Director: Terence Verity
Music: Leighton Lucas, conducted
by Louis Levy
Editor: Edward Jarvis
Photographed at Elstree Studios
Principal Actors:
Marlene Dietrich (Charlotte
Inwood)
Jane Wyman (Eve Gill)
Michael Wilding (Inspector
Wilfred Smith)
Richard Todd (Jonathan Cooper)
Alastair Sim (Commodore Gill)
Dame Sybil Thorndike (Mrs. Gill)
Patricia Hitchcock (Chubby
Bannister)
and Joyce Grenfell, Miles
Malleson, André Morell

STRANGERS ON A TRAIN (1951)

101 minutes
Production: Alfred Hitchcock,
Warner Brothers
Screenplay: Raymond Chandler and
Czenzi Ormonde, based on the
novel by Patricia Highsmith
Adaptation: Whitfield Cook
Director of Photography: Robert
Burks
Special Photographic Effects: H. F.
Koene-Kamp
Art Director: Edward S. Haworth
Sets: George James Hopkins
Editor: William H. Ziegler
Music: Dimitri Tiomkin, conducted
by Ray Heindorf
Costumes: Leah Rhodes
Location Work: Washington, D.C.
Forest Hills, N.Y., New York City
Principal Actors:
Farley Granger (Guy Haines)
Ruth Roman (Ann Morton)
Robert Walker (Bruno Anthony)
Leo G. Carroll (Senator Morton)
Patricia Hitchcock (Barbara
Morton)
Laura Elliot (Miriam Haines)
Marion Lorne (Mrs. Anthony)
Jonathan Hale (Mr. Anthony)

I CONFESS (1952)

95 minutes
Production: Alfred Hitchcock,
Warner Brothers

Screenplay: George Tabori and William Archibald, based on the play *Nos Deux Consciences* by Paul Anthelme

Director of Photography: Robert Burks

Art Director: Edward S. Haworth

Sets: George James Hopkins

Editor: Rudi Fehr

Music: Dimitri Tiomkin, conducted by Ray Heindorf

Costumes: Orry-Kelly

Technical Consultants: Father Paul la Couline, Inspector Oscar Tangvay

Location Work: Quebec

Principal Actors:

Montgomery Clift (Father Michael Logan)

Anne Baxter (Ruth Grandfort)

Karl Malden (Inspector Larrue)

Brian Aherne (Willy Robertson, the attorney)

O. E. Hasse (Otto Keller)

Dolly Haas (Alma Keller, his wife)

Roger Dann (Pierre Grandfort)

Charles André (Father Millais)

DIAL M FOR MURDER (1954)

123 minutes

Production: Alfred Hitchcock, Warner Brothers

Screenplay: Frederick Knott, adapted from his stage play

Director of Photography: Robert Burks, (3-D, Naturalvision)

Color: Warnercolor

Art Director: Edward Carrère

Sets: George James Hopkins

Music: Dimitri Tiomkin

Costumes: Moss Mabry

Editor: Rudi Fehr

Principal Actors:

Ray Milland (Tony Wendice)

Grace Kelly (Margot Wendice)

Robert Cummings (Mark Halliday)

John Williams (Chief Inspector Hubbard)

Anthony Dawson (Captain Swan/Lesgate)

Patrick Allen (Pearson)

George Leigh (William)

George Alderson (the detective)

Robin Hughes (police sergeant)

REAR WINDOW (1954)

112 minutes

Production: Alfred Hitchcock, Paramount

Screenplay: John Michael Hayes, based on a novella by Cornell Woolrich

Director of Photography: Robert Burks

Color: Technicolor

Special Effects: John P. Fulton

Art Director: Hal Pereira

Sets: Joseph McMillan Johnson, Sam Comer, Ray Moyer

Editor: George Tomasini

Music: Franz Waxman

Costumes: Edith Head

Assistant Director: Herbert Coleman
Technical Adviser: Bob Landry
Principal Actors:
James Stewart (L. B. Jeffries)
Grace Kelly (Lisa Fremont)
Wendell Corey (Detective Tom
　Doyle)
Thelma Ritter (Stella, the nurse)
Raymond Burr (Lars Thorwald)
Judith Evelyn (Miss Lonelyheart)
Ross Bagdasarian (the composer)
Georgine Darcy (Miss Torso, the
　dancer)
Jesslyn Fax (sculptress)
Rand Harper (honeymooner)
Irene Winston (Mrs. Thorwald)

TO CATCH A THIEF (1955)

97 minutes
Production: Alfred Hitchcock,
　Paramount
Second Unit Direction: Herbert
　Coleman
Screenplay: John Michael Hayes,
　based on the novel by David
　Dodge
Director of Photography: Robert
　Burks, (VistaVision)
Photography Second Unit: Wallace
　Kelley
Color: Technicolor
Special Effects: John P. Fulton
Process Photo: Farciot Edouart
Art Director: Hal Pereira
Sets: Joseph MacMillan Johnson,
　Sam Comer, and Arthur Krams

Music: Lyn Murray
Editor: George Tomasini
Costumes: Edith Head
Location Work: South of France
Principal Actors:
Cary Grant (John Robie)
Grace Kelly (Frances Stevens)
Charles Vanel (Bertani)
Jessie Royce Landis (Mrs. Stevens)
Brigitte Auber (Danielle Foussard)
Rene Blancard (Commissioner
　Lepic)
John Williams (insurance
　inspector)

THE TROUBLE WITH HARRY
(1956)

99 minutes
Production: Alfred Hitchcock,
　Paramount
Associate Producer: Herbert
　Coleman
Screenplay: John Michael Hayes,
　based on the novel by John
　Trevor Story
Director of Photography: Robert
　Burks, (VistaVision)
Special Effects: John P. Fulton
Color: Technicolor
Art Directors: Hal Pereira, John
　Goodman
Sets: Sam Comer, Emile Kuri
Music: Bernard Herrmann
Editor: Alma Macrorie
Costumes: Edith Head
Location Work: Vermont

Principal Actors:
Edmund Gwenn (Captain Albert
Wiles)
John Forsythe (Sam Marlowe)
Shirley MacLaine (Jennifer,
Harry's wife)
Mildred Natwick (Miss Gravely)
Mildred Dunnock (Mrs. Wiggs)
Jerry Mathers (Tony, Harry's son)
Royal Dano (Calvin Wiggs)
Phillip Truex (Harry)

THE MAN WHO KNEW TOO MUCH (Second Version) (1956)

120 minutes
Production: Alfred Hitchcock,
Paramount, Filmwite
Productions
Associate Producer: Herbert
Coleman
Screenplay: John Michael Hayes
and Angus McPhail, based on a
story by Charles Bennett and
D. B. Wyndham-Lewis
Director of Photography: Robert
Burks (VistaVision)
Color: Technicolor
Art Directors: Hal Pereia, Henry
Bumstead
Sets: Sam Comer, Arthur Krams
Music: Bernard Herrmann
Lyrics: "Que Sera, Sera"
("Whatever Will Be")and "We'll
Love Again" by Jay Livingston
and Ray Evans; "Storm Cloud

Cantata" by Arthur Benjamin
and D. B. Wyndham-Lewis,
performed by the London
Symphony Orchestra conducted
by Bernard Herrmann
Editor: George Tomasini
Costumes: Edith Head
Location Work: Morocco, London
Principal Actors:
James Stewart (Dr. Ben McKenna)
Doris Day (Jo McKenna)
Daniel Gélin (Louis Bernard)
Brenda de Banzie (Mrs. Drayton)
Bernard Miles (Mr. Drayton)
Ralph Truman (Inspector
Buchanan)
Magens Wieth (the ambassador)
Alan Mowbray (Val Parnell)
Hilary Brooke (Jan Peterson)
Christopher Olsen (little Hank
McKenna)
Reggie Malder (Rien, the assassin)
Carolyn Jones (Cindy Fontaine)

THE WRONG MAN (1957)

105 minutes
Production: Alfred Hitchcock,
Warner Brothers
Associate Producer: Herbert Coleman
Screenplay: Maxwell Anderson and
Angus McPhail, based on "The
True Story of Christopher
Emmanuel Balestrero" by
Maxwell Anderson
Director of Photography: Robert
Burks

Art Director: Paul Sylbert

Sets: William L. Kuehl

Music: Bernard Herrmann

Editor: George Tomasini

Location Work: New York

Technical Consultants: Frank O'Connor, District Attorney, Queens County, New York, and George Groves, Sergeant, New York City Police Department, Ret.

Sound Engineer: Earl Crain, Sr.

Principal Actors:

Henry Fonda (Christopher Emmanuel Balestrero)

Vera Miles (Rose, his wife)

Nehemiah Persoff (Gene Conforti)

Anthony Quayle (O'Connor)

Harold J. Stone (Lieutenant Bowers)

Charles Cooper (Matthews, a detective)

John Heldabrand (Tomasini)

Richard Robbins (Daniel, the guilty man)

VERTIGO (1958)

120 minutes

Production: Alfred Hitchcock, Paramount

Associate Producer: Herbert Coleman

Screenplay: Alec Coppel and Samuel Taylor, based on the novel *D'entre les Morts* by Pierre Boileau and Thomas Narcejac

Director of Photography: Robert Burks (VistaVision)

Process Photography: Farciot Edouart and Wallace Kelly

Special Effects: John Fulton

Color: Technicolor

Art Directors: Hal Pereira, Henry Bumstead

Sets: Sam Comer, Frank McKelvey

Editor: George Tomasini

Music: Bernard Herrmann, conducted by Muir Mathieson

Costumes: Edith Head

Titles: Saul Bass

Dream Sequence: Designed by John Ferren

Location Work: San Francisco, San Juan Bautista, Muir Woods, Mill Valley

Distributor: Paramount

Principal Actors:

James Stewart (John "Scottie" Ferguson)

Kim Novak (Madeleine Elster, Judy Barton)

Barbara Bel Geddes (Midge Wood)

Henry Jones (the coroner)

Tom Helmore (Gavin Elster)

Raymond Bailey (the doctor)

Ellen Corby (hotel manager)

Konstantin Shayne (Pop Liebl)

and Lee Patrick

NORTH BY NORTHWEST (1959)

136 minutes

Production: Alfred Hitchcock, MGM

Associate Producer: Herbert Coleman
Screenplay: Ernest Lehman
Director of Photography: Robert Burks (VistaVision)
Color: Technicolor
Special Photographic Effects: A. Arnold Gillespie and Lee LeBlanc
Art Directors: Robert Boyle, William A. Horning, Merrill Pye
Sets: Henry Grace, Frank McKelvey
Music: Bernard Herrmann
Editor: George Tomasini
Title Design: Saul Bass
Location Work: Manhattan Long Island, Chicago, Mount Rushmore
Principal Actors:
Cary Grant (Roger Thornhill)
Eva Marie Saint (Eve Kendall)
James Mason (Phillip Vandamm)
Jessie Royce Landis (Clara Thornhill)
Leo G. Carroll (the professor)
Philip Ober (Lester Townsend)
Josephine Hutchinson (Vandamm's sister)
Les Tremayne (auctioneer)
Phillip Coolidge (Dr. Cross)
Patrick McVey (Chicago policeman)
Edward Platt (Victor Larrabee)
Robert Ellenstein (Licht)
Martin Landau (Leonard)

Adam Williams (Valerian)
Edward Binns (Captain Junket)
and Ned Glass, Malcolm Atterbury

PSYCHO (1960)

109 minutes
Production: Alfred Hitchcock, Paramount
Screenplay: Joseph Stefano, based on the novel by Robert Bloch
Director of Photography: John L. Russell
Art Directors: Joseph Hurley, Robert Claworthy
Sets: George Milo
Music: Bernard Herrmann
Title Design: Saul Bass
Editor: George Tomasini
Assistant Director: Hilton A. Green
Costumes: Helen Colvig
Photographed at Universal Studios
Location Work: Phoenix, Arizona, San Fernando Valley, California
Principal Actors:
Anthony Perkins (Norman Bates)
Janet Leigh (Marion Crane)
Vera Miles (Lila Crane)
John Gavin (Sam Loomis)
Martin Balsam (Milton Arbogast)
John McIntire (Sheriff Chambers)
Lurene Tuttle (Mrs. Chambers)
Simon Oakland (Dr. Richmond)
Frank Albertson (Cassidy)
Patricia Hitchcock (Caroline)

THE BIRDS (1963)

119 minutes
Production: Alfred Hitchcock,
  Universal
Assistant to Mr. Hitchcock: Peggy
  Robertson
Screenplay: Evan Hunter, based on
  a story by Daphne du Maurier
Director of Photography: Robert
  Burks
Color: Technicolor
Special Effects: Lawrence A.
  Hampton
Pictorial Designs: Albert Whitlock
Special Photographic Adviser:
  Ub Iwerks
Art Directors: Robert Boyle and
  George Milo
Sound Consultant: Bernard
  Herrmann
Electronic Sound: Remi Gassman
  and Oskar Sala
Bird Trainer: Ray Berwick
Editor: George Tomasini
Location Work: Bodega Bay,
  California; San Francisco
Distributor: Universal
Principal Actors:
Rod Taylor (Mitch Brenner)
Tippi Hedren (Melanie Daniels)
Jessica Tandy (Mrs. Brenner)
Suzanne Pleshette (Annie
  Hayworth)
Veronica Cartwright (Cathy
  Brenner)
Ethel Griffies (Mrs. Bundy)
Charles McGraw (Sebastien Sholes)
Ruth McDevitt (Mrs. MacGruder)
Elizabeth Wilson (waitress)
Malcolm Atterbury (Deputy Al
  Malone)
Karl Swenson (drunk)
Lonny Chapman (Deke Carter)
Doodles Weaver (a fisherman)
Doreen Long (hysterical woman in
  restaurant)
and John McGovern, Richard
  Deacon, William Quinn, Joe
  Mantell

MARNIE (1964)

130 minutes
Production: Alfred Hitchcock,
  Universal
Assistant to Mr. Hitchcock: Peggy
  Robertson
Screenplay: Jay Presson Allen,
  based on the novel by Winston
  Graham
Director of Photography: Robert
  Burks
Color: Technicolor
Art Director: Robert Boyle
Sets: George Milo
Editor: George Tomasini
Music: Bernard Herrmann
Distributor: Universal
Principal Actors:
Tippi Hedren (Marnie Edgar)
Sean Connery (Mark Rutland)
Diane Baker (Lil Mainwaring)
Martin Gabel (Sidney Strutt)
Louise Latham (Bernice Edgar,
  Marnie's mother)

Bob Sweeney (Cousin Bob)
Alan Napier (Mr. Rutland)
Bruce Dern (the sailor)
S. John Launer (Sam Ward)
Mariette Hartley (Susan Clabon)
Meg Wyllie (Mrs. Turpin)

TORN CURTAIN (1966)

128 minutes
Production: Alfred Hitchcock,
  Universal
Assistant to Mr. Hitchcock: Peggy
  Robertson
Screenplay: Brian Moore
Directors of Photography: John F.
  Warren, Hein Heckroth
Art Director: Frank Arrigo
Sets: George Milo
Special Effects (mattes): Albert
  Whitlock
Editor: Bud Hoffman
Music: John Addison
Principal Actors:
Paul Newman (Professor Michael
  Armstrong)
Julie Andrews (Sarah Sherman)
Lila Kedrova (Countess Kuchinska)
Tamara Toumanova (ballerina)
Wolfgang Kieling (Hermann
  Gromek)
Ludwig Donath (Professor Gustav
  Lindt)
David Opatoshu (Mr. Jacobi)
Mort Mills (farmer)
Carolyn Conwell (farmer's wife)
Arthur Gould-Porter (Freddy)

TOPAZ (1969)

125 minutes
Production: Alfred Hitchcock,
  Universal
Assistant to Mr. Hitchcock: Peggy
  Robertson
Screenplay: Samuel Taylor, based
  on the novel by Leon Uris
Director of Photography: Jack
  Hildyard
Color: Technicolor
Special Photographic Effects (mattes):
  Albert Whitlock
Art Directors: John Austin,
  Alexander Golitzen, Henry
  Bumstead
Editor: William Ziegler
Music: Maurice Jarre
Costumes: Edith Head
Second Unit Location Work:
  Copenhagen, Wiesbaden, Paris,
  New York, Washington
Principal Actors:
Frederick Stafford (André
  Devereaux)
Dany Robin (Nicole Devereaux)
Claude Jade (Michele Picard)
Michel Subor (François Picard)
Michel Piccoli (Jacques Granville)
Philippe Noiret (Henri Jarré)
John Forsythe (Michael
  Nordstrom)
Karin Dor (Juanita de Cordoba)
Per-Axel Arosenius (Boris
  Kusenov)
Sonja Kolthoff (Mrs. Kusenov)
John Vernon (Rico Parra)

Roscoe Lee Browne (Philippe
   Dubois)
Tina Hedstrom (Tamara Kusenov)
John Roper (Thomas)
Anna Navarro (Carlotta Mendoza)
Lewis Charles (Pablo Mendoza)

FRENZY (1972)

116 minutes
Production: Alfred Hitchcock,
   Universal
Assistant to Mr. Hitchcock: Peggy
   Robertson
Screenplay: Anthony Shaffer, based
   on the novel *Goodbye Piccadilly,
   Farewell Leicester Square* by
   Arthur La Bern
Director of Photography: Gil Taylor
Color: Technicolor
Art Directors: Robert Laing,
   Sydney Cain
Editor: John Jympson
Music: Ron Goodwin
Sets: Simon Wakefield
*Photographed at Pinewood Studios
   and the London Streets*
Principal Actors:
Jon Finch (Richard Blaney)
Alec McCowen (Inspector Oxford)
Barry Foster (Bob Rusk)
Barbara Leigh-Hunt (Brenda
   Blaney)
Anna Massey (Babs Milligan)
Vivien Merchant (Mrs. Oxford)
Billie Whitelaw (Hetty Porter)
Bernard Cribbins (Felix Forsythe)

Clive Swift (Johnny Porter)
Jean Marsh (Monica Barling)

ALFRED HITCHCOCK'S FAMILY PLOT (1976)

120 minutes
Production: Alfred Hitchcock
Assistant to Mr. Hitchcock: Peggy
   Robertson
Assistant Director: Howard Kazanjian
Screenplay: Ernest Lehman based
   on the novel *The Rainbird
   Pattern,* by Victor Canning
Director of Photography: Leonard J.
   South
Special Effects (mattes): Albert
   Whitlock
Art Director: Henry Bumstead
Sets: James Payne
Editor: Terry Williams
Music: John Williams
Costumes: Edith Head
Location Work: San Francisco and
   Los Angeles
Principal Actors:
Karen Black (Fran)
Bruce Dern (Lumley)
Barbara Harris (Blanche)
William Devane (Adamson)
Cathleen Nesbitt (Julia Rainbird)
Ed Lauter (Maloney)
Katherine Helmond (Mrs.
   Maloney)
William Prince (Bishop)
Nicolas Colasanto (Constantine)
Marge Redmond (Vera Hannagan)

False Starts

In addition to his feature films, Alfred Hitchcock also worked in various production capacities on a series of silent films for the American company, Famous Players-Lasky, the forerunner of Paramount, at their Islington studio. Hitchcock designed title cards for a series of silent films, from 1920-1922, including:

"The Call of Youth," "Beside the Bonnie Briar Bush," "The Great Day," "The Princess of New York," "Tell Your Children," and "Three Live Ghosts."

None of the films have survived.

Hitchcock had false starts as a director on:

NUMBER THIRTEEN (1922)

The film, a two-reeler, was abandoned before it was completed and is now lost.

ALWAYS TELL YOUR WIFE (1922)

When the director Hugh Croise was unable to continue, Hitchcock took over. But this film too, was abandoned before completion.

Hitchcock then returned to general production capacities:

WOMAN TO WOMAN (1923)

Producers: Michael Balcon, Victor Saville, John Freedman
Director: Graham Cutts
Scenario: Graham Cutts and Alfred Hitchcock
Sets: Alfred Hitchcock
Assistant Director: Alfred Hitchcock

THE WHITE SHADOW (1923)

Producers: Michael Balcon, Victor Saville, John Freedman
Director: Graham Cutts
Scenario: Michael Morton, from his play
Sets: Alfred Hitchcock
Editor: Alfred Hitchcock

THE PASSIONATE ADVENTURE (1924)

Producer: Michael Balcon, for Gainsborough
Director: Graham Cutts
Scenario: Alfred Hitchcock and Michael Morton, from a novel by Frank Stayton
Sets: Alfred Hitchcock
Assistant Director: Alfred Hitchcock

THE BLACKGUARD (1925)

Producer: Michael Balcon, for Gainsborough, a co-production

with Ufa, shot in Berlin at the Neubabelsberg Studios
Director: Graham Cutts
Scenario: Alfred Hitchcock, from a novel by Ramond Paton
Sets: Alfred Hitchcock
Assistant Director: Alfred Hitchcock

THE PRUDE'S FALL (1925)

Producer: Michael Balcon, Victor Saville, John Freedman for Gainsborough
Director: Graham Cutts
Scenario: Alfred Hitchcock, from a play by Rudolph Besier
Sets: Alfred Hitchcock
Assistant Director: Alfred Hitchcock

In 1930 Hitchcock was a participating director in "Elstree Calling," a filmed revue that was made to introduce and promote sound pictures. Several directors under the supervision of Adrian Brunel, including André Charlot, Jack Hulbert, and Paul Murray in addition to Hitchcock, directed parts of the film. Hitchcock's contribution was a running gag in which a primitive television set, that was supposed to broadcast the acts of "Elstree Calling," refused to work.

During World War II, in addition to his feature films, Hitchcock made:

BON VOYAGE AND ADVENTURE MALGACHE (MADAGASCAR ADVENTURE) (1944)

Two short films made in England for the British Ministry of Information. Both films were shot in French with French casts and crews. They were intended to be shown in liberated parts of France to acquaint French citizens with the work of the Free French resistance movement. Hitchcock made both films as part of the war effort.

Television Films

In 1955 Hitchcock began the television series, "Alfred Hitchcock Presents," and produced 365 episodes over the next ten years. During that time he directed twenty episodes, for his own series and for others:

BREAKDOWN (1955)

30 minutes, CBS
Written by: Francis Cockrell and Louis Pollock
Cast: Joseph Cotten.

Cotten, a man who disdains tears, has a terrible car accident and is presumed to be dead. In fact, he's paralyzed but completely aware of the people standing over him, treating him like a corpse. Most of the production is done in a voice-over of Cotten's thoughts, a device that's both theatrical and inexpensive, a great Hitchcock combination. As Cotten is being prepared for burial, he sheds a tear, and that shows he's alive.

REVENGE (1955)

30 minutes, CBS
Written by: Francis Cockrell and A. I. Bezzerides, from a story by Samuel Blas
Cast: Ralph Meeker, Vera Miles.

Miles has been attacked, so she and her husband, Meeker, drive through town looking for the assailant. Miles sees him on the street and says, "That's him," and Meeker takes bloody off-camera revenge. Then on the way home she sees another man on the street and says, "There he is."

THE CASE OF MR. PELHAM (1955)

30 minutes, CBS
Written by: Francis Cockrell, from a story by Anthony Armstrong.
Cast: Tom Ewell, Raymond Bailey, Kirby Smith

Ewell is a well-to-do businessman whose life is taken over by a double. His schemes to outwit the double come to nothing and finally the real

Mr. Pelham is called the imposter, and it drives him mad.

BACK FOR CHRISTMAS (1956)

30 minutes, CBS
Written by: Francis Cockrell, from a story by John Collier.
Cast: John Williams, Isobel Elsom

Williams kills his wife and buries her in the cellar. He goes off on a holiday, pleased with himself, until he gets a letter from a company his wife hired to excavate the basement. Everything in the cellar will be dug up before he's "back for Christmas."

WET SATURDAY (1956)

30 minutes, CBS
Written by: Marian Cockrell, from a story by John Collier.
Cast: Sir Cedric Hardwicke, John Williams, Tina Purdom

Sir Cedric tries to shift the blame for a murder his daughter has committed onto someone else. Transference of guilt is a favorite Hitchcock theme of course and here Sir Cedric winds up partly guilty himself.

MR. BLANCHARD'S SECRET (1956)

30 minutes, CBS
Written by: Serett Rudley, from a story by Emily Neff.

Cast: Mary Scott, Robert Horton, Meg Mundy, Dayton Lummis

Scott, a mystery writer, looks out her window to keep an eye on her neighbors, in the manner of "Rear Window." Her overheated imagination leads her to believe that a neighbor has killed his wife. Surely the weakest of Hitchcock's TV films.

ONE MORE MILE TO GO (1957)

30 minutes, CBS
Written by: James P. Cavanagh, from a story by F. J. Smith
Cast: David Wayne, Louise Larrabee, Steve Brodie

Wayne murders his wife and puts her body in the trunk of his car. A helpful State Trooper stops him because of a broken tail light. The cop insists on fixing it, even it if means opening the trunk.

THE PERFECT CRIME (1957)

30 minutes, CBS
Written by: Sterling Silliphant, from a story by Ben Ray Redman.
Cast: Vincent Price, James Gregory

Gregory, a lawyer, accuses Price, a detective, of sending an innocent man to his death. To stop that kind of talk, Price bakes the lawyer's body in a pottery oven, turning the remains into a vase, which he then displays.

FOUR O'CLOCK (1957)

60 minutes, (for the TV series "Suspicion"), NBC
Written by: Francis Cockrell, from a story by Cornell Woolrich
Cast: E. G. Marshall, Nancy Kelly, Richard Long, Jesslyn Fax

Marshall, a watchmaker, suspects his wife is unfaithful. He rigs a time bomb to blow up the wife and her lover. But burglars break in and tie Marshall up. The bomb doesn't go off, but the tension of thinking it will drives Marshall mad.

LAMB TO THE SLAUGHTER (1958)

30 minutes, CBS
Written by: Roald Dahl, from his own story
Cast: Barbara Bel Geddes, Harold J. Stone, Allan Lane

Bel Geddes kills her husband with a frozen leg of lamb. The police investigate, looking for the murder weapon. While they search, she cooks the evidence and feeds it to the cops. One of the most popular and enduring of Hitchcock's television films.

DIP IN THE POOL (1958)

30 minutes, CBS

Written by: Robert C. Dennis and Francis Cockrell, from a story by Roald Dahl

Cast: Keenan Wynn, Louise Platt, Phillip Bourneuf, Fay Wray, Doreen Lang

Wynn, a compulsive gambler, and his wife, Fay Wray, are on a cruise. He bets all his remaining money that he can estimate the ship's speed. To win the bet, Wynn jumps overboard, sure that will slow the voyage down. The witness he was counting on to yell, "Man overboard!" turns out to be blind.

POISON (1958)

30 minutes, CBS

Written by: Casey Robinson, from a story by Roald Dahl

Cast: Wendell Corey, James Donald

In a jungle outpost, Donald insists a poisonous snake has slithered into his bed. Corey laughs and accuses him of being drunk, telling him the snakes are far away. Then Corey is bitten.

BANQUO'S CHAIR (1959)

30 minutes, CBS

Written by: Francis Cockrell, from a story by Rupert Croft-Cooke

Cast: John Williams, Kenneth Haigh, Max Adrian, Reginald Gardiner

Williams, a police inspector, hires an actress to play the ghost of a murdered woman, as a ploy to frighten a suspect into confessing. It works. The ghost is very frightening and the murderer confesses. Then the actress hurries in, apologizing for being late.

ARTHUR (1959)

30 minutes, CBS

Written by: James P. Cavanaugh, from a story by Arthur Williams

Cast: Laurence Harvey, Hazel Court, Patrick Macnee

Harvey, a chicken farmer in New Zealand, isn't interested in marrying Court. He kills her, grinds up the body, and dumps the remains in the chicken feed he sells. His customers all remark on how improved they find the feed.

THE CRYSTAL TRENCH (1959)

30 minutes, CBS

Written by: Sterlng Silliphant, from a story by A.E.W. Mason

Cast: James Donald, Patricia Owens, Werner Klemperer

Donald is a young husband who is buried in an avalanche. His widow waits forty years for the snows to shift so she can claim the body. She comes as an old woman, faithful to her memories, and discovers that when her husband died, he was wearing a locket with a picture of another woman.

INCIDENT AT A CORNER (1960)

60 minutes, 1960 (Ford Star Time), NBC
Written by: Charlotte Armstrong from her own story.
Cast: Paul Hartman, Vera Miles, George Peppard, Bob Sweeney, Leora Dana, Philip Ober, Jack Albertson.

An argument between a school crossing guard and a woman school official is retold from several vantage points, in the style of "Rashomon." A poison pen letter is meant to connect the otherwise incompatible strands of the plot.

MRS. BIXBY AND THE COLONEL'S COAT (1960)

30 minutes, 1960, NBC
Written by: Halsted Welles, from a story by Roald Dahl
Cast: Audrey Meadows, Les Tremayne

Meadows has been given an elegant fur coat by her lover, the Colonel. In order to keep the coat without making her husband suspicious, she pawns it and tells him she found the ticket. Playing into her hands, he offers to take the ticket and find out what it will yield. Then he comes home with a cheap, tattered coat and of course she can say nothing. Later, when she goes to his office, she sees his attractive young secretary wearing the elegant fur. An odd and very entertaining mixture of Hitchcock and Feydeau.

THE HORSEPLAYER (1961)

30 minutes, NBC
Cast: Claude Rains, Ed Gardner, Percy Helton, Kenneth MacKenna

Rains is a Priest who notices that Gardner is giving a lot of money to the church, because, Gardner says, it helps him win at the track. Rains gives the man church money to bet, in the hope that the church can be repaired with the winnings. Then, filled with remorse, he prays his horse won't win. Gardner puts the money on "place" so the Priest's prayers are answered but the church still gets its new roof.

BANG! YOU'RE DEAD
(1961)

30 minutes, NBC
Written by: Harold Swanton, from
   a story by Margery Vosper
Cast: Biff Elliott, Lucy Prentiss,
   Billy Mumy, Steven Dunne

A little boy, Mumy, plays with what everyone assumes is a toy pistol. He goes about his house and neighborhood pointing it and saying "Bang!" In fact the gun belongs to his Uncle and has two live bullets in it. The Uncle retrieves his pistol before anything substantial happens. Hitchcock always said he regretted the explosion in "Sabotage" that killed the child and other bus passengers. Maybe he was trying to compensate for that, but the ending here is tepid.

I SAW THE WHOLE THING
(1962)

60 minutes, NBC
Written by: Henry Slesar and
   Henry Cecil
Cast: John Forsythe, Kent Smith,
   Evans Evans, John Fiedler,
   Philip Ober, Claire Griswold.

A courtroom drama in which Forsythe is on trial for a hit-and-run accident. The accident is shown from the point of view of several witnesses, each of whom claims to have "seen the whole thing." After Forsythe is convicted, we learn that it was his wife who was actually driving the car. The point is both that witnesses are unreliable and, because this is a Hitchcock film, albeit a minor one, guilt is more transferable than a witness's testimony.